THE CARRIER
EXCITING. EXPL

CARRIER

The North Korean Navy has captured a U.S. Intelligence ship in international waters. They dare Washington to retaliate. The U.S. response? The ultimate military power play . . .

VIPER STRIKE

A renegade Chinese fighter group punctures Thai airspace— the spearhead of a giant invasion force streaming across the Burmese border. The skies are about to blow wide open . . .

ARMAGEDDON MODE

India and Pakistan are on the verge of nuclear destruction, and Carrrier Battle Group Fourteen must shift into Armageddon Mode—the ultimate battle by land, air, or sea . . .

FLAME-OUT

After a hard-line military takeover, the Soviet Union is reborn. Norway is invaded. Finland is crushed. And the President orders Carrier Battle Group Fourteen to smash the Soviet strike force at all costs . . .

MAELSTROM

The Soviet occupation of Scandinavia continues as Carrier Battle Group Fourteen struggles to keep up in conventional weapons combat, and avert all-out war . . .

COUNTDOWN

Carrier Battle Group Fourteen must launch marine and aerial assaults to prevent the deployment of Russian Typhoons. They are the largest submarines in the world. And they may have nukes . . .

AFTERBURN

As the Russian Civil War rages on, Carrier Battle Group Fourteen is ordered to the Black Sea as a show of American strength. But if the U.S. thinks they can sail into traditionally Russian waters without a fight, they're dead wrong . . .

CARRIER

Book Eight
ALPHA STRIKE

Keith Douglass

J

JOVE BOOKS, NEW YORK

CARRIER 8: ALPHA STRIKE

A Jove Book / published by arrangement with
the author

PRINTING HISTORY
Jove edition / February 1997

The Putnam Berkley World Wide Web site address is
http://www.berkley.com/berkley

ISBN: 0-515-12018-9

A JOVE BOOK®
Jove Books are published by The Berkley Publishing Group,
200 Madison Avenue, New York, New York 10016.
JOVE and the "J" design are trademarks
belonging to Jove Publications, Inc.

PRINTED IN THE UNITED STATES OF AMERICA

10 9 8 7 6 5 4 3 2 1

PROLOGUE
Friday, 21 June

1400 local (Zulu -7)
Guazhong Advanced Aviation Test Facility
China

Mein Low swore as the adversary Chinese Sukoi-27 Flanker vanished into the blinding glare. He could almost feel the other pilot yanking his aircraft into a hard, gut-wrenching turn, bringing his guns to bear on Mein Low's advanced prototype F-10 fighter while the sun hid his turn.

In combat the lines between men and aircraft blur until the difference between them disappears. My vision—the radar. My will—the weapons. And so it is for him as well. We both know only one of us will land after this knife fight.

The sky flashed metal, slightly above him at ten o'clock. The Flanker pilot had underestimated the width of his cloak of invisibility, exposing one wingtip. The attack geometry flashed into Mein Low's mind.

Bleed off air speed, turn, and drop in behind me for the killing shot. But now that you've exposed your direction of turn, you've lost the advantage of uncertainty. And you will lose this engagement as well!

Mein Low jerked the F-10's nose up to thirty degrees above the horizon and rolled to the right, keeping his eyes glued to the approaching Flanker. The seat fell away slightly from his back as the faster and more maneuverable F-10 slowed rapidly. Fifteen hundred feet later, Mein Low was inverted, craning his neck back to stare down at the Flanker desperately trying to turn away from him.

Too late. The Flanker had given up too much precious airspeed in his last maneuver. As the Flanker drew parallel beneath him, Mein Low completed the roll, dropped the nose of the aircraft down, and dove into a killing position behind the slower aircraft.

The Flanker bobbed and jinked, and the turbulence from his jet's engines battered the F-10. Mein Low's hand clamped down around the control stick. His weapons selector switch was already toggled to guns. The F-10's cannon spat out six thousand rounds per minute, stitching the Flanker's side.

The other aircraft's canopy exploded in shards, and the metal framework peeled back from the rest of the airframe. He caught a glimpse of the other pilot, crumpled and bloody in the cockpit, before leaking fuel met hot metal. Mein Low jerked his fighter into a tight turn just as the Flanker exploded into a bloody red-orange fireball.

Only one more test. Five miles from the training field, a Grumble surface-to-air missile waited, the final obstacle to full funding of the F-10 program—*his* program—and his promotion to Wing Commander. Defeat it, and Mein Low would vault up the ladder of power and prestige in the Chinese army.

The radar threat indicator screamed a warning microseconds before the missile symbol blipped onto the heads-up display in the cockpit. Mein Low shoved the throttle on the F-10 forward, dumping raw fuel into the jet's engine. In seconds, the aircraft muscled its way through the shock waves that battered the aircraft at Mach .9 and accelerated past Mach 1.

Against a Mach 3 missile, the fighter's supersonic speed was almost irrelevant. Still, the point of the operational exercise was to prove the capabilities of the next-generation Chinese fighter operating at the edge of its envelope.

Let them tell the Flanker pilot, now spread across five miles of desert with his aircraft, that it was just an operational test!

The missile closed to five miles.

Mein Low twitched his finger, activating the countermeasures toggle on the stick. Four gentle thumps shook the aircraft as a combination of flares, chaff, and electromagnetic decoys shot out of the belly slots. The pilot stabbed the preload button on his G-suit. As soon as he felt the pressure on his extremities increase, he threw the sleek jet into a hard breaking turn, tensing every muscle in his torso to augment the effects of the constrictive flight suit and force increased blood flow to his brain.

Cold sweat soaked his flight suit as he fought against unconsciousness. He *would* enter the next cycle of life knowing whether or not he'd succeeded, not blindly exiting this life without ever knowing the results!

Time slowed to a crawl. He had all eternity to watch the deadly white missile grow larger, the tiny oscillations in its flight stilled as the Front Dome radar tracker and illuminator seeker head zeroed in on the jet, so close now he imagined he could see the invisible pulses of energy radiating out from its nose.

Suddenly, the missile twitched. Its nose dropped a few inches as it shifted its aim.

It worked! Cold joy filled Mein Low, and time resumed its normal speed. A white flash of death streaked past him and impacted the cluster of decoys behind and below the F-10.

Turbulence from the blast almost accomplished what the missile had failed to do, knocking the jet nose down and tail high. The F-10's air speed plummeted into the stall region in seconds, and Mein Low's vision narrowed to a tiny pinpoint of light.

The barely conscious pilot fought the jet back into stable flight, regaining control five thousand feet above the barren plains. With stall warning buzzers and threat indicator alarms still ringing in his ears, he automatically turned the jet toward the airfield.

Fifteen minutes later, he was on the deck. A wave of cheering technicians, scientists, and engineers swamped the fighter the second it stopped its rollout. The crowd pulled Mein Low from the cockpit and carried him on their shoulders to the hangar. By the time his feet finally hit the tarmac, his hands had stopped shaking.

Still dazed, he raised his right hand to the crowd. The assembled mass fell silent.

"Today," he said, surprised his voice remained steady, "we regain control of our skies. Your hard work and dedication have given your country the next generation in fighter aircraft. With it, I pledge to you restoration of our historic rights over the South China Sea. Each victory in the air is not ours—it is yours!"

He raised his hand again, and let the roar of the crowd wash over him.

CHAPTER 1
Saturday, 22 June

0810 local (Zulu -7)
South China Sea
Tomcat 205

Bird Dog slammed the stick to the right, rolled the F-14 Tomcat over onto its back, and craned his neck back to stare down through the canopy at the South China Sea fifteen thousand feet below. From that altitude, the whitecaps were mere fly specks on the dark blue water. A gash of silver cut east to west across the sea, the last remnants of the aircraft carrier's wake. He hung suspended between sky and water for ten seconds, blood pounding in his head, and then rolled the Tomcat back into level flight.

Angels fifteen, CAVU,[1] and a Tomcat strapped to my ass—life doesn't get any better than this! If it doesn't trip the Master Caution Light or yell at me over tactical, it's not worth worrying about. Not as long as I'm up here.

Lieutenant Curt "Bird Dog" Robinson was long overdue for a little slice of heaven. In the last three weeks of Navy life, he'd learned that being an F-14 pilot was a lot more complicated than they'd told him it would be. It wasn't the flying—no, not

---

[1] Clear Air Visibility Unlimited

that at all. That was the only thing that was sweet about being a junior nugget in VF-95, the sharpest fighter squadron onboard *USS Jefferson*. It was all the other stuff. The paperwork, the endless administrative details that occupied far too much of his waking hours, and the problems that plagued his work center, the Aviation Electricians Branch.

A weary sigh came over the ICS. "You want to let me know the next time, asshole?" Lieutenant Commander Charlie "Gator" Cummings, his Radar Intercept Officer (RIO) asked. "What if I'd been taking a leak? And wasn't this briefed as a straight and level mission?"

"I *was* straight and level," Bird Dog said hotly, sidestepping the issue of whether or not he should have alerted his backseater before rolling the Tomcat inverted. "What wasn't straight and level about that?"

"Upside down?"

"So? No one told me I couldn't. They just said straight and level. And, if you had any judgment at all, you'd have to agree that that was about the straightest, levelest inverted flight you've ever been privileged to experience!"

Another deep sigh was the only response from the backseater.

Automatically, Bird Dog kept up his scan, glancing down at the cockpit instrumentation every few seconds and then back up at the horizon. The line between water and empty air blurred into haze in the distance. He concentrated on the hard throb of the Tomcat's engines, the familiar growl radiating into his body at every point that it touched his ejection seat. Now, if his backseater would just stay quiet, maybe he could escape back into that perfect union of man and aircraft where nothing mattered but airspeed and altitude.

No such luck.

A metallic flash off to his right brought him back to reality. Irritated, Bird Dog toggled the communications button. "Jeez,

Spider, give me a little airspace! What's the matter, afraid you're going to get lost?"

"Sorry." His wingman slid back and away from Bird Dog's aircraft.

"Better," Bird Dog mumbled. He tapped the throttle forward slightly, increasing his airspeed just enough to pull ahead and put Spider out of view.

"Ten minutes, Bird Dog," Gator announced.

"I know, I know. You think I've been somewhere else for the last hour?"

His backseater fell silent again.

Bird Dog sighed and tried to recapture the euphoria he'd been feeling a few minutes earlier. The daily look-see presence patrol over the Spratly Islands in South China Sea was the most boring, useless waste of the powerful fighter's capabilities that he'd ever seen, but at least he was flying instead of playing Navy. Flying he could do. It was the Navy business that went along with it that was giving him problems.

Below him, the Spratly Islands were spread over an area about the size of Montana. The cluster of sandbars, rocks, and occasional islands was a key flash point in the South China Sea and the Far East. China, Vietnam, Malaysia, and the Philippines all laid claim to the area and the rich oil-bearing seabed below it. Lately, both China and Vietnam had started building "fishing camps" on the islands. The presence of tanks and guided missile emplacements in "fishing camps" indicated that both nations were expecting a little more than economic competition.

"First rock coming up," Gator said a few minutes later.

"Okay, okay. Anything around?"

"Nothing new. I probably would have told you if there were."

Bird Dog winced at the chilly note of reproach in his RIO's

voice. Not only was Gator a friend, he was also considerably senior to Bird Dog.

"Sorry, Gator," he said finally. "Just in a bad mood today, I guess."

"Happens. Best get your head out of your ass and fly this mission, though. If I tell you to move, I want to see some action up front."

"Yeah, yeah. Like anything's going to happen. We've been circling this pile of rocks for days, and nobody's ever shown up to play with us. And it ain't like there's anything on those rocks that's going to shoot at us."

"You really think you're immortal? 'Cause if you do, you can let me off at the next pit stop."

"No, I know they've got Stingers. But why in the hell would they shoot one at us? We're not at war with anyone. I don't even know what we're doing here!"

"National security, Bird Dog. Didn't you read the OPORDER? We're supposed to keep China from making a grab for the islands."

"Like it's any of our business anyway. Who cares whether the Chinese or the Vietnamese or the Malaysians end up owning these islands?"

"You'll care, if China throws everybody else out by force. No way we could let her start establishing a regional hegemony, and that's what will happen if she gets her hands on that oil."

Bird Dog moaned. Not only was he required to fly straight and level—no aerobatics, no fooling around—in the world's best fighter, but he had to listen to lectures on world politics at the same time.

"One minute away from Mischief Reef, thirty seconds to Island 203," Gator added. "T-54 tank, probably some Stingers with it."

"Got that, Spider?" Bird Dog said over the radio circuit. One short click acknowledged the transmission.

Great. Now even his wingman wasn't speaking to him.

0820 local (Zulu -7)
Island 203
Spratly Islands, South China Sea

Chu Hsi crawled out of the tank and stretched. He glanced around, hating the naked vulnerability of his post. Fifteen years in the Chinese army, most of those as part of a tank crew, had ingrained in him an instinctive longing for maneuverability that was the key to survival in land warfare. Trapped on this rock, barely out of the reach of the sea, his tank rusting under the constant mist of sea spray and his instincts screaming reflexive warnings about his immobility, Chu Hsi could only wonder at the thinking of his superiors.

The rock had no name, and was barely even far enough above water to be called an island. Twenty meters long and eight meters wide, its ragged peak protruded only two meters above the waves. Two weeks earlier, a transport helicopter had deposited the T-54 Russian-made tank and its two-man crew on the rock. Perched squarely in the middle of the rock, tilted and uncomfortable ten degrees off plumb level, his tank looked forlorn and abandoned.

Doctrine called for maintaining a continual alert status and radio watch, though he'd never known—nor bothered to ask—why. Mischief Reef, five miles away and barely visible through the haze and the fog, was the command post for this area of the South China Sea. Its elaborately constructed bamboo-and-corrugated-sheet-metal main camp perched on an island six times the size of Chu Hsi's rock.

The Mischief Reef camp was three stories tall, the lowest

floor almost twenty feet above the island's surface. While the island itself might be able to boast of more surface area than Chu Hsi's rock, most of it was awash in the sea. Even the drinking water there had a faintly salty taste. The stilts were necessary to keep the structure away from the ever-hungry ocean.

From a distance, the structure looked like it might teeter and fall into the warm South China Sea at any moment, but appearances were deceiving. Centuries of practice had given the Chinese the ability to construct deceptively strong buildings out of little more than bamboo, twine, and wire. The two-inch-diameter poles were woven together in such an intricate interlace that the resulting building could withstand almost anything short of a typhoon.

Chu Hsi held up one hand to block the sun and gazed longingly at the larger camp. Life was easier there, certainly. On his last trip to the base camp, he'd seen the catchment basins used to collect rainwater. One of the soldiers had told him that they were allowed two gallons of water every week just for bathing, a luxury Chu Hsi's crew would have to forego for the three weeks of their tour on the rock. By the time their tour was up, the salt that collected on their skin would have started to chafe open sores around their collars. Only changing socks every three days kept their feet from disintegrating into molding, festering tissue.

A distant roar reached his ears, barely audible above the noise of the waves lapping at his rock. Chu Hsi scanned the horizon, finally locating the source.

More aircraft. Probably the Americans again, he thought. He called his gunner. The daily overflights by aircraft and the hourly radio checks with the Mischief Reef camp were the only relief from terminal boredom.

His gunner popped his head out of the tank, and then pulled himself up to join Chu Hsi on the deck.

"Back again, yes? Maybe someday we can make life more interesting for them. I have just the toy to do it with!"

"You really believe you could hit an American fighter with that device?" Chu Hsi laughed. "About as much chance as us hitting it with this tank!"

"You wait." The gunner looked pointedly at his Stinger, and hefted it to his shoulder. The Stinger, a US-built shoulder-launched infrared guided surface-to-air missile, had proved its reliability in every combat theater in the last fifteen years. It had been the primary reason for the Soviet defeat in Afghanistan. Chu Hsi had seen the demonstrations, and was impressed. But he wasn't about to tell his gunner that.

"I won't hold my breath."

The two men watched the aircraft grow larger, impossibly fast. The light gray shapes were hard to see in the ever-present haze that clung to the surface of the warm sea, but the contrails that formed in the warm air were clear.

"F-14. I will make the report."

"Which is so necessary," Chu Hsi sneered. "As though our superiors on the next island can't see and hear it just as clearly as we can."

The gunner paused, half in and half out of the tank. "It is a requirement. You are aware of that."

Chu Hsi waved him down, suddenly tired of baiting the gunner. Useless entertainment, since nothing ever pierced the gunner's humorless devotion to operational requirements. The sheer boredom of sitting in a tank on a rock in the middle of the ocean would probably kill both men before anything else.

The American aircraft disappeared over the horizon. Chu Hsi took a step back toward the open hatch. The minutes until the next hourly radio report stretched interminably before him. Chu Hsi sighed.

The two Tomcats made several passes over the two rocks, descending to five thousand feet for a better look. "Nothing new, as far as I can tell," Bird Dog said finally. "Same old rusty tank, same little fellow sitting on top. And the same old gun emplacements on Mischief Reef. Okay, enough of this shit!"

"Now that we've had our look-see, you ready to head for home?" Gator asked.

Bird Dog didn't answer.

"Come on, Bird Dog, let's just head back to the carrier, nice and easy," Gator coaxed.

"In a minute. Let's take a quick trip around the battle group first. Just for the hell of it," Bird Dog said, too casually.

"Don't do this to me again," Gator warned. "No flyovers on the cruiser, you hear me? They got downright hostile the last time you did that without asking them. You're going to convince them to send a missile up our ass next time, instead of just locking us up like last time."

Bird Dog shoved the throttle forward and felt his ass sink into the hard seat. Around him, the comforting scream of the twin engines deepened. He held his hand on the throttle for a moment, reveling in the sheer power of the vibrations there. Sweet and even, reassuring reminders that every bit of this finely tuned machine was running perfectly.

"We're not going to do a flyover," he said softly. "Not this time. But somebody ought to remind them to watch out for friendlies. That damned CIWS locked me up last time. I don't appreciate it. Not one little bit."

The Phalanx Mark 15 20-mm CIWS—pronounced see-whiz—was the Close-In Weapons System, a ship's last defense against a fast-moving inbound missile. Its J-band radar tracked both incoming targets and the gatling-gun stream of bullets it fired, self-correcting its aim. Theoretically, the Block I version on the *Vincennes* could fire 4,500 rounds each minute within two seconds of detecting an incoming object that matched its threat parameters.

"What're you going to do, Bird Dog?" Gator asked, a sudden note of concern in his voice. "Don't go screwing with that ship. CAG already reamed you out for the flyover, and he'll castrate you if he catches you dicking around out here."

"Hang on!" Bird Dog said, and punched the throttle forward into afterburner. He nosed the aircraft down, letting gravity add speed to the power generated by the afterburners.

Bird Dog leveled out at five hundred feet, increasing his speed to .8 Mach. At 480 knots, the aircraft was traveling eight miles every minute. The cruiser was thirty-five miles away, and would have a surface radar range of approximately thirty miles against a decent target. Bird Dog hoped he'd dropped off their radar screens when he'd descended.

"Damn it, Bird Dog! You're trying to kill me, aren't you? I swear to God, one of these days I'm punching out! I'll let *you* try to explain why you got back to the ship minus your backseater!"

Bird Dog watched the ocean streak by below. One more minute.

Six miles from the cruiser, Bird Dog yanked back on the stick and stood the screaming jet on its tail. He let it claw for altitude, and felt the slight decrease in pressure against the back of the seat as his speed fell off. At six thousand feet, he leveled off and continued on toward the cruiser.

"There," he said, satisfied. "CAG can hardly gig me for a flyover if I'm at angels six, can he?"

"Oh, no, hardly a flyover. You idiot! Are you trying to give that ship a hard-on for you?"

"What? Me?" Bird Dog said innocently.

"Asshole," Gator muttered. "You know exactly what they thought, and CDC is going to be screaming in my ears any second. Disappear off everyone's radar, come in fast and low and pop up—you know what they thought!"

"That I was a sea-skimmer missile popping up on them? Oh, surely not, Gator! Not that finely trained bunch of black shoes that tried to sic CIWS on me last week! After all, they're watching the scopes, tracking the friendlies. They *had* to know it was me, didn't they? I mean, we *talked* to them last week about not causing a blue-on-blue engagement. Surely they're paying more attention this time!"

"If I had any sense, I would have punched out an hour ago and taken my chances with the sharks! Better them than CAG."

"So touchy," Bird Dog murmured. "You RIOs never have the right stuff. You know that, Gator?"

His backseater sighed and gave up.

Twenty miles from the carrier, something blipped into existence on the RIO's radar screen for two sweeps. "Hold on, I got—wait, it's gone," Gator said.

The note of excitement in Gator's voice cut through Bird Dog's daydream of a perfect world where pilots flew every day and every trap was a three-wire. "Got what, Gator? *What?*" Bird Dog demanded.

"Nothing now," his RIO said, frustration edging his voice. "I thought I saw a high-speed blip break out of the ocean clutter. Just for a second—it's gone now."

"I saw it, too," Lieutenant Commander Joyce Flynn, Spider's RIO, chimed in. Nicknamed Tomboy, the diminutive redheaded Naval Flight Officer had been one of the first women assigned to a combat squadron.

"What the—what do you mean, a blip?" Spider demanded.

"Just that. A couple of hits on the AWG-9, then it disappeared."

"Sea clutter. Ain't nothing out here high speed," Bird Dog said. He shrugged, and felt a moment of sympathy for the two Radar Intercept Operators. If the presence patrol missions were boring for a pilot, they were doubly so for the RIO. Few radar contacts, nothing to track or shoot at, and not even the simple pleasure of flying to make up for it. Even if there had been adversary air, Bird Dog wouldn't have been inclined to worry. He took it as an article of faith that there wasn't an aircraft built or a missile launched that could touch a Tomcat. RIOs always worried too much.

"You're probably right. Nothing in the LINK on it," Gator said uneasily. The AWG-9 had its problems with look-down capability, a problem partially remedied on the later versions of the F-14 and somewhat improved on the F/A-18. "Then again, this area'd be out of range of the surface search radars off the ships. And it's awful calm down there to be generating much sea clutter. We got time to swing back and take another look?"

Bird Dog glanced at the fuel gauge. "Nope, not unless you really need to. We stay around too much longer and *Jeff*'s gonna have to launch a Texaco. Then we'll catch it when we get back."

"No, not solid enough for that," Gator answered. "Probably just sea clutter, like you said. Still . . ."

"How about we drop down a little lower while we head back to the boat?" Bird Dog asked. "You take a quick look around on the turn. Maybe it's a fishing boat or something."

It was, he thought, the least he could do for the RIO, who'd suffered through an occasional barrel roll or period of inverted flight to break up Bird Dog's own boredom. Chasing down sea clutter ghosts would give them both a break from the monotony of straight and level flight.

A high-pitched whine, barely audible at the edge of his perception, caught his attention. Chu Hsi paused, halfway out of the tank. Was it barely possible that there might be another aircraft in the area? Some unexpected event to relieve the unending tedium?

He scanned the horizon, turning in a circle, looking for the source of the noise. He selfishly said nothing to the others, keeping this experience all for himself. Then *he* would be the one with the new experience to relate, rather than having to share it with the humorless gunner.

A hint of movement on the horizon caught his attention. Too small and too low to be an aircraft, unless it were driven by a suicidal pilot, the shape skimmed over the tops of the waves, barely clearing the water. It was impossible—no! He'd watched the American aircraft during their entire transit, and he would have seen anything leave their wings.

Four seconds had passed since the flash had caught his attention. Chu Hsi opened his mouth to yell at the rest of the tank crew.

The missile streaked in from the horizon, traveling at Mach 4, about 2400 miles an hour. The first guttural scream barely had time to start out of Chu Hsi's throat before the missile hit his tank.

The fuel and ammunition flashed the interior of the tank into a searing hell, reducing the gunner inside to ash and cinders. A split second later, shards of shrapnel shredded Chu Hsi into barely recognizable chunks.

Fragments of tank, island, and men exploded outward and upward on the crest of an explosive fireball. Responding to the inexorable insistence of gravity, the debris eventually hung in midair for a split second, two hundred meters above the water, before beginning its descent back into the warm waters of the South China Sea.

Had he still been alive, Chu Hsi would have been pleased to see that the Spratly rock he hated so much no longer existed.

0829 local (Zulu -7)
Tomcat 205

"Holy shit!" Gator screamed over the ICS. "Shit, Bird Dog, get this baby turned around! Helluva explosion back there!"

"Tell me about it!" Bird Dog said, fighting a blast of turbulence that shook the aircraft from behind. "Whatever it was, it shook the hell out of the atmosphere!"

Bird Dog thumbed the switch over to the tactical frequency reserved for aircraft to combat direction center communications. "Homeplate, Viper 205. You see that?"

"Roger, Viper 205. Say state?" the Operations Specialist, or OS, on board *USS Jefferson* responded. The OS had been monitoring Bird Dog's mission continually on the radar on board the carrier.

Reflexively, Bird Dog reeled off his fuel status and then said, "What the hell was it?"

"We don't know. Tanker airborne in ten mikes for Viper flight. TAO requests you swing back over those islands and take a look."

Bird Dog threw the Tomcat into a tight left turn and said, "Roger, on my way. I'm gonna need gas in about thirty mikes, sooner if I have to go buster."

"On its way now, Tomcat 205."

What the hell was it? And where did it come from? If it'd been aimed at us, would we have seen it? Of course we would.

Lost down in the sea clutter, it can't touch us. It'd have to gain altitude to reach a Tomcat, and we'd have plenty of time to react. Ain't nothing can reach out and touch a Tomcat, nothing!

But if they were so damned invulnerable, why the hell was his stomach clutched in a knot and his heart beating faster than the thrum of the Tomcat? And why the hell did he have to pee so bad?

Three minutes later, Bird Dog slowed to three hundred knots, after Gator assured him that there was no hostile activity in the area. His RIO's voice had lost all traces of his earlier good mood and was now flatly cool and professional. Bird Dog knew Gator's face would be glued to the soft plastic hood surrounding the radar screen, his hands moving nimbly by rote over the different shaped knobs and dials that controlled the display. His own heartbeat had slowed to almost normal, and he felt the easy invulnerability he'd always felt flying.

The air caught the aircraft and buffeted it slightly as the Tomcat's wings automatically swept forward into the low-speed configuration. The additional wing area increased lift and enabled the Tomcat to stay aloft at slower speeds.

"See anything, Bird Dog?" Gator asked. His RIO's head would stay buried in the scope until they were certain there were no other contacts around.

"Not me. How about you, Spider?"

"Just the Mischief Reef tree house. Nothing else. That's the problem. Five minutes ago, there was another rock out here, one with a T-54 and Stingers. Damned tough to see anything at this speed, but I know it was there." Even at three hundred knots, the surface of the ocean flashed by too quickly for close observation.

"This is a job for a Viking or a helo," Bird Dog agreed. "Let's see what Mother can scare up for us. Homeplate," he continued, switching from ICS to the tactical circuit, "Viper 205. We need a slow-mover out here. Suggest we tank, and then provide cover for supporting units."

"Roger, understand. Wait one." The OS monitoring the two Viper aircraft fell silent, and the hiss of static filled the circuit. A few moments later, the distinctive two-tone warble of a secure circuit being activated cut through the static.

"Viper 205, you're cleared to tank. Vikings are airborne in fifteen mikes, along with SAR."

"SAR? What for?"

A new voice cut in on the circuit. "Viper flight, TAO. The only thing that could have blown up out there are those rocks. Just in case anyone made it out, SAR will cover."

Well, great. What the Tactical Action Officer really meant, Bird Dog knew, was that since no one had any idea of what had hit the rocks or where it'd come from, no one could tell him whether there was another one on the way.

So just to be on the safe side, they're launching SAR. Just in case they have to pull my happy little ass out of the drink. Like I don't know that, even if they won't say it that way.

0840 local (Zulu -7)
Fifty miles east of Island 203
Tactical Flag Command Center
USS Jefferson (CVN 74)

"What the hell *was* it? Come on, people, I need some answers!" Rear Admiral Matthew Magruder, commander of carrier group 14, stared at the tactical display in the tactical flag command center, usually called TFCC. No signs of trouble there, with every aircraft and surface ship positively identified as neutral or friendly. "And what's that damned Aegis cruiser doing *this* time?"

"Don't know, Admiral," the TFCC watch officer said. He pulled one of his radio headset earphones away from his head so that he could hear the admiral better. "An explosion of some sort. *Vincennes* requested permission to go take a look. From the looks of the screen symbology, she didn't wait for permission to change course."

The tall admiral gazed at the screen impassively. His slate-gray eyes were set in the expression of permanent neutrality that had earned him the call sign "Tombstone" at his first F-14 squadron. The shortened version of it, "Stoney," was an even more accurate description of his usual expression. Aviators who'd flown with him for years swore that they'd seen him smile before, but the TFCC watch team had their doubts.

"Tell *Vincennes* I said to get her Aegis ass back into screen position," Tombstone ordered. "Until we know what that was, I don't want her charging off into the unknown and leaving the carrier unprotected. I'll be in Supp Plot."

Supplemental Plot was the high-security intelligence module next door to TFCC. Tombstone ducked out of TFCC, into the common vestibule the two spaces shared, and was inside Supp Plot in four steps. He nodded to the enlisted Intelligence Specialist, or IS, guarding the door, and was met by the watch officer, Commander Busby.

"You crypto guys got any information on this?" Tombstone asked.

"No hard data, Admiral, but there are several possibilities," Commander Busby said. "The Chinese might be using the island as a depot for material they don't want to risk underneath their Mischief Reef tree house. Mix volatile compounds with bad safety practices, and you've got the right conditions for spontaneous combustion. Or there might have been a fire in the tank. Not a likely explanation. A diesel fire alone wouldn't cause a fireball that big."

"Any evidence to support either theory? That rock's been photographed more times that Cindy Crawford. No signs of oil drums or construction of any bunkers that I've seen."

"No, Admiral. That brings me to the second possibility. A missile."

"From where? More importantly, who shot it? There was nothing in the area except Tomcat 205."

"Submarine, maybe. Could be a land-launched sea-skimmer, too. That would explain the blip the RIOs saw. Breaking those things out on the radar picture is chancy at best. They get lost in the sea clutter. But on a nice day like this, sea state one, there's a possibility of detecting one," Busby said.

"Same problem as your first theory. We've had no contact on any submarines, and no HUMINT on any deployed in this area. And you're talking about a hell of a long range for a sea-skimmer—couldn't have been shot from land," Tombstone said.

"Not according to current intelligence, no. But the range is within the capability of a U.S. Tomahawk."

"Which they don't have. That we know about."

"That we know about," the intelligence officer echoed. "But the theory fits the facts that we *do* have."

"Set Condition Two," Tombstone ordered. "Until we figure out what caused this, I want every eye peeled for hostile activity. I'll be in TFCC if you need me." *And all the more reason to keep the Aegis in close. That blasted cruiser's been more of a pain in the ass than any other ship in the battle group. Killington would choose this particular time to do it, too!*

When you got right down to it, he decided, Captain Jake Killington, Commanding Officer of the *USS Vincennes*, had been a marginal pain in the ass for the entire cruise. *Vincennes* was often not where she was supposed to be, off doing something more interesting than protecting the carrier or pursuing some tangential interest of her CO. They'd expended more "giant tomatoes," the inflatable targets used for surface gunnery practice, and more five-inch shells than all the other ships put together. To top it off, after the last onboard conference with Killington and his operations officer, the flag mess chief had reported that two gallons of ice cream and a silver sugar-and-creamer set were missing.

Back in TFCC, Tombstone stared at the symbols crawling across the big-screen display. *Wonder if those pilots know how lucky they are? My list of things to worry about was a lot shorter when I was just a pilot. Sure, it'd been dangerous, but it was just me, my RIO, and my wingman.*

The more senior Tombstone got, the more people depended on him to make the right decisions to keep them from getting killed. On top of that, he barely got a chance to fly enough to stay qualified. Flying actual combat missions was out of the question. The whole battle group, over ten thousand men and a billion dollars worth of equipment, was his responsibility now, not just a couple of aircraft or even one squadron's worth.

Add to that worrying about new Chinese weapons systems, ones the intelligence communities might have missed . . . Tombstone stared at the screen. "If they *do* have something equivalent to the Tomahawk—then we've got a serious problem. If the *Vincennes* is half as capable as she thinks she is, it might be enough—just barely. Get me a secure line to Commander, Seventh Fleet. I have a feeling he's not going to be too happy about this."

1015 local (Zulu -7)
Tomcat 205

It couldn't have been more than a minute after I saw them. The guy standing outside the tank, one just getting out. One second they were there, then BOOM! It seems like they ought to have known they were going to die. That'd be only fair—some sort of premonition, or something. Bird Dog tried to concentrate on the deck of the carrier, repressing the train of thought that was making him distinctly uneasy.

After taking on more fuel from the KA-6 tanker, Bird Dog and Gator had circled overhead for two hours while slow-flying S-3B conducted a detailed search of the area where Island 203 had been located. Neither the Lockheed Viking nor the SH-60F helicopter had found anything of interest, although both reported an oil slick and small amounts of floating debris in the area. There was no trace of the two men Bird Dog had seen earlier on the rock.

The flight of Tomcats headed back to the carrier. Spider trapped first, catching the three-wire neatly. Finally, it was Bird Dog's turn to descend from the Marshall stack and make his approach.

The controlled crash that passed for a successful landing on an aircraft carrier stimulated the highest readings of blood pressure and muscle tension of any profession ever measured. For Bird Dog, moving his hands, feet, and eyes in the intricate patterns necessary to land, coupled with the expected stress, always acted like a strong dose of caffeine. Time slowed down—except when the approach went wrong—and he found his mind racing over myriad details unrelated to the landing.

"Wave off, wave off!" the LSO yelled over the circuit. "Go around, Viper 205. Let's give it another shot. And this time, when I say you're high and fast, I damn well better see you bleeding off some frigging airspeed and altitude! You got that, Bird Dog?"

"Roger," Bird Dog acknowledged, suppressing the impulse to swear at the landing signals officer. He hadn't been high on final approach to the carrier; he *hadn't*! What the hell did the LSO know? *He* wasn't flying this Tomcat!

The LSO was stationed on the port side of the aircraft

carrier, slightly below the level of the flight deck and in front of the meatball. It was his job to guide the landing aircraft into the perfect approach profile, supplementing the visual clues that the Fresnel lens, or meatball, provided to the approaching pilot. Too high or too low, and the pilot's lineup with respect to the meatball would make the lighted signal appear red. In the groove, at the right altitude and range from the deck, and the meatball glowed green. The meatball provided guidance, but the LSO, an experienced aviator himself, was the final word on whether an approach was safe or not.

"Take it easy, Bird Dog," Gator said quietly. "Little off, that's all. You'll snag it next time."

"Asshole's got it in for me," Bird Dog muttered. "I was good for at least the four-wire, if not the three. No way I was high—no way!"

"Okay, Okay," Gator said soothingly. "These guys are just human. They make mistakes like the rest of us."

Gator's well-intentioned words irritated him even more. Until this afternoon, when something had streaked undetected below him to smash the rock into gritty mud, Bird Dog hadn't really believed he was just human. He was a *Tomcat pilot*, for Chrissake! Invulnerable in the air, entitled by birthright to be arrogant on the ground. Immune to the dangers of wrestling his aircraft back onto the pitching deck of the carrier, and perpetually blessed by the gods of the air.

Until now. On final approach, he'd suddenly realized how small the deck of the carrier looked, and how fast it was coming at him. His skin had prickled as it'd occurred to him what the rough nonskid on the deck could do to the skin of his aircraft, and he'd felt the tiniest quiver of—of what? Nervousness? God, could he be *afraid*?

Bird Dog swallowed hard and forced himself to concentrate on his instruments. He rejoined the Marshall stack, the aircraft circling on the port side of the carrier waiting for their turn to land.

Nothing was different, nothing, he insisted to himself. This was just another landing on the carrier, something he'd done at least two hundred times before.

"Piece of cake, Bird Dog," Gator said when they finally broke out of Marshall and started their final approach. Bird Dog felt sweat bead on his forehead as he listened to the LSO and his RIO. The pitching deck rushed up at him, and he ignored the flash of unfamiliar emotion that threatened to distract him.

"Three-wire!" Gator crowed as the F-14 slammed onto the deck. "Good trap, buddy!"

Bird Dog felt the tension seep out of his body as he lifted the tailhook and released the thick steel cable. He taxied slowly toward the yellow-shirted flight deck supervisor, wondering what the hell had gotten into him up there, acting like he'd never trapped on the carrier before.

Well, whatever it was, it was gone now. And the bitch of it was, he still had to pee.

CHAPTER 2
Saturday, 22 June

Commander Hillman Busby glanced around the CVIC briefing room, mentally taking muster. All his key players were there. The junior officers and the chief petty officers had snagged the few chairs still left out from the morning brief. The rest of the enlisted men and women packed into the room leaned against walls or perched on plotting tables.

"Okay, people. Time to do some magic. We need some answers—or at least some informed intelligence estimates," Busby said.

The Carrier Intelligence Center, or CVIC as it was commonly known, was the information fusion center for Carrier Battle Group 14. Pronounced "civic," it was home to the battle group intelligence officers, enlisted Data Systems Specialists (DS) and Intelligence Specialists (IS) ratings that kept track of the world. CVIC tapped into the most advanced message and information processing computers in the U.S. Navy's vast array, and was capable of monitoring circuits so highly classified that even admitting they existed was a federal felony.

For all its resources, CVIC couldn't create probabilities,

27

estimates, or analysis without data. It was completely dependent on information fed to it by other sources: national assets, satellites, debriefing reports from the CIA, and tactical sensors such as the SLQ-32(V4) ESM sensors installed on the ships in the battle group.

The dependence on outside information was at the heart of Commander Busby's dilemma. Admiral Magruder wanted intelligence's best estimate of the cause of the explosion earlier that morning, and there was simply no data. Even with all his electronic wizardry, Busby knew no more now than he had when he was standing his watch in supp plot.

At thirty-five, Busby had been in the Navy long enough to know that admirals were not the most patient bosses. While Admiral Magruder had a good reputation for fairness, it wasn't likely that he was going to appreciate what Busby had to tell him.

Which was absolutely nothing.

Busby sighed and ran his hands over his head. His hair was trimmed Marine-close to his head, his skull clearly visible through the pale blond fringe. For a moment, he considered shaving his head completely. Blond hair, blue eyes, and pale skin detracted from his personal idea of how an intelligence officer should look as a steely-eyed professional in daily contact with secret spies and highly classified information. And his nickname, given to him at his first squadron as an ensign and boot air intelligence officer, didn't help either.

Who wanted to get a prelaunch briefing from an officer nicknamed "Lab Rat"?

Well, after he talked to Admiral Magruder, he might not have to worry about his haircut. The Admiral was likely to rip off his head, along with several other sensitive body parts. He sighed again and stared at the yellow legal pad. The information he *could* give the Admiral was remarkable only in its lack of usefulness.

Item: The Chinese, along with five other nations, claimed

ownership of the Spratly Islands. The Spratly Islands were barely worthy of the title "island," since most of them were almost completely submerged, bare tips of rocks poking mere feet above the surface of the South China Sea.

Item: The ocean bed surrounding the Spratly Islands was one of the richest remaining oil fields in the world.

Item: Yesterday, one of the islands disappeared, along with the tank that had been perched precariously on it. Tomcat 205 and other battle group sensors had detected a massive explosion in the area.

Item: All of the Chinese submarines were accounted for, at least according to the satellites.

Item: The Chinese, although world-famous for the dangerous Silkworm sea-skimmer, were not known to possess a long-range cruise missile similar to the U.S. Tomahawk.

Busby studied the list for a moment and then doodled a question mark next to the last two items. He was long on questions, short on answers. For an intelligence officer, it was damned irritating.

1215 local (Zulu +12)
Operations Center
Commander, Seventh Fleet
Honolulu, Hawaii

"So Tombstone's on the front line again," Vice Admiral Thomas Magruder said. As Commander Seventh Fleet, he had operational command of every Navy asset west of the international date line. Right now, that included his nephew's battle group. "I should have known getting promoted to Rear Admiral wouldn't change his luck. When did this happen?"

"Thirty minutes ago, sir. The battle group sent the on-scene Tomcat back to take a look at the area, and then launched some

S-3B's to get a closer look. The helos followed them in after the Tomcats tanked," the watch officer replied.

"And you mean to tell me that we don't know what caused it? With a full battle group in the area, as well as satellite coverage? What about nuclear data? Any indication that it was something besides a conventional war shot?" the admiral asked.

"KH-11 was down, sir, but other sensors indicate that there was no nuclear involvement. It seemed like a good time for routine maintenance, according to the SpaceCom watch officer I spoke with. With a battle group in the area, and no hostilities imminent . . ." the watch officer let his voice trail off.

Space Command in Colorado controlled all "national assets," the highly classified network of satellites, sensors, and other sources of information that were deemed too important to national security to be under the jurisdiction of any single service. While they were generally responsive to requests for information and observation scheduling, it was not unusual for them to take satellites down for maintenance without warning. Absent a request for special coverage, the electronic security whizzes in the secret "black" programs there felt it was better to avoid the risk of letting *anyone* know when the satellites weren't looking. That had been decided in coordination with the Air Force in a series of budget battles.

The Air Force, the most junior of all the military services, coveted all the satellite programs. Senior Air Force staffers continually pointed out that the outer reaches of the earth's atmosphere were still within their area of expertise. Space-based sensors, weapons—indeed, anything that flew—ought to belong to them. In one series of white papers, they'd argued that satellites could be used as forcefully in a "presence mission" as any carrier battle group.

Satellites in presence missions. Vice Admiral Magruder snorted in disgust. According to the officers that wore light blue suits, the mere rumor that a satellite was focused on a particular region would give a two-bit dictator reason to worry. They'd immediately stop slaughtering their own populations in the name of ethnic cleansing and become peaceful members of the world community.

For some strange reason, the rest of the military community failed to agree that a satellite could be as visible a symbol of U.S. intentions as a carrier battle group or amphibious task force sitting within view of the coast. While all services agreed that air superiority was a necessary precondition for a successful land campaign, no service except the Air Force believed that air power could eliminate the need for ground combat.

What would the "Air Farce" want next? Satellites flying in formation like F-14's? A satellite equivalent of "Top Gun" school? Vice Admiral Magruder smiled at the thought and wondered if he could hornswoggle some junior Air Force officer into seriously proposing the concepts. The resulting flame war and embarrassment would be worth watching. Now that he was safely out of the Pentagon and back in an operational command, the political machinations and aspirations of others were a good source of flag-level jokes.

No, despite the invaluable information that satellites provided, they were far too vulnerable and weather-dependent to replace the Navy in presence missions. Besides, assuming that satellites would serve as a deterrence to hostilities depended on one assumption of doubtful validity—that the country supposedly being deterred *knew* that satellite was there. And for the third-world countries that currently teetered on the edge of violence, that was a mistake.

On the other hand, China was hardly a technological backwater. While its society was rigidly stratified, with millions of people living in unimaginable poverty, the most populated country in the world had devoted a large percentage of her GNP to military advancements. Along with her purchases from Russia, Japan, and Korea, she was quickly developing a high-tech military-industrial complex of her own. Analysts at highly classified briefings had speculated that China's international intelligence network was becoming a significant concern, particularly in light of the United States' relatively lenient policy of granting political asylum to almost any Chinese national who claimed it. Undoubtedly, China had the means for determining when U.S. satellites were providing surveillance on the area, and Vice Admiral Magruder wouldn't rule out the possibility that they were also tapped into the satellites' maintenance schedule. Maybe satellites *could* deter the burgeoning regional—and soon, international—power.

But deterrence required understanding *why* a country was doing whatever it was doing, and unraveling the chain of logic that underlay China's political and military decisions was an almost futile task. Steeped in centuries of military tradition, and following the tenets of such brilliant military-political thinkers as Sun Tzu, the Chinese agenda was undoubtedly a subtle one.

"Get me a secure line to General Emberfault," the senior Magruder said, referring to the Chairman of the Joint Chiefs of Staff. "He's probably already gotten reports on this from other sources, but I want him to hear it from us. It's *my* battle group that's on the line out there, and I need to know what I can do to protect it."

1215 local (Zulu -7)
CVIC
USS Jefferson

"I didn't see it myself, Admiral, but I sure felt the blast." Bird Dog Robinson shifted uneasily in the hard plastic chair. The buzz of adrenaline from the bolter and his trap was starting to fade, leaving him feeling dopey and slow. He was tempted to rest his elbows on the government-issue table and support his head with his hands. He was still in his flight suit, although he'd ditched his ejection seat harness in the Handler's office on his way down to CVIC for debriefing. Despite the air conditioning in his Tomcat and in CVIC, dried sweat glued his Nomex shirt to his back, and it was starting to itch. With the Admiral sitting in on the debriefing, a fresh trickle of sweat had started down the middle of his back.

"I thought I saw a blip of something, Admiral," Gator volunteered. "Tomboy saw it, too, but it was there and then gone so fast, I can't be certain. Could have been a sea-skimmer, though—the speed seemed right, from what I can remember."

"We'll take another look on the mission tapes. None of our surface ships picked up anything, not even the Aegis. Not that that decides it one way or the other. You boys had the advantage of altitude." Rear Admiral Magruder frowned slightly. "The perennial look-down problem of the AWG-9 surfaces again. The F/A-18 Hornets and the F-14F have gone a long way toward correcting the deficiency, but the versions of the F-14 we're still flying in the Fleet have a tough time on low-altitude contacts."

The Admiral glanced back at the debriefing sheet Bird Dog had filled out. "The rock—anything unusual about it?" the Admiral asked.

Bird Dog looked down, unable to meet the eyes of the Commander of the Carrier Group. The Admiral's voice had a hard-edged impatience to it. If the lack of information irritated him, what would the highly decorated pilot say if he knew how Bird Dog felt during that last trap? He shifted again in his seat, certain that Admiral Magruder would be as disgusted with him as he was with himself.

"Nothing. Still just a rock with a tank on it. I thought I saw a couple of guys standing on the tank, but we were still fairly high. If they were waving and cheering for the American way of life, I missed it," Bird Dog said.

Immediately, he wished he could recall the words. Fear did that to him, for some reason. His mouth opened before he thought, and inappropriate words came tumbling out before he could think. But this was a serious matter, and the admiral had a reputation for being a serious guy. Someday, Bird Dog's smart-ass mouth was going to get him in trouble.

"Sorry, Admiral," he mumbled, and stared at his shoes.

Tombstone stared at him silently for a few moments. Then he said, "You remind me of my old wingman, Batman. Same sense of humor, and same sense of timing. I bailed him out more than once in briefings." The barest trace of a smile twitched at the corner of the admiral's mouth. "Lieutenant Commander Flynn? You saw this contact, too, I understand?" Tombstone asked the tiny redheaded RIO.

"Yes, Admiral. The AWG-9 just got a couple of hits on it, barely enough to paint a trace. Whatever it was—if both paints were even the same target—it was going like a bat out of hell. Then again, it could have just been two clots of sea clutter that happened to pop up one right after the other." She shook her head. "I can't give you a solid answer, sir. I'm sorry."

"What's your gut feeling about the contact?" Tombstone pressed. "You've got good eyes, Tomboy. You were trained by the best, after all."

A smile flashed across her face, quickly replaced by the more serious look of a professional naval aviator called on to make a decision. Too often in the intricate game of radar detection and classification the final call on whether a contact was hostile or not depended on the judgment of the officer on the scene.

Tombstone had good reason to trust Tomboy's judgment. During her first cruise, she'd been his RIO on countless occasions when he was CAG of Air Wing 14. Despite her markedly female appearance on the ground, Tomboy was a hard-line, top-notch RIO in the air.

"My gut says it was a missile, Admiral," she said in a clipped, incisive voice. "My radar painted something that looked like skin. It looked solid, and it looked like the same contact on both sweeps. I'd call it an actual contact, not a ghost. And there's supporting information for that as well."

"A Chinese outpost getting blown out of the water a few minutes later is pretty solid correlation," the Admiral agreed. "What worries me is the lack of detection on a launching platform."

"Do the Chinese have anything like our Stealth program, Admiral?" Gator asked. "That could be one possibility. An aircraft that we didn't detect launched a missile."

"Several of the intelligence officers have suggested that possibility," Tombstone acknowledged. "There are a couple of problems with that explanation, though.

"First, if the missile had been air-launched, it would probably have been from a reasonable altitude. We'd have had a better detection on the missile, if not the aircraft. We know it's not a stealth missile because you two *did* get a couple of hits on it. From the sounds of the contact, the reason for the intermittent detection was low altitude, not stealth technology.

"Second, a non-stealth missile on a stealth aircraft would destroy the low radar profile of the aircraft. Third, if it were air-launched, we'd probably have seen a seeker head of some sort," he said, referring to the normal terminal guidance method of most air-launched missiles. "And finally, there's no evidence that China has made much progress on a stealth program. They're still buying fighter aircraft from the Russians, and Russia's not about to sell their nearest regional threat their latest in advanced technology."

"So it had to be launched from something else," Bird Dog

said thoughtfully. "A submarine, maybe. Or it could be a Chinese version of our Tomahawk missile."

"Those are also possibilities, but they require us to make some assumptions about their technology. According to our intell, the Chinese don't have a long-range land-launch strike missile, nor do their subs carry one. Remember, the Chinese navy is still strictly a brown-water force, not a blue-water like ours."

Tomboy shrugged. "Well, whatever it is that they *don't* have, it sure made a hell of an explosion out there."

Tombstone questioned the four aviators for a few more minutes. Finally, convinced that they knew nothing else about the incident, he dismissed them. His eyes followed Tomboy as the aviators left the debriefing room. The baggy flight suit was pulled taut across her upper back and fell into loose folds around her slender hips, concealing her figure. From what he remembered of their last liberty together, that was a damned shame. A trickle of pure lust ran through his body, making him uncomfortable because of the sheer incongruity of feeling it while looking at a RIO in a flight suit. Still, despite her call sign, Tomboy was nothing if not completely female.

"That pilot—he sounds just like Batman did at that age," Tombstone said reflectively.

CAG chuckled. "I see it, too. How'd you ever get him to quit playing hotshot with those Soviet Bears?"

"I didn't—not really. He'd still be at it if he were out here."

Batman, known more formally as Captain Edward Everett Wayne, was a Top Gun-trained F-14 pilot. He'd joined the VF-95 Vipers as a lieutenant nugget when then-Lieutenant Commander Tombstone Magruder was on his second—or was it third?—cruise. He'd been hardheaded and impulsive, and had almost gotten himself in serious trouble hotdogging with a Soviet Bear reconnaissance aircraft. Later, once it hit home with him that he was killing men along with aircraft in the sky, he'd started to doubt his ability in combat. Tombstone had served as his sounding board.

In subsequent cruises, Batman and Tombstone had seen combat in Norway and Pakistan. The hotheaded young pilot had grown into one of the most superbly proficient aviators Tombstone knew.

Now Batman was flying something new, a platform that was forcing him to grow in new and not entirely pleasant ways: a desk in the Pentagon. Tombstone had read recently that Batman was heading up the development on JAST, the Joint Aviation Strike Technology program.

"What about these explosions? Washington's not going to be happy if we don't have some response planned," Tombstone said to Captain Cervantes, his CAG.

The title of CAG was a holdover from the days when a Carrier Airwing was called a Carrier Air Group, and was commanded by a Commander. These days, CAG was a full Navy Captain and the position carried considerably more power—as well as seniority—than the Air Group commander had. But the old handle was so firmly embedded in carrier aviation culture that Tombstone doubted it would ever disappear. Besides, CAG was a hell of a lot better acronym than CAW.

His current CAG, Captain Peter Cervantes, was an F-14 driver like Tombstone. They'd known of each other for years, although they had always seemed to be assigned to different coasts and had never worked together. CAG's reputation within the tight-knit fighter community was golden, though.

"Until we know what that strike was, I'd consider us in harm's way out here. And if they have a little cruise missile surprise to worry the surface ships, it makes me wonder what they've got cooked up for us that we don't know about," CAG said.

"My thoughts exactly. Stingers I'm not that worried about. But what if there's something else?"

"We can start by shifting more of the surveillance patrols to the F-18 squadrons, and keeping an E-2C up around the clock. Let's use what we've got."

"Tomcats aren't going to like that," Tombstone said thoughtfully.

"They'll have to live with it. In this particular scenario, the Hornet's the best bet. I hate admitting it as much as you do. An AWACS would be even better," CAG replied.

AWACS, short for Airborne Warning and Control System, was military slang for the E-3 Sentry surveillance aircraft. A modified Boeing 707, it carried extensive mission avionics packages for long-range targeting information and identification. The 11,800-pound rotodome measured thirty feet in diameter, and was mounted on two struts on top of the aircraft. Its AN/APY-2 slotted, phased-array antenna and APX-103 IFF interrogator provided excellent coverage of large areas of ocean. But it had two fatal drawbacks, as far as Tombstone was concerned—it was owned by the Air Force, and it couldn't be deployed from an aircraft carrier.

"The odds of us getting one aren't great. Too few friendly land bases nearby. Plus, we'd have to coordinate fighter protection for it," Tombstone said.

"I know, and I'm not counting on it. Let me tinker with the flight schedule for a few hours, then run some ideas by you. We've got enough power to take care of ourselves."

"Okay, CAG. Keep me posted." Tombstone resisted the impulse to quiz CAG on his plans. When Tombstone had been CAG, his admiral had given him considerable free rein in running his airwing, even to the point of moving his flag to a cruiser and leaving CAG Magruder as the senior officer present on the carrier. It was one of the eternal challenges of getting promoted—learning to keep one's hands off one's former jobs.

"Roger that, Admiral. I'll get back to you ASAP." CAG pulled his 230 pounds up out of the hardback CVIC chair. "Hitting the flight deck today for a run, Admiral? We're going to have four open hours later today."

Tombstone smiled. "Tell me that again after you get through revamping the flight schedule, and after Seventh Fleet gets back to us. I have a feeling that the flight deck's going to be a bit busier than we originally planned!"

Bird Dog threaded his way aft through the maze of passageways to his stateroom, avoiding the heart-to-heart chat his backseater had insisted they needed to have. Gator was a good RIO and an even better all-round officer, he thought. His advice undoubtedly would have proved helpful. But there were just some things a man had to sort out for himself.

Nothing that day had turned out like he'd thought it would. He'd lost it on his first pass at the carrier, and then mouthed off to the Admiral. Besides that, the VF-95 Executive Officer was on his tail about overdue enlisted evaluations, and islands were blowing up out of the sea when he got near them. Hell, the battle group had been so hyped up over the rock exploding that CAG hadn't even gotten around to chewing him out for screwing with the Aegis cruiser.

On top of everything, he had a host of problems to sort out with his work center, the AE Branch. No, he concluded, life as a naval aviator was not a whole lot like it'd been advertised.

He remembered the day he'd first reported to the carrier. Sure, he'd been on carriers before during qualifications, but this was different. This was *his* carrier, the one that'd be his home for his first deployment. He had stared up at the tower that loomed over the deck, wondering for a moment if he would ever be sitting up there as Air Boss or Mini Boss.

The petty officer running the desk in logistics had given him terse directions to the Admin and Berthing offices. Bird Dog had hauled his gear down six decks to turn in his orders, pick up a check-in sheet, and get a room, and then back up six decks to his stateroom. He'd tossed his duffel bag on the unoccupied bunk and set out to locate the VF-95 squadron Ready Room.

Fifteen minutes later, he'd met the VF-95 XO and been introduced to Chief Franklin, the chief petty officer in charge of his squadron branch. After over three years of training commands and Navy schools, Bird Dog had finally arrived at his first Fleet squadron.

"You're getting a good group of people, Lieutenant," Chief Franklin had said as they shook hands.

The Chief seemed to fill the wardroom. Two inches taller than Bird Dog, and at least thirty pounds heavier, the senior enlisted man in the AE Branch was corded with muscle, a massive, powerful presence. A regular at one of the *Jefferson*'s three weight rooms, Bird Dog guessed. His dark hair, edged with gray, was clipped short. He looked older than his rank suggested, his face worn into grooves by the long hours, constant stress, and deprivations of life at sea. A hint of resigned good humor played around his dark eyes, which were circled with white where flight deck goggles had shielded his skin from the sun.

Perhaps it was his imagination, but Bird Dog felt as if the Chief were eyeing his shiny bright railroad tracks, as the lieutenant collar devices were known, with a jaundiced eye. "You're getting smart twidgets. We've got damned few discipline problems, pretty decent morale, and some strong petty officers. We keep 'em flying right steady—not often one of our birds will be down for an electrical gripe," the chief said.

"That's good to hear, Chief," Bird Dog said heartily. "I'm sure we'll get along fine."

"If there's anything you need, Lieutenant, you can reach me down in the Chiefs Mess. I'll introduce you to the troops tomorrow at quarters, if that's okay. I imagine you've got a lot of settling in to do. This your first cruise?"

"Sure is. I'm damned glad to be out of the training pipeline, too. Three years, and I'm finally getting to my first ship."

"We'll do everything we can to help you get used to the way things run around here, sir. You got any questions, you just ask. Nothing wrong with not knowing something, sir. There's a lot they didn't teach you in Aviation Officer's Candidate School."

"Thanks, Chief. Maybe we could get together a few minutes before quarters? I'd like to go over my priorities for the Branch with you."

"Your pri—uh, sure, sir. Whatever you say."

Bird Dog had watched the chief leave, puzzled by his reaction. Wasn't that what he was supposed to be doing as a Branch Officer? Setting the right tone, leading the men and women assigned to him to great achievements? Somehow, he got the impression the Chief didn't think that was in Bird Dog's job description.

Now, two months later, his relationship with Chief Franklin had cooled to slightly above freezing. Bird Dog had made several suggestions about how the branch might work more efficiently. At first, Chief Franklin had resisted, taking hours to explain *why* things were set up as they were, and what problems Bird Dog's changes would cause. Bird Dog had finally ordered the Chief to implement the changes, and given the Chief some literature on Total Quality Leadership to read.

Since then, the Chief had been formal and polite. All of Bird Dog's suggestions were implemented immediately, without discussion or argument from the Chief.

Within days, the Maintenance Officer was chewing on Bird Dog's butt in public for disrupting standard operating procedures in the department. When Bird Dog visited the branch work spaces, the chatter and joking between the enlisted men and women responsible for all the electrical gear on the birds died away. It took Quality Assurance inspectors longer to get around to certifying electrical branch repairs, and Chief Franklin had just dumped a two-foot-high stack of repair part inventories on his desk, with a note attached saying that the Chief was sure the pilot might have some input for the latest parts requirements request. While Bird Dog's peers seemed to spend more time in the rack than they did in their work centers, Bird Dog's in box was filling up at an alarming rate.

The problems just convinced Bird Dog that Electrical Branch was even more in need of his personal attention than he'd originally thought. And as for Chief Franklin, Bird Dog hoped that a little more of an officer's leadership would bring the man around to the new Navy way of doing things.

CHAPTER 3
Tuesday, 25 June

Captain Wayne studied the satellite imagery carefully, and then compared it with the one from the day before. No doubt about it—the South China Sea was missing one rock.

"Son of a bitch," he breathed, as he leafed through the rest of the briefing package. Even after his months at the Pentagon, the capabilities of satellite surveillance still stunned him. Pictures of events happening over five thousand miles away were hand-carried to his desk by an armed courier before the on-scene commander even had time to figure out what had happened.

"Not a chance anyone survived that blast long enough to drown, Batman," Admiral Dunflere said. "Hell of a way to go. It's not like that boat could even fight back."

Both men shivered slightly. The idea of being trapped in a small boat, at the mercy of almost any other platform, was repulsive to any fighter pilot. At least in the air they'd die fighting back.

"Where was this, Admiral?" Batman asked his boss. "Anywhere near Mischief Reef?"

"Five miles to the south," Admiral Dunflere replied. "That

whole area's thick with reefs, shoals, and rocks. The Vietnamese outposts are damned near within spitting distance of the
Chinese ones. That battle group commander must be sweating
some water space management problems just trying to keep
from going aground. And if he has to maneuver worrying about
sea-skimmers . . . better him than me. Interesting tactical
situation, don't you think? Suggest anything to you?"

"That's Stoney's battle group, you know," Batman remarked
casually. "Old friend of mine from way back."

"He's on the scene," the admiral agreed pleasantly. "Helluva
coincidence."

"If you're thinking what I'm thinking, it's more than that.
Stoney's got a sea-skimmer problem, and we've got a new toy
that might just make his life a little easier. Course, we'd make
the same offer to any on-scene commander, but it sure does
make it easier if it's Stoney."

"Great minds think alike," his boss said, and grinned. "Why
don't you give your old lead a call, and see how life's treating
him? Let's get a response before we start generating message
traffic—I want us all singing in the same key on this before we
go public."

"Roger, copy, Admiral. If I know Stoney, he's going to be
awful glad to see his old buddy about now."

"As glad as any operational commander *ever* is to see
someone from Washington," the Admiral replied.

Wednesday, 26 June,
0700 local (Zulu -7)
Flight Deck
USS Jefferson

"AE Branch! Atten-hut!" the Chief snapped.

Bird Dog walked toward the eighteen technicians assembled
in three neat ranks for morning quarters. Some were in

dungarees with chambray shirts or green pullovers while others wore coveralls. A scruffy-looking lot, he thought as he approached them. Although Bird Dog had been on the carrier for almost a month, he was still struggling with names and faces of the technicians who worked in AE—Aviation Electricians—division.

Appearances were important, he reminded himself. He'd taken extra care with his uniform that morning, even polishing the gold belt buckle to a brilliant shine to convey the impression of leadership, of a sharp, polished officer. By God, it was time for a change in attitude in AE Branch. These people would know they didn't have a slacker for a Branch officer.

Unfortunately, the enlisted personnel didn't seem to care. At least half of the men hadn't bothered to shave. While some of them might not even *need* to shave on a regular basis, three petty officers sported rough-looking stubble. The five women in the Branch particularly dismayed him. He'd expected the women to take a little more pride in their appearance. Two of them had long hair straggling out from underneath their cranials, and one wore the grimiest looking coveralls he'd ever seen.

Bird Dog returned the Chief's salute, trying to conceal his dismay. They must be testing him, he thought. Trying to see how far they could go with him. Well, he wouldn't stand for it!

"Personnel inspection, Chief," he snapped.

The Chief looked startled. "Sir, we're setting flight quarters in thirty minutes. The FOD walk-down—"

"How long can it take with fifteen people?" Without bothering to see if the chief followed him, Bird Dog began pacing down the row of assembled sailors.

"Haircut," he said shortly, as he looked the first sailor over carefully. "That goes for just about all of them, Chief."

"Yes, sir," the Chief said.

He walked slowly down the first line, then the second.

Halfway through the third rank, he came to the young female sailor in grimy coveralls. The top of her head barely came up to his wings, and her short blond hair was in disarray.

"Why isn't this sailor wearing a cranial, Chief?"

"Uh, sir—Shaughnessy?"

"Forgot it, Chief," she said. Her voice was so low Bird Dog had to strain to catch it. "It's in the line shack." A Southern drawl drew the five words out into a paragraph.

"Your bird a go this morning?" the Chief asked, ignoring Bird Dog impatiently shifting his weight from foot to foot beside him. The huge Chief, darkly bronzed by the sun and immaculately attired in sharply pressed khakis, towered over the small blond woman. For some reason, the odd contrast between the Chief and the airman annoyed Bird Dog even more than Chief Franklin's attitude. Wasn't *anything* the way it was supposed to be in the Navy?

"Yes, Chief." The corners of the young airman's mouth twitched upward. "Found the problem about ten minutes ago. A circuit breaker—can you believe it?"

"No shit? Good work! Which one was—?"

"Ahem. The personnel inspection, Chief," Bird Dog said.

The Chief glanced down at him as though seeing him for the first time. "Sorry, sir," he said after a moment. "You know how it is, trying to get all the aircraft FMC just before flight quarters. We've been having problems with that bird for two days now. Shaughnessy thought it might be a bad circuit breaker, not resetting correctly. Sounds like she was right."

"Fine, but there's no excuse for ignoring safety regulations, Chief. She's on the flight deck, she wears a cranial from now on."

"Aye, aye, sir," Chief Franklin said. "Want her to go get it now?"

Bird Dog hesitated. Something in the chief's voice made the rough tarmac under his feet feel like a slippery slope. "Up to you, Chief," he said, trying to inject a decisive note into his voice. "As long as we're clear that my first priority for AE Branch is safety."

"Aye, aye, sir," the Chief said again.

Bird Dog paced down to the end of the row, and then returned to the front of the ranks. The Chief followed him.

"AE Branch—parade rest!" Bird Dog snapped. The sailors hesitated for a split second, glanced at each other, and then fell into the more relaxed stance. "I will now read the Plan of the Day."

Suddenly, a voice boomed over the flight deck. "Would you people like an engraved invitation? The rest of the airwing would be pleased to have you join us for a FOD walkdown—that is, of course, assuming it's convenient?"

Bird Dog looked up, bewildered.

"Air Boss, sir," the Chief said. "If I could make a suggestion—this might be a real good time to dismiss the troops and buster down to the ass end of this bird farm. Air Boss likes to sit up in Pri-Fly and watch FOD walkdown. He's a little touchy in the mornings."

"Very well," Bird Dog replied, trying very hard to convince himself that he was in control of the situation. "Take care of it, Chief." He snapped off a salute in response to the Chief's, executed a smart about-face, and started walking briskly toward the island.

"Not so fast, mister," the voice boomed out again. "Get your little khaki butt down to the stern. Officers and chiefs aren't excused from FOD walkdown."

Bird Dog stopped dead. He could feel his face turning a brilliant shade of red. He looked aft and saw that his branch was already joining the line of sailors strung across the flight deck. Damn Chief Franklin! He could have warned me, he thought angrily.

"NOW!" the speaker roared.

Bird Dog settled into a jog—hoping it was a dignified one—and headed for FOD walkdown.

2330 local (Zulu -7)
Admiral's Cabin
USS Jefferson

"Of course I'm here! Just where the hell else did you think I would be, Batman? It may be after midnight, but you've been in Washington too long. You've forgotten what life at sea is like and the hours we keep." Tombstone glanced down at the receiver and noted that Batman was calling on the secure, encrypted circuit. "To what do I owe the pleasure of this call?"

"Just looking out for my old lead, shipmate. Doing my small part for the war effort back here in the Pentagon." Batman's voice sounded slightly murky. Not surprising, since it had been encrypted, bounced off two satellites, and then de-encrypted before being piped into the plain vanilla telephone receiver now pressed to Tombstone's ear.

"It's good to hear your voice, Batman. But quite frankly, your timing sucks. I've got a couple of situations going on down here, and—"

"I know all about it, old buddy. That's why the Batman is calling. Think I've got something cooked up back here that might be of some small assistance to you."

Tombstone snorted. "Like what? Another one of those point papers the Pentagon feeds on? Some help that'd be."

"Better than that. How'd you like to have a couple of hotshot look-down shoot-down aircraft out there?"

"I've got Hornets and E-2C's. Not to mention the Tomcats."

"Don't try to con me, Tombstone. Our Tomcats aren't what you need, not until the next upgrade hits the Fleet. I've got something that will outclass even those lawn-dart Hornets. Would you buy a Tomcat with the latest JAST technology?"

"JAST? The Joint Aviation Strike Technology stuff? I thought that was years away from being operational!"

"In production models, yes. But I just happen to have a couple of prototypes hidden out for special occasions. Nothing I'd like better than to see if these airframes can live up to the manufacturer's warranty."

"But Batman, we're not talking about a range exercise out here. Somebody's doing some real live shooting."

"All the better. I'd rather see what these turkeys can do in real operating conditions instead of on the range. Listen, Stoney, this is important. Not only for your battle group, but for the Navy as well. With the push on to go joint, JAST is going to be the technology of our next fighter aircraft, and we'll be living with it for decades. If it works, fine. If it doesn't, I want to know that now, before we're committed."

"So what do you want *me* to do?"

"Give me some deck space and berthing. I'll send you two JAST, plus flight crews and technicians."

"Who's gonna fly them?"

There was a moment of silence on the line, and then Batman chuckled. "Oddly enough, there're only three pilots completely checked out on this bird and her electronics. Unfortunately for the Pentagon, one of them happens to be me."

"Anything to get out of the Pentagon, huh?"

"It's not that bad, once you get used to the fact that a full-bird Captain is barely qualified to make coffee around this place. Trade places with you any day."

"Okay, okay, come on out. I'll let CAG know his air wing just got a little bigger and stranger."

"Expect a COD and our airframes in three days. It'll take a little while to arrange the tanking and refueling, but we're on our way."

Tombstone replaced the receiver and stared thoughtfully at it. From what he'd heard of the problems with JAST technology, he wasn't all that convinced the modified Tomcats would be that much help. But Batman seemed convinced an op-test was essential to evaluating the performance of the aircraft, and Stoney had to agree with him on that. If the Navy was going to be stuck with the aircraft, it might as well make sure they worked first.

JAST was a comprehensive program aimed at building the finest strike force in the world. Its mission was to develop technology and equipment to outfit aviation strike programs for every branch of the service. Key to its requirements were programs related to low observability—the follow-on term for what had initially been called "stealth" technology—and black box avionics that would dramatically increase both attack capabilities and interoperability with other services' data systems.

Tombstone took the frequent press releases and the JAST announcements on the World Wide Web with a grain of salt. Too many programs over the past twenty years had been touted as the ultimate marriage of man and machine, as the final word in complete integration of all weapons systems.

There were two problems with building the ultimate joint strike system. First, no matter how advanced the technology the United States developed, someone would eventually develop a counter to it. The Aegis seaborne weapons systems were a prime example. Even with a radar as sensitive as the SPY-1 system, the ships still had to be wary of mines and submarines.

Second, there was one factor that developers always seemed to overlook. Clausewitz, the nineteenth-century German general and theorist, had given the most accurate name to the phenomena that plagued every combat force and confounded every tactical decision: the fog of war. No matter how sophisticated, how elegantly planned and calculated, something would always go wrong during a military campaign. War-fighters that relied on the latest technology too much failed to plan for the inevitable foul-ups that were part of life.

Still, he admitted, there were some improvements that could make a great deal of difference in the Tomcat's capabilities. And if Batman was vouching for the JAST Tomcats, they were worth taking a look at.

Who knows? We might even have a chance to make some suggestions about these queer turkeys before they go into production. A little Fleet testing could make the difference between another Pentagon project that sticks us with a politically correct and technologically screwed-up platform that just won't work.

He picked up the receiver to the carrier telephone lines and dialed CAG's number. After all, what was the use of being an admiral if he couldn't roust a mere Captain out of bed?

CHAPTER 4
Thursday, 27 June

"Still awake back there?" asked Lieutenant Commander Steve "Rabies" Grills. The Viking S-3B aircraft was at eight thousand feet, her engines droning monotonously.

"Just barely. If you'd turn the vacuum cleaner down a little lower, we could get some sleep," the TACCO in the backseat complained.

"Awful surly for mere passengers," the copilot said.

Rabies looked at his copilot and winked. "Regardless of what these fine jet engines *sound* like, I'll have you know this jet is *not* a vacuum cleaner. It is a tactical military jet—and a damned fine acoustic chamber. In fact, since you backseaters are being so uncomplimentary, I may just have to prove it to you."

"Come on, Rabies, no aerobatics. I had the pork chops for lunch," the TACCO whined.

"I was thinking of singing a few bars of my latest work for you. I call it 'She Left Me For A Dump Truck, But I Ain't Dumping You,'" Rabies said gleefully. "And you're really going to like the second verse. Hell, *everybody* likes country

53

music—you just don't know you do yet! By the time this
cruise is over, you'll be begging me to share my music with
you."

"Come on, sir, this is officer business!" said AW1 Fred
Harness, the enlisted technician in the other backseat. "I was on
last cruise with you. Why do I have to suffer, too?"

The Lockheed S-3B ASW aircraft banked into a gentle turn
to the left. Originally built during the Cold War era as a
submarine hunter-killer, the aircraft had been upgraded into the
"B-bird" in the early 80s. In addition to its acoustic processing
suite and ESM capabilities, it was a superb surface surveillance
and command and control platform. Armed with the APS-137
ISAR radar and Forward Looking Infrared Radar (FLIR), the
S-3B could carry Harpoon antiship missiles, Mk-46 torpedoes,
and sixty sonobuoys.

Today, Hunter 701 was on an ASW (Anti-Submarine Warfare) mission, with secondary tasking as SUCAP (Surface
Carrier Air Patrol). Anything that floated on or under the water
was fair game, at least until the carrier could determine what
platform had caused the two explosions. Its radar and FLIR
were designed to detect snippets of periscopes protruding up
from the depths, and the S-3B's look-down capabilities far
exceeded that of the F-14.

ASW, however, was not the most exciting of taskings. It
was, thought Rabies, somewhat akin to watching grass grow.

The S-3B held a crew of four, two pilots in the forward two
seats and a TACCO and an enlisted Aviation Anti-Submarine
Warfare Specialist (AW) in the two backseats. The TACCO
was a Naval Flight Officer trained in managing the intricate
battle problem and sensors. The AW ran the acoustic sensor
suite, monitoring the sonobuoys and Magnetic Anomaly De-
tector (MAD) boom that trailed fifteen feet behind the aircraft.
While the S-3B lacked the flashy sleek lines of the fighter
community, her long endurance, ability to operate at slower

speeds, and remarkable flexibility made her much more than an ASW aircraft.

And, Rabies thought, at least she was a jet. He cleared his throat and said, "Okay, all together now. Just follow the chords—C major, F major, then E flat. Just imagine Waylon playing along with us. *Ohhhhh, she may have dumped me, but I'm never dumping you. She may have been untrue, but—*"

"Rabies, come back around south," the TACCO interrupted. "We're getting out of range of buoy seventeen, and Harness thought he heard something interesting."

"Harness, don't you be lying to the TACCO just to get me to quit singing," Rabies huffed. "A little culture ain't going to hurt you none."

"No shitter, sir—I got something interestin' sniffing around that buoy," Harness replied. Not that he wouldn't have invented something if he'd been certain it would get the commander to quit singing. Harness, who suffered from having perfect pitch and a keen appreciation for classical music, had gotten desperate enough to do just that on previous flights.

"Interesting? As in submarine interesting?" Grills felt a small surge of adrenaline.

"Probably just a whale farting," Harness replied. "Still, I'd like to monitor the buoy a few minutes longer."

"Never hurts to be safe. South it is." Rabies put the aircraft into a steeper turn back toward their original course.

"Okay, that's—shit, sir, we got one!"

"You gotta be kidding!" the TACCO said.

"No, sir, diesel submarine engine sounds. Looks like almost all the engine components! Hold on, look at—there it is! I've got a probable snorkel mast, bearing one-eight-three, range four miles! Picking up FLIR, too."

Rabies stood the aircraft on its side, banking back toward the bearing Harness had indicated and using the turn to descend.

They'd been monitoring the buoys at seven thousand feet, but a snorkel mast from a submarine warranted a closer look.

"Classify this contact probable Kilo-class diesel submarine, snorkeling," Harness announced.

Ahead in the water, Rabies saw the distinctive feather of disturbed water streaking away behind a large black pipe. "Make it visual identification. Wonder if this bad boy's been launching any missiles at tanks lately?"

"Let's get some practice. This is a drill, gentlemen. Setting up for deliberate attack," the TACCO said, entering the steering coordinates for the pilot. The pointers and courses popped up on Grill's display.

"Roger, got it. We don't need a MAD run with VID. And gentlemen, please note that this is a simulation. It wasn't our tank that got blown off the island, and we're not killing a submarine today," Rabies said.

While the pilot maneuvered into position for an attack, his copilot updated the carrier on the tactical situation, talking with the Destroyer Squadron Commander, or DESRON, onboard the carrier. The DESRON, a senior Captain with extensive surface ASW experience, inhabited the 08 level of the carrier, five decks above the Combat Direction Center. While the carrier had its own ASW module located directly off CDC, Hunter 701 had been chopped at launch to the DESRON for command and control.

"Surface, you sweet little bastard," Rabies heard Harness mutter. "Just come on up all the way, baby, just for me. You wanna get some sun on that sail, let me get a good look at you!"

Uncannily, as though in response to the prayers of the technician, a sleek black hull emerged from the water. The sea ran off the submarine's hull, cascading back into the warm water and creating a foamy froth around the hull. Two additional masts emerged from the still-dripping sail, and a small radar dish unfolded.

Fascinated, Rabies dropped his altitude another five hundred feet. At one thousand feet, he slowly circled the submarine.

"Oh, yeah," Harness crooned. "That's it, baby. Sir, can you get me in a little closer? First picture of the cruise is in the bag, and I'd like it to be a good one!"

Suddenly, part of the submarine's sail slid back, and a small launcher emerged.

Rabies slammed the throttles forward hard, taking the nimble jet to full military power. His earlier fascination had just been replaced by clear, cold dread.

"What the hell?" the TACCO said, as his head slipped out of the radar mask and hit the back of his headrest.

"SAMs! Shut up for a minute, and let me get us the fuck out of here!" Rabies snarled.

He'd seen the intelligence reports, but had never seen a report of an operational surface-to-air missile on a submarine. Facts and figures flooded into his mind, gleaned from countless intelligence briefs and his own extensive studies. It was estimated that some of the Kilos carried a follow-on to the S/A-Grail missile, a shoulder-launched or small-launcher-controlled antiair missile. With its infrared guidance system, the submarine version of the SAM was a fire-and-forget weapon. The missile probably had a range of no more that six nautical miles, he knew. It could probably do at least Mach 1, or about six hundred knots. The S-3B could do 440 knots on a good day. Downhill.

Rabies poured on the speed, not bothering to seek altitude. It wouldn't help. If he couldn't outrun it, then his only hope was to wait until it got close, and try a hard braking maneuver with chaffs and flares, hoping to coax the missile into overshooting its intended victim or going after the decoys.

His copilot was talking in clipped, short sentences to CDC,

ignoring the frantic demands from the DESRON for information. With a missile on his tail, Hunter 701 needed to talk to other aviators, not the surface officers who were nominally in control of her operations.

Rabies leaned forward against the straps that held him in the ejection seat, as though he could force more forward speed out of the jet by sheer willpower. They were too low eke out a few more knots by trading altitude for speed. Irrelevantly, it crossed the pilot's mind that there was a damned fine song in those words somewhere. Now if he could just live long enough to write it.

1745 local (Zulu -7)
Combat Direction Center (CDC)
USS Jefferson

"Get those alert five Hornets off the deck! That Hoover needs some missile cover. And get the alert S-3's rolling, too," the TAO snapped at her assistant. She reached for the microphone that would put her in touch with the officer of the deck, six levels above her on the bridge of the carrier. Before she'd finished, the TAO heard the 1MC blaring, "Flight quarters, flight quarters. Launch the alert five Hornets. Now, flight quarters." The sound of Hornet engines turning immediately thrummed through the ship, as the alert fighters waiting on the catapult prepared to launch.

CDC was the nerve center of the carrier. Originally called Combat Information Center, or CIC, the new name was a reflection of the changing ways that a carrier battle group controlled the ebb and flow of war at sea. The main compartment was dominated by a wall-sized blue screen that displayed every contact held by every sensor in the battle group. The CDC officer and the Tactical Action Officer, or TAO, sat side by side at desks in front of the display. Around them, enlisted technicians monitoring aircraft manned radar and data consoles. In a separate room immediately behind the TAO, another group of watch standers managed the ASW problem, coordinating their tactics over the bitch box with the DESRON five decks above their module. At one end of the compartment, two parallel rows of consoles were reserved for Tracker Alley, the group of Operations Specialists that correlated and deconflicted the radar inputs from every ship and aircraft in the battle group.

"What're they loaded with?" the TAO asked, as she watched the Hornets power up on the catapults.

"Two Sidewinders, two Sparrows, plus a cluster bomb on the Hornets. Harpoon only on the alert Vikings, although the airborne Viking has two torpedoes. We're out of luck if 701 loses him and the sub dives," the watch officer replied.

"That S-3 is out of luck if she doesn't. And the Hornets aren't going to be wild about going in, either."

Suddenly, the speaker over the TAO's head came to life. "Homeplate, Hunter 701. Looks like the SAM has fallen off. We're RTB."

Twenty-two people in CDC simultaneously let out the breaths they'd been holding. Freddie, the traditional handle for the operations specialist controlling an ASW aircraft, answered for them all, relief evident in his voice. "Roger, Hunter 701. Say state."

"Four thousand pounds. We're fine, Freddie, enough gas for a couple of passes."

"Hunter 701, contact Pri-Fly," the OS said, adding the flight control frequency.

The speaker hissed as Hunter 701 left that circuit to contact the Air Boss who would control its return to the carrier.

"Close one," the TAO muttered.

"Too close," the CIC watch officer responded. "I guess now we know what launched those other two attacks."

Maybe. And maybe not, the TAO thought, glancing at the surface warfare officer who was her assistant. *Never heard of a SAM being targeted at a land-based or a ship. SAMS are antiair weapons. Still, it might be possible, so better safe than sorry.*

If the submarine *had* launched the other two attacks, the mystery was solved. And if it hadn't—well, the carrier still had something to worry about.

CHAPTER 5
Thursday, 27 June

1100 local (Zulu +5)
The United Nations

Battle-ax, thought T'ing. He'd just learned the meaning of the word from one of his aides. It suited the ambassador from the United States. She was two inches taller than he was and twenty pounds lighter, but her iron demeanor and uncompromising insistence on the American view of the world made the word fit her too perfectly. *Pity that American women don't age more gracefully. A Chinese woman is perpetually of a certain age, until she suddenly grows old and dies. That is the way it should be with women. The American compulsion to thrust them into every arena ages them too quickly.*

Still, battle-ax or not, Ambassador Sarah Wexler was the only opponent that concerned him on the Security Council. The little charade he was about to play had been carefully crafted for her alone.

"It is regretful that I must make this complaint on such short notice, but events leave my peace-loving country few alternatives," the Chinese ambassador said silkily. T'ing paused for a moment and surveyed the members of the Security Council. The Russian ambassador already knew what China would say, the result of a carefully worded briefing earlier that day. Both

countries had played political games with the United States for
too long not to understand the rules.

"The Council understands that sometimes circumstances
require immediate action. Please, continue," the Russian ambassador, currently chairman of the Council, said solicitously.

"Very well. It is our hope that this distinguished body can
intervene immediately to short-circuit what appears to be an
escalating state of affairs immediately off our coast." T'ing
kept a careful watch on the ambassador from the United States.
Surely she must have some hint of the subject he was about to
broach! But her face wore the carefully schooled blank look of
polite attention so characteristic of professional diplomats.

"At approximately eight o'clock yesterday morning, American forces conducted an unprovoked and completely unlawful
attack on Chinese land located in the South China Sea—the
area the United States refers to as the Spratly Islands. This
action resulted in the deaths of two Chinese servicemen, as
well as the destruction of government property." A murmur
filled the room as the aides to the various ambassadors
conferred in whispers with their bosses.

Ah-ha! That got her attention, he thought, as he watched the
American ambassador's color deepen. She opened her mouth
to speak, then paused as an aide tugged on her jacket from
behind.

"Mr. Chairman," the American ambassador began, her eyes
blazing as fury flooded her face.

"I am not finished, Mr. Chairman," T'ing interrupted smoothly.
"The rules do entitle me to complete my complaint before the
aggressors are allowed to responded, I believe?"

"Of course, Ambassador T'ing. Ms. Wexler, please hold
your comments until the ambassador is through," the Russian
chairman said blandly.

"Since there is always the possibility that the American
forces are carrying nuclear weapons, we have taken the

precaution of declaring an exclusion zone in the South China
Sea. This action is necessary to protect Chinese lives and the
security of our good neighbors who border this historic bay."
And take that, *Madam*, he thought viciously.

"I have in my possession radar data and other military
information that will show the necessity of this action. At the
time of the attack, the only military forces in the area were
from the American warships. We believe that a circling fighter
aircraft known as an F-14 may have been the launch platform.
Naturally, portions of these documents are classified, but I
have taken the liberty of making as much of that data available
to the Council as is consistent with our national security,"
T'ing concluded.

"A horrible story, Mr. Ambassador, and one you can be
assured the Council will investigate thoroughly," the Russian
said. "Ms. Wexler, has the United States any possible excuse or
explanation for this blatant imperialistic attack?"

The American ambassador stood, slowly unfolding her lanky
frame from the chair. She glanced at some notes written on
small cards and then tossed them on her table. She surveyed the
faces around the room—one friendly, two decidedly hostile,
and the remainder as carefully bland as her own had been
minutes earlier.

"Mr. Chairman, fellow delegates, the ambassador from
China is sadly misinformed. It is true that an American task
force was in the area, exercising its freedom of navigation on
the high seas. The South China Sea, despite China's claims, is
not subject to the whims of one nation's control, nor is there a
basis for this supposed exclusion zone that China wishes to
impose.

"I received this morning," she continued, "a report for-
warded from the on-scene commander. He states that there was
an explosion in his vicinity yesterday morning, probably the
result of an undetected cruise missile fired at an island. A

thorough search for survivors was made, as well as for the source of the missiles, and none was found."

"How kind," China's ambassador said viciously, "to first annihilate a target and then go through the motions of looking for survivors!"

"If I may continue?" she snapped, glancing at the Russian, who nodded abruptly.

"Neither the United States nor any force or unit under her control was responsible for these attacks. Mission tapes and displays will be made available to the Council to support that claim, to the same extent that China makes her data available.

"Finally, no American force deployed anywhere, other than ballistic missiles submarines on routine patrol, is armed with nuclear weapons. This includes the task force in the international waters of the South China Sea. The United States deplores the existence of these weapons throughout the world, and is in full support of and compliance with all arms limitations treaties. China has no reason to doubt our assertions in this regard."

"Just one reason, Madam Ambassador," the Chinese ambassador said, pitching his voice low to capture the attention of the audience and still the ever-present whispers. "And that is the best reason of all—past experience. *Of all the nations in the world that possess nuclear capabilities, the United States is the only country ever to have used them.*"

Satisfied, the ambassador from China leaned back in his chair, a look of deep concern and outrage carefully pasted on his inscrutable features. Of all the charges, both false and true, that could be made against the Americans, that one fact was irrefutable.

Somehow he thought most of the other nations might see it the same way.

"Ugly fuckers, aren't they?" the Air Boss said to his assistant, the Mini Boss. The two were seated in their large elevated chairs in Pri-Fly on the O-10 level, directing the careful symphony of actions it took to get any aircraft on board the carrier. Tensions—and interest—were running high, and the tower was crowded with looky-loos wanting to get a first glimpse of the two modified F-14 JAST aircraft.

"Bigot," replied the Mini Boss mildly. The Air Boss was an F/A-18 driver, and his ribbing almost automatic. "If you flew a *real* fighter like the Tomcat, you'd have some basis for comparison. Nothing about your Hornets that would make any man's heart beat faster."

"Ask the MiG pilots about that," the Air Boss drawled. "Seems to me I remember bailing out a couple of Tomcats not long ago."

The Mini Boss studied the aircraft taxiing away from the wire seven decks below him. The first JAST F-14 had taken one touch and go, and then gracefully slammed to a stop on the first approach, catching the three-wire handily. There'd been a moment of concern when the second JAST bird had boltered its first pass, touching too far down the flight deck to snag a wire. Still, the pilot had snagged the two-wire on his second pass. Not too shabby—there wasn't a pilot in the air wing that hadn't boltered from time to time. Even the eminent Carrier Group Commander, Rear Admiral Tombstone Magruder, had had his share of bad passes.

At first glance, the JAST aircraft looked like any other F-14. A closer look revealed small but significant differences.

First, the radar dome. It was larger, extended further under the belly of the aircraft. The Mini Boss squinted and then picked up his binoculars. He followed the aircraft down the flight deck toward the catapults. "Different antennas, it looks like. And the pitot tubes look funny—longer, a little skinnier maybe. And the skin. She looks like she's rippled, almost."

"Supposed to be low observability. I read that those shallow-angle variations reflect radar off in funny directions. Composites just under the skin absorb some of the radar energy, too. But most of the differences are in the black boxes. If JAST can do even half of what the contractor claims, it's a good deal," the Air Boss said.

"*If* it can! They claim the avionics are practically sailor-proof. Maintenance ought to be happy about that."

"Nothing's ever been built that a sailor can't screw with," the Air Boss replied. "Besides, I'm pretty happy with the Hornet as it is."

"It'll be a great fighter—as soon as they come up with an AVGAS hose long enough to keep it permanently plugged into a tanker." The Mini Boss smirked. The Hornet had a much smaller fuel capacity than the Tomcat. While the reduced weight gave the Hornet added maneuverability, the constant whining of Hornet pilots for tankers was a standing joke that the Tomcat drivers invariably found hysterically funny. The Hornet aviators weren't as amused.

"We'll have our chance to check these babies out pretty carefully. If they can solve this mystery about the cruise missiles, that'll be enough. My stereo likes staying dry, and I don't want to think about what a new cruise missile can do to our happy little home here."

"You're not feeling safe and secure with Aegis nearby?" the Air Boss said casually.

The Mini Boss shot him a sharp glance. They hadn't discussed it, but every senior officer on the ship knew that Rear

Admiral Magruder was less than happy with the Aegis cruiser. Rumor had it that the CO had received a serious ass-chewing on his last visit to the carrier. Even the mess decks were abuzz with gossip concerning the disappearance of ice cream from the flag mess.

"If Aegis doesn't see it, it isn't there," the Mini Boss said finally. "Isn't that what they claim?"

"Then I guess the last attack was just spontaneous combustions, because Aegis sure as hell didn't see what caused it," the Air Boss replied. He raised his binoculars and pointed them at the passengers disembarking from the COD. "Well, will you look at that! That COD's got more modifications than the JAST birds!" the Air Boss exclaimed. The Mini Boss followed his line of sight, and then trained his binoculars in the same direction.

"Not bad," he said grudgingly. "But anything looks good halfway through deployment. Any woman that's not an aviator," he amended hastily.

"That's one of the reporters," an enlisted air traffic controller, or AC, offered. "Saw her listed on the manifest for the COD."

"Reporter, huh? Wonder what brought her out here, the JAST birds or the tactical events? Hey, what's her name? Anyone we'd have heard of?" the Mini Boss asked.

The AC picked up a clipboard, and ran his finger down the list of names. "Here it is. Pamela Drake, from ACN. I've heard of her."

The Air Boss and Mini Boss exchanged a telling look. So had they, but not from watching television. Unless they were completely mistaken, Miss Drake was Rear Admiral Magruder's long-standing heartthrob. Rumor control, monitored by the petty officers that handled all mail going off and coming on the carrier, said that the two were no longer an item. Speculation had run rampant on the mess decks about the future of the relationship.

"If you thought things were getting interesting out here before," the Air Boss said quietly, "just stand by."

CHAPTER 6
Thursday, 27 June

A light tap sounded on Tombstone's door, the one that led to the flag briefing room and TFCC. The chief of staff, usually referred to as COS, stuck his head into the admiral's quarters. "The new birds are on deck. Thought you'd want to know."

"Come on in, COS. I saw them coming in on the Plat," Tombstone replied, referring to the closed-circuit TV that monitored the flight deck. "Sounded like plain old Tomcats landing to me."

COS pushed the door open and entered the combination office/living room of Tombstone's cabin. He glanced at the paperback book open on the coffee table. "Didn't know you were a Western history buff, Admiral."

"Ah, that. My boss gave it to me at my going-away party. He said that since my call sign was Tombstone, I ought to know a little about the story of Tombstone, Arizona, and the shoot-out at the OK Corral and all. That was Wyatt Earp's last fight, you know."

"I *do* know that, actually. When I was a kid, I read everything I could get on the Old West. It was an escape, I guess. Growing up in Chicago, there wasn't that much open space. Somehow, the idea of going for days without seeing another person, riding across the ranges with your trusty horse and six-shooter, seemed like the best life in the world."

"Know what you mean. I never got a pony when I was a kid, but I got a Tomcat when I grew up."

"At least airspace is still as unlimited as the old Texas ranches were," COS said.

"Except that now the Chinese are starting to act like the farmers that wanted to put up fences. Maybe my old boss was right. He said the nature of conflict remained constant over the centuries." Tombstone glanced down at the pile of paperwork on his desk and grimaced. "Wonder if Wyatt Earp had to deal with this much paperwork. It looks like I won't get to even *see* one of the new birds for another two hours. Why is everything that ends up on my desk either impossible or screwed up?"

"Because I take care of the easy decisions before they get to you, Admiral. That is what's left over."

"All right, all right. Anything here that can't wait a few hours?" Suddenly, the urge to break free from the confining spaces below decks shook him. How long had it been since he'd flown? At least two months, back when *Jefferson* was still in transit. With the recent events in the South China Sea, there was absolutely no excuse for the admiral in command of an entire battle group to be airborne. The risk was simply unacceptable.

Back when he'd been a young hotshot pilot, he'd pulled countless hours of alert five duty, sitting in his Tomcat in every kind of weather, waiting for the word to launch that rarely came. Then, it'd seemed the worst sort of tantalizing tedium— deck-bound in an aircraft preflighted, armed, and fueled for flight. If someone had told him that he'd look back on alert five longingly, he would have thought they were insane.

"Nothing easy, but nothing urgent, Admiral," the Chief of

Staff said easily. "Of course, safety is always our top concern on *Jefferson*. Wouldn't hurt to have another set of eyes take a look at those tie-down chains, I imagine. Set a good example for the flight deck crew, too, seeing how their admiral had his priorities in order."

Tombstone looked sharply at the man, but could detect no trace of humor. It was true, of course, that working on the flight deck was the most dangerous and physically demanding job on the carrier. The young men and women who spent most of their waking hours waltzing between vast, sucking jet engines, whirling helicopter blades, and dangerous propellers became almost oblivious to the constant danger. It never hurt to remind them that their admiral knew what they were up against.

"Is the admiral in?" Tombstone heard someone say out of sight behind the Chief of Staff. Tombstone recognized the voice and groaned. The Communications Officer. He silently pointed at the opposite door, the one that opened out onto the flag mess, and quietly slid out from behind his desk and headed for it. With any luck, the Chief of Staff could handle whatever it was that the communications officer wanted while Tombstone snuck out the back door.

As he put his hand on the doorknob, he glanced back and saw the Chief of Staff reading a message. The expression on COS's face made him pause.

"I'll see he gets this immediately," COS said, and shut the TFCC door in the COMMO's face.

Is there any chance I'll get to see sunlight in the near future? Sometimes I think that the Communications Officer has my quarters bugged. Tombstone sighed and walked back across the room.

"I can handle this, but you need to know what it is." His Chief of Staff handed him the message. The paper was still warm from the copy machine in Comms.

FROM: COMSEVENTHFLT

TO: CARGRU14

SUBJ: FREEDOM OF NAVIGATION OPERATIONS

1. CHINA RECENTLY INCREASING TENOR OF CLAIMS THAT SOUTH CHINA SEA VICINITY SPRATLY ISLANDS SUBJECT TO TERRITORIAL CLAIMS. IN LIGHT OF RECENT EVENTS, ESSENTIAL THAT THE UNITED STATES ESTABLISH CLEAR EVIDENCE OF INTENTIONS.

2. CARGRU14 WILL COMMENCE FREEDOM OF NAVIGATION (FON) OPERATIONS VIC SOUTH CHINA SEA IMMEDIATELY UPON RECEIPT. FORWARD OPERATIONAL INTENTIONS TO ORIG WITHIN EIGHT HOURS.

FON ops were intended to establish the right of any nation to travel in and operate on, under, and above international waters. The rest of the message laid out the general geographic area *Jefferson* was to patrol and ordered CVBG 14 to forward his intentions to Seventh Fleet immediately. Tombstone scrawled his initials on the message to indicate that he'd read it.

"I'll have our response planned and the message drafted for your signature when you return," the Chief of Staff said, and opened the door for Tombstone to leave. Gratefully, the Commander of CARGRU14 escaped toward the flight deck.

The Chief of Staff watched him go, amused. A surface warfare officer himself, he understood but never completely sympathized with the longing aviator admirals always felt for their aircraft. Every one that he'd ever worked with eventually seemed to wilt when kept below decks and away from the cockpit for too long.

Part of the COS's job was to keep the Admiral functioning at peak performance. If that included making sure he got to play hooky from his desk once in a while, then it was up to the Chief of Staff to make sure the Admiral got an occasional flight deck fix.

However, the CARGRU operations officer, also a pilot, was

several years junior to COS. Humming quietly to himself, COS walked across the passageway and passed the message on. Not *every* aviator on the carrier was going to get an immediate look at the JAST birds.

1710 local (Zulu -7)
Flight Deck

Technicians and flight decks personnel crowded around the two aircraft, a rainbow of colors splashed against the dark, gritty gray of the flight deck nonskid. Each jersey color denoted the wearer's role in the complex ballet that made up flight deck operations: brown for plane captains, red for ordnance techs, purple for fueling crews, and green for maintenance technicians. A few yellow shirts worn by the catapult officers and the aircraft handlers that directed the flow of traffic across the deck were sprinkled through the crowd.

The Brown Shirts crowded close to the aircraft, taking righteous possession of it now that it was shut down on the deck. At the perimeter of the crowd, aviators in green flight suits tried to edge their way closer. But sometimes rank just didn't count. The enlisted technicians ignored them, forming an unyielding phalanx of backs that blocked the aviators from the aircraft.

All but one aviator.

The crowd parted to let Rear Admiral Magruder approach the aircraft. He walked up to it and ran one hand over a side panel, reflexively checking to see if the panel was dogged down tightly. The smooth paint gleamed, untarnished by months of sitting on the flight deck exposed to the elements like the other birds under his command. That would change soon, he knew. He touched it lightly and felt the odd ripples in the airframe's skin.

"Admiral! They look good, don't they?" How long had it been since he'd heard that voice, Tombstone thought. It could have been centuries, and he knew he'd still remember it. He'd heard it too many times, on too many dangerous patrols—and it'd saved his life more than once. One of the things an aviator never forgets is the voice of his regular wingman. Tombstone turned around.

"Captain Wayne," he said, reaching out to shake Batman's free hand. Neither man saluted, since they were uncovered, although a helmet dangled from Batman's left hand. "Good to see you again! Was that you that boltered?"

Batman smiled. "Not on your life, Admiral. That was Mouse, there," he said, gesturing toward a pilot surrounded by a flock of enlisted technicians. "Just a youngster out of Pax River. Three cruises under his belt, though, and a damned fine reputation as a test pilot. I caught the three-wire—think I got an okay from the VF-95 LSO."

Aircraft landings were graded okay, marginal, or fault. An okay pass was a clean trap, with the aircraft snagging one of the arresting wires without major problems on the approach or landing. A Marginal grade indicated some weaknesses in the landing that could have resulted in a mishap, while a fault was an evolution entirely below standards with great potential for disaster. Grading was conducted by the LSOs, or Landing Signals Officers, who were stationed off to the port side of the flight deck, slightly below on a catwalk.

"Who else did you bring with you?" Tombstone asked, scanning the crowd for unfamiliar faces. "We'll have to wait on the formal introductions, I guess. Looks like your boys want to show off their new toys."

"Well, there's Mouse, of course. He's a lieutenant commander, lead test pilot on the program. His RIO is that ugly fucker over by the nosewheel. Lieutenant Connally Dershowitz. They call him Bouncer. You can see why."

"No kidding," Tombstone replied. The RIO Batman pointed out must be barely within the height and weight standards for flying Tomcats. "What's he run, about two hundred and fifty pounds?"

"About that. He bench presses around four hundred pounds. I wouldn't want to piss him off. We've got one other pilot-RIO team as well. They flew out on the COD."

"Where's your RIO?"

"I was hoping to talk to you about that. Right after I talked to you, I found out the dumb bitch broke her leg. I let her have a couple of days of leave, to catch the last trace of snow out in Aspen, and she pulls this shit."

"So you're short a RIO. Damn, Batman, bad enough that I have to provide AVGAS and water for your boondoggle—now you want to cadge a RIO out of my Air Wing as well? Besides, I thought this hotshot stuff was too complicated for a mere Fleet Tomcat aviator."

"The backseat's not so bad," Batman argued. "A few improvements, but nothing a sharp RIO can't catch on to in a few lessons. Bouncer can talk her through it in a few hours."

"Her?"

Batman had the good grace to look slightly ashamed. "Yeah, well—you see, it's like this, Admiral. I've gotten used to flying with a female backseater. Bulldog—that's my regular RIO—broke me of a number of bad habits in the last six months. I was just thinking that there's enough going on for a pilot that it'd be counterproductive to have to get used to a male voice in my ear, seeing's how I'm all trained up to expect some sweet young thing cooing about missile ranges."

"You said your RIO was called *Bulldog*?"

"Well, she doesn't exactly coo. Don't tell her I said that if you ever meet her, okay? But this *is* going to take a smart RIO to catch on quick. I was hoping you might let me borrow Tomboy."

"You want AVGAS *and* my own RIO?" Tomboy still flew every qualification flight Tombstone managed to squeeze into his schedule. Since she'd been his RIO in combat, it seemed only natural. Unwillingly, though, Tombstone found that he understood what Batman meant about having to get used to new voices from the backseat. And Tomboy was one of the smartest RIOs he'd ever come across. She'd had as much, if not more, combat experience than any man in her squadron.

"You can ask her," Tombstone said finally. "If she says yes, and on the condition that she stills flies with me when I go up, you can borrow her. Understood?"

"Roger that, Admiral!" A strange expression played across Batman's face. "Um, I'll look out for her, Tombstone. You know? I mean—well—if she's *your* RIO—"

"She's just an aviator, Batman," Tombstone said, answering the question that Batman would not dare ask directly. "Now how about these queer Tomcats?" he continued, intentionally changing the subject.

Batman nodded and looked relieved. Message received and rogered for, Tombstone thought.

"What do you think?" Batman said, gesturing to the aircraft.

"Nice paint job. If it works as good as it looks, we can keep you busy."

"Let me show you the radome. We'll put some power on her, and I'll show you what the new avionics look like." Batman led Tombstone around to the nose of the aircraft with a proprietorial air.

"Hold it! Great shot!" Tombstone heard someone say. Irritated, he glanced back toward the voice. He'd be damned if one of his Public Affairs Officers, or PAOs, was going to turn one of his few moments of freedom into a photo opportunity. The cruise book would have to go without recording this historic event.

He caught sight of the photographer and groaned. Somewhere on his desk, he was sure, was a message detailing the composition of the small civilian press pool that had arrived with the two JAST birds on the COD. It was one thing to tell his own PAO staff to get stuffed—another thing entirely to offend the civilian media.

As the photographer knelt on the flight deck to steady his camera, another figure came into view. Tombstone felt a red flush creep up his neck and caught the trace of amusement on Batman's face.

"You could have told me, asshole," he hissed at his former wingman.

"And miss this look on your face, Admiral? Oh, no, Stoney, I don't think so. Besides, I thought you told me you had a hotshot staff? Didn't they brief you on the press?"

"Damn it, Batman, I want to see your ass in my cabin as soon as you get these birds tucked in and tied down!"

A woman stepped forward and held out her hand. "Hello, Tombstone—or should I say, Admiral Magruder?" she said warmly, pitching her voice low so that no one else could catch the words. "It's been a very long time."

He said the only words that came to mind. "Welcome aboard, Miss Drake." From the amused look on her face, she knew exactly what that meant.

2000 local (Zulu -7)
Flag Briefing Room

The demands of planning a response to the FON message kept him from seeing Pamela Drake again immediately, but Tombstone was irritated to find that she was constantly on his mind. He ignored the vivid recollections of her that kept crowding in, distracting him from the brief in progress, but thoughts of the round fullness of her heavy breasts, the smooth, flat lines of her belly gently flaring to the boyish hips, kept intruding. There'd been times when they were together that he could barely tell where she ended and his own body began, so closely locked together had they been. He shook his head, trying to clear his thoughts, and glanced at the other officers surrounding the cloth-covered briefing table. Not a one of them would believe that their Admiral, with his legendary reputation for an impassive face and calm demeanor, was sitting there thinking about the last time he'd made love to Miss Pamela Drake.

The lights in the briefing room came up as the intelligence officer finished the slide show portion of the brief. Two ISs darted forward and started unrolling a small-scale chart taped to the top of the chalkboard. It displayed the South China Sea and the littoral countries that bordered it. Running from east to west, a rectangle bisected the middle of the South China Sea.

"Okay, here's what we recommend, Admiral. This box takes us east to twelve miles off the coast of Vietnam, then due west back out to the Spratly Islands. One day in, another day back out. A little longer if we linger on Vietnam's coast." Busby used a pencil-sized laser pointer to trace out the proposed course.

"It accomplishes what Seventh Fleet wants us to do, without getting us too far from the Spratly Islands. I like that. Doing FON ops off China's coast, moving up north further, might be what they had in mind, though," Tombstone remarked. He stared at the narrow rectangle on the chart. Something about it seemed familiar—no, not familiar, but it reminded him of something else he'd seen recently.

"We thought of that, Admiral, but we don't recommend it at this time. There has to be some connection between the political maneuvering in the UN and what we've witnessed down here. The Chinese are just too accomplished at this game for it to be coincidence. Moving north to China's coast puts us two days away from the Spratly Islands," the CARGRU operations officer answered.

What is it, damn it? Why do I get an uneasy feeling just looking at the box? It's not any particular operation that I can remember. The only thing I can think of is that deuced fjord we once used to hide the carrier in up around Norway, but that's not it either. Those double lines around the box—is that it?

"A more northern oparea would put us in the vicinity of the Paracel Islands," Tombstone said, stalling for time while he tried to let whatever random association his mind had made float to the top of his thoughts. "If something odd is going on in the Spratly Islands, I'd lay odds that the Paracels are having their share of unexplained events as well."

The Paracels were a small group of islands located in the northern half of the South China Sea. Slightly more prominent and stable than the tiny Spratly chain, the islands were also claimed by China, with Vietnam and Taiwan disputing their ownership. China was two hundred miles to the north of the Paracels, and Vietnam slightly closer to the west. Taiwan was almost six hundred miles to the northeast.

"We might gather some information, but we'd also be mounting a more direct challenge to China's exclusion zone," the CARGRU Operations Officer chimed in. "It's one thing to be eight hundred miles to the south of her coast, another to be cruising around the twelve-mile limit. Our best guess is that Seventh Fleet—as well as his bosses—isn't quite ready to push China that hard. From the box Commander Busby is proposing, we can still reach out and touch the Paracels anytime we need to. Keeping the battle group around the Spratly Islands and testing the twelve mile limit with Vietnam seemed like a good compromise between doing FON and not limiting our options in the South China Sea."

"Additionally," Busby added, "Vietnam is currently in a state of flux."

"When in the last fifty years has it *not* been?" Tombstone said. "But you're right—Vietnam knows that whatever her relationship with the United States, she will have to live with China as her neighbor. With all the issues surrounding normalization of relations with Vietnam, it might not hurt to remind them that the United States has the power to intervene in Southeast Asia's backyard. Okay, let's go with this plan. Starting tomorrow morning."

"CAG," Tombstone said, turning to Captain Cervantes. "Let's talk about that flight schedule. I want to make damned sure we're not sending the wrong signals at any point. And make sure your pilots understand how critical the twelve-mile limit is. Under *no circumstances* are they to go wandering off inside it—in fact, just for safety's sake, let's set the limit at fifteen miles for aircraft. We can creep up to the twelve-mile limit a lot more safely at fifteen knots with surface ships than at four hundred knots with an aircraft."

The CAG looked slightly put out. *As I would in his shoes,* Tombstone thought. Still, he was not prepared for what followed.

"I'll brief the aircrews personally, Admiral. But we'll also need to make sure the surface ships are just as careful. Not all of the battle group," CAG said, picking his words carefully, "has always understood how critical that limit is. A shoot-out is the last thing we need."

For a moment, Tombstone was tempted to dismiss CAG's remarks as simply evidence of the rivalry that had always existed between aviators and the "shoes." He glanced around the room and saw a number of officers studiously examining the deck. Then it hit him.

Vincennes. Early on in her career, the cruiser had shot down that airbus in the Persian Gulf. Evidence was now surfacing that *Vincennes* might have been inside Iran's territorial waters when she'd fired. If the real truth about her location had ever been fully determined, it was classified at the highest levels.

"All of our assets will be very clear on my orders, CAG. And thank you for bringing up that point."

And now I know what it was I was trying to recall. The shoot-out at the OK Corral in Tombstone, Arizona. Wyatt Earp's last battle. The diagram I saw last night had those same double lines marking off the boundaries of the corral, tracing out Earp's path to the showdown.

Tombstone had never been superstitious, and he wasn't about to admit that the strange coincidence of the graphics in a book and the diagram of a FON box had anything in common. This was no calculated warning, no psychic premonition. It was merely more evidence that the human brain was hardwired in ways that might never be fully understood.

Just the same, whatever else he could roll downhill to his staff and the COS, the matter of the *Vincennes* required his personal attention and the weight of the stars on his collar to back up his orders. Sometime in the next sixteen hours, Rear Admiral Magruder was going to have to have a very serious talk with *Vincennes*.

CHAPTER 7
Friday, 28 June

The moment came eventually, as Tombstone knew it would. He stepped out of his cabin and into the Flag Mess. Pamela was standing next to the coffeepot, carefully pouring the thick, hot brew into an insulated plastic coffee cup, holding the lid wedged between two fingers.

"Care for a cup, Admiral?" she asked politely. Her eyes took him in carefully, noted his discomfort, and flashed amusement.

"Thank you, Miss Drake." He held out his own mug, emblazoned with the VF-95 squadron insignia. He dreaded the moment when she would finish pouring the coffee, when he would have to decide whether to stay and talk with her or retreat to his cabin.

Damn it! It's my ship, my battle group! My world, the one she wouldn't share me with. If anyone ought to be squirming, it's her. He took a deep breath finding some nerve in his anger.

"Miss Drake is an old friend," he remarked to no one in particular. "I think we have a lot to catch up on, don't we, Miss Drake? Care to join me in my cabin for a few minutes?"

"Thank you, Admiral. Yes, it has been a long time, hasn't it?"

Tombstone opened the door to his quarters and held it for her to enter. He glanced back into the Flag Mess. The four staff officers seated there pointedly had other things to do, other places to look, than at their admiral.

Great. So much for my reputation. If she leaves in less than five minutes, they'll say she turned me down or I was after a quickie. And any longer than five minutes will assuredly make the grapevine just as quickly.

Well, there was no avoiding it. Hadn't been since the moment Pamela had set foot on his flight deck. And he would be damned if he'd let himself think about her in any way other than strictly professional.

Pamela was a senior correspondent for ACN. If she hadn't wanted to come on this assignment, she wouldn't have. Wondering about whether or not she'd known he was here, and whether or not there was any personal motive behind her presence, wasn't acceptable. It had to be cleared up here and now.

The last time they'd seen each other, they'd finally come to the realization that there was no future to their relationship. That understanding, along with Tombstone's growing attraction to Tomboy, had seemed to end it. Then what was Pamela doing here, he wondered. Just another assignment? Or second thoughts?

He followed Pamela into his cabin and let the door click shut behind them.

Pamela was already seated on the couch in the starboard side of his cabin. Her coffee cup sat on the table in front of it.

"I can offer you a real coffee cup, if you prefer," he said, for lack of anything else to say. "Something without a lid and a football team logo on it."

"Thanks, Stoney, but this is fine. I went to a lot of trouble to remember to bring it. Those paper ones the Flag Mess usually has—I always spill something somewhere."

He sat down in the comfortable chair that sat at right angles to the couch. "It's good to see you again," he said, slightly surprised at himself. He somehow expected that breaking their engagement would have miraculously broken the compelling attraction that had always existed between them. It hadn't, though. He felt the familiar sense of urgency and expectancy, a taut, demanding urge to bridge the gap between them. His fingers remembered silky hair slipping through his hands and cascading over his chest, the delicate texture of skin on skin, and the lush curve of her body from hips to chest.

"How's the admiral business?" Her voice, casually friendly, contained no hint that she was remembering him in the same way. He forced himself back to reality, abandoning the memories almost regretfully.

"Busy. I haven't flown in months. And ACN—you're still their star, from what we see out here," he said, matching her conversational tone. Just two old friends who'd once been something more, catching up on old times, he decided. He decided to relax. He could do this—he could.

"I have my moments with them. It's a full-time commitment still." Her eyes met his, and he felt her carefully assess his mood. Damn, he'd almost forgotten how she always could seem to read his thoughts!

Despite his best intentions, he felt the first tinges of a flush creep up from his neck toward his cheeks and heard a voice that sounded exactly like his own ask, "That answers my question, then. I was wondering if there were any other reason for you taking this assignment."

Her answer came quickly, as though she'd rehearsed an answer. "Like getting a chance to see you? That was part of it, I admit. I'll never turn down that opportunity."

"You already did," he said. He heard the anger and hurt in his voice and swore silently.

"I turned down marriage and commitment, not you. Oh,

Stoney, we've been through this a thousand times! It never would have worked! My schedule with ACN keeps me on the road at least half of the year. Between trips, I'm either trying to recover from jet lag or fighting off the latest foreign bug I've caught."

"Alone." It was almost a question.

"Alone, yes. But not obsessed with wondering when the chaplain is going to knock on my door and tell me I'm a widow. Stoney, the places you go, the flying, the killing, what you do for a living—it's too much. I could deal with the flying, if it were for a civilian airliner, but not the continual combat. Every time some pissant little spot on the globe decides to act out its fantasies of world domination, you're in the middle of it. I'd never be able to do what I do for worrying about you."

"And you don't worry now?"

"You know I do. But for the most part, I simply try to forget you exist. But pass up the chance to see you again—no, I couldn't do that."

It was his turn to study her. The brilliant green eyes, sleek dark hair—a few faint lines had crept up around the corners of her eyes since the last time they'd met. Otherwise, she could have been the same young reporter he'd first met and fallen in love with back when he was a lieutenant commander.

"I almost wish you had," he said finally.

The buzz of his telephone saved him from having to explain. He picked it up and said, "Admiral."

"Admiral, sorry to bother you. I thought you'd want to know that the *Vincennes* is setting flight quarters to launch her helo. You asked their CO to see you this afternoon, I believe."

Tombstone was faintly grateful to the cruiser CO for giving him a graceful way to terminate his visit. "Thank you, COS. I'll be right out."

He replaced the receiver in its cradle and remained standing next to his desk. "Pamela, it's been good to see you again. I won't deny that. But knowing how things stand between us, I think you'll understand if I don't spend too much time with you."

He saw her face go stiff and wondered if a similar trick of expressions had been what'd earned him his call sign, Tombstone. "I understand completely, Admiral. You're not willing to settle for what I can offer. Let's just leave it at that, shall we?" She picked up her cup and walked to the door, her stiff back stilling the sway of her hips to a gentle twitch.

"I hope I can," he said softly as he watched her go.

0930 local (Zulu -7)
Admiral's Cabin

Captain Killington, Commanding Officer of the *USS Vincennes*, arrived thirty minutes later. Tombstone stayed seated at his desk as COS showed the man into his office. He motioned to a chair in front of his desk.

As the surface warfare officer settled into the sturdy Navy chair, Tombstone looked him over carefully, searching for the key to the man's character. Their professional paths had crossed several times, but Tombstone knew little about the man personally. The Aegis CO had assumed command of *Vincennes* only two months before the deployment, when the prior Commanding Officer suffered a stroke at sea one night. As a result, he'd missed most of the workup and exercise schedule that would have given Tombstone a chance to assess the man.

Captain Killington was several inches shorter than Tombstone, with a solid, massive build. His hair was light brown, with no trace of gray or thinning, carefully trimmed and brushed back from his face. His eyes were an almost colorless shade of brown, one that would either be called hazel or warm spit.

According to his professional reputation, he was an aggressive operator, one who clearly envisioned stars on his collar in the not-too-distant future. Most of his shore-duty tours had been in DC rather than in the Fleet. The other surface warfare officers regarded him as a politician who believed himself to be a warrior.

Tombstone held out his hand, and Captain Killington took it firmly. For a moment, Tombstone wondered whether the man would try to apply hard pressure and make him wince. Surely he wouldn't be that stupid around the man who signed his fitness reports, and who would make recommendations that might affect whether or not he would eventually wear stars.

"Thanks for coming over on short notice, Captain," Tombstone said.

"My pleasure, Admiral. I was prepared for the request." Killington smiled smugly and patted a manila folder he carried.

"Oh, really?" For a moment, Tombstone felt off-balance. "And why was that?"

"Well, it was obvious to me, Admiral, based on your last orders. Conducting these FON ops is going to take us to the edge of Vietnamese territorial waters. I knew you'd want to know what steps we were taking, what precautions we'd recommend in constrained waters. That's why I had my staff—" *You idiot, you don't have a staff! I have a staff—you have your normal complement of department heads and divisions officers*, Tombstone thought,"—prepare these charts. Of course, we're prepared to address any obvious contingencies as well."

"I see. And by contingencies, you mean . . . ?"

The Aegis CO leaned forward in his chair, his voice dropping lower. "We're going to be in mighty close, Admiral. We could be closer."

"Closer than twelve miles?"

"Not officially."

"I see," Tombstone said for the second time.

Now I understand why I heard my uncle use that phrase so often. Back when he sat in this chair, he must have learned it was a good way to buy time when you're trying to deal with an idiot! He could have told me that when he came to my change of command. Just a little family admiral secret, passed down from the man who is now Seventh Fleet to his favorite nephew.

"I'm glad you came prepared, Captain. That will make this entire meeting more fruitful. May I see your briefing charts?" Tombstone held out his hand.

"I can explain each one if—"

"Just the charts, if you please."

Reluctantly, the surface warfare officer handed over the manila folder.

Tombstone leafed through the printouts and diagrams. Part of the information was indeed useful—descriptions of additional precautions the battle group should take to detect missile dangers from the coastline, pop-up aircraft, and neutral traffic. It was the last two diagrams that worried him. They contained detailed descriptions of possible shore targets along the coast, as well as a range chart showing increased early alert warning capability if the Aegis were to proceed into six miles off the coast.

"According to this, you'd be in full view of anyone on the coast," Tombstone remarked.

"They'll be able to see us anyway. Even twelve miles away, the carrier will be visible. The masts of the smaller ships, too."

"And you're recommending this as an OPPLAN?"

"I'm recommending it as an approach to exerting our rights of innocent passage. The law lets us intrude into their territorial waters if we're in transit between two international waters and not conducting military operations."

"But you would be, according to this. Conducting military operations, I mean."

"They'd never be able to prove it. I'd leave my helos airborne, with orders to bingo to the carrier for refueling."

"Well. Captain, you've certainly put some thought into this," Tombstone said, anger starting to grow. CAG had been right—the Aegis was potentially more of a problem than CAG's aircrews. "And I appreciate your initiative in sharing it. So let me explain my intentions to you, just so we're all in sync with this.

"The Aegis," Tombstone continued, "is an extremely valuable battle control platform. Your capability to manage the air war, as well as the assets of the other cruisers in the battle group, is vital in conflict. What I am concerned about is whether or not you are incompetent, stupid, or absolutely fucking insane."

Killington had started to beam at Tombstone's words. His mouth dropped open at the last sentence, and his face froze into an incongruous mask of self-approval and shock.

"But—" he started.

"Shut up and listen if you want to stay in command for more than another three seconds. *We are not at war, Captain!* My message contained no secret message that you should run through your secret decoder ring. We are simply going to patrol back and forth in the box I've laid out for you, *staying outside the twelve-mile limit!* And the first time I catch your happy little ass and your boat closer than fifteen miles away from the coast, I'm going to helo over to your ship, walk up on your bridge, and publicly castrate you. And *then* I will relieve you of your command. Do you understand me, you idiot?"

The Aegis CO choked out a "Yes, Admiral."

"From now on, I am going to be taking particular note of the operations involving *Vincennes*. Every time I look at the screen in combat, I'd better see your ship so tightly in the middle of her screen position that it'd take a crowbar to pry you loose. There had better never be a question in my mind about what you are doing, where you are going, or what you are thinking. Is that absolutely clear, Captain?"

This time, Killington could only nod.

"Get back to your ship. Don't let this happen again."

The Aegis CO rose and walked to the door. In the few steps that it took him to get there, he regained a portion of his composure. With his hand on the doorknob, he turned back toward Tombstone.

"I thank the admiral for taking the time to instruct me in basic rules of engagement for this part of the world. Be assured, Admiral—I won't forget our conversation." His face was carefully neutral during his statement.

"Get out, before I change my mind and relieve you now," Tombstone said in a deadly quiet tone.

CHAPTER 8
Saturday, 29 June

"We will be increasing the size of the garrison here immediately," Mein Low said. "Your logistics officer will meet with mine to discuss the details."

"May I ask why?" Bien forced a neutral tone into his voice. The ten Chinese Flankers currently on "temporary assignment" to Vietnam were already straining the resources of the small training base.

"Increased training opportunities," the Chinese officer replied. "Your men have made excellent progress in air combat. It is time to take the next logical step in this evolution and begin experimenting with squadron-level tactics rather than one-on-one combat. To support that, I need more than one squadron here."

"I will have to discuss this with my superiors, of course," Bien said politely. "It will take some time to make preparations for more aircraft."

"The next squadron will arrive next Tuesday," Mein Low said, as though his Vietnamese counterpart had not spoken.

"I'm not certain—"

"Four days from now, Bien." Mein Low fixed Bien with an impassive, vaguely threatening look.

So finally the Chinese show their hand! Bien thought. *I warned the government against this very scenario. Once China has a presence inside a country, they can be very difficult to dislodge. They are the perpetual unwanted houseguests who far overstay their welcome—haven't we at least learned that during the last twelve centuries? And to refuse this additional deployment will be an invitation for them to extend their presence by force.*

The politicians who were eager to consolidate their recent gains in power had been eager to take advantage of the advanced airpower training the Chinese had offered. Bien's concerns had been dismissed as old-fashioned, his fears as paranoia.

"In addition to more advanced training for your countrymen," Mein Low purred, "there will be other exciting opportunities to advance your regional security. Our squadrons will also be deploying to Malaysia and Brunei, to assist their programs. Within months, you will have the capability to make the South China Sea an impenetrable fortress. Never again will you see the Americans invading your soil, destroying your unity! With our help, you will be invulnerable."

I heard those arguments six months ago, when your first aircraft arrived. It was that very concept that sold the politicians on this entire evolution—that we would develop the capabilities to withstand another American invasion. But if the Soviets were difficult masters, how much worse the Chinese will be!

But there was nothing to be won jousting with the Chinese commander, not when his own politicians failed to see the dangers. Bien bowed politely, leaving Mein Low's office deeply worried about the future of his country's independence.

1100 local (Zulu -7)
Hornet 401
Spratly Islands, South China Sea

Most of the battle group wheeled to the west, steadied on a course of three hundred, and headed toward the coast of Vietnam. *Jefferson* turned into the wind, generating thirty-five knots of wind across the deck, and set flight quarters.

Inside Hornet 401, Major Frederick Hammersmith, call sign Thor, cycled his stick forward, back, and then side to side, testing his aircraft control surfaces. He watched the Yellow Shirt and nodded when he got a thumbs-up. He shoved the throttle forward, coming to full military power. The Hornet vibrated eagerly as he went to afterburners.

Thor returned the Yellow Shirt's salute and settled the small of his back against what passed for a lumbar support pad in his seat. Two seconds later, the steam-driven catapult screamed forward, accelerated the Hornet to 130 knots in just under four seconds, and threw it off the forward end of the carrier.

The Hornet dropped sickeningly. Thor felt the usual second of sheer terror, wondering whether he had enough airspeed to fly. Of all the things that could go wrong in carrier aviation, a "soft cat" was his personal nightmare.

With gas and a combat load of weapons, a Hornet weighed 49,244 pounds. In order to loft it into the air, the steam piston below the flight deck had to be charged to the correct pressure. Too little, and the fighter would simply dribble off the bow of the ship, unable to claw its way into the air. Too much, and the catapult might snap his wheel strut off, and the rest of the aircraft would do a final impersonation of a NASCAR stock car crash, probably sweeping the handler and several other technicians off the flight deck as well.

Marine F/A-18 squadrons had been deploying off of carriers for several years now, as more and more often amphibious ships were married up with carrier battle groups for those strange conflicts the Pentagon insisted on calling "military operations other than war" or MOOTW. The strange acronym was pronounced "moot-wah." Monitoring the precarious political situation around the Spratly Island fell into that nebulous mission.

Seconds after the cat shot, Thor felt the Hornet grab air and steady up. As his speed increased, he hauled back on the stick to gain altitude. Leveling off at five thousand feet, he waited for his wingman to join him.

Thirty seconds later, Hornet 307 snuggled up to him on the right. James "Killer" Colburne waved. Thor clicked his radio once and pointed left, to the west. Killer nodded and followed 401 into a gentle turn.

Thor waited until they were steady on course and then made his next call.

"Redcrown, Jigsaw One checking in."

"Roger, Jigsaw One, we hold you, flight of two," the Operations Specialist on the Aegis cruiser said. The brief exchange told Thor and his wingman that their IFF transmitters were working, and the Aegis would be able to distinguish them from enemy aircraft if necessary.

Thor clicked his mike once in response and then settled down for a routine CAP mission. Whatever had tried to shoot at the Viking the previous day would find that shooting at a Hornet—and a Marine one, at that—was a whole different ball game. Especially one that carried a few cluster bombs snugged up on the center pylon.

Vincennes, Tombstone noted, was meticulously locked into the center of her screen position. After the initial flurry of maneuvers, she settled in fifteen thousand yards dead ahead of the carrier. Tombstone doubted that life was very pleasant for the officers and crew of the Aegis cruiser.

An hour later, Thor was shifting uneasily in his ejection seat. "Jeez, my back's already aching," he complained to Killer over tactical. "Twenty minutes to get out here, and forty minutes of clockwise circling. Just for the fun of it, I'm going to go the other direction for a while."

"That's what we get for being disciplined. If we were in the Navy, we'd be able to have some fun out here."

"Yeah, but we're not. Thank God for that, anyway. Still, the colonel's obsessed with neat little circles in the sky. It's getting to be a pain. Man flies a jet, he oughta be able to have some fun with it."

"Guess he doesn't see it that way."

And the Colonel *did* see what his pilots were up to while on CAP. Thor had seen his commanding officer park his tail end in CDC and watch a scope, watching his pilots cut neat, symmetrical circles in the sky.

"Take a leak. That helps sometimes," his wingman offered.

Thor snorted. "I'd just as soon wait. Wish Grumman built these birds instead of McDonnell-Douglass. At least they have the common sense to put relief tubes in their aircraft. I hate these damned piddle packs." MD's solution to the inevitable calls of nature was a small plastic Baggie with elastic on one end. Might as well use a Coke bottle, Thor thought, disgusted.

Suddenly, the E-2C Hawkeye NFO's voice cut in on the radio static. "Homeplate, Snoopy 601. Strangers, bearing 318, range 130 miles. Negative mode four IFF."

Unidentified aircraft, ones that did not broadcast the IFF modes and codes that would mark it as a friendly military aircraft. For a moment, Thor was interested. It was, he immediately decided, probably a commercial airliner, heading southwest and hugging the coast. He waited. So far, there was nothing on his own radar.

"Roger, Snoopy. Hold that contact on course 135, speed four hundred."

Well, this was getting interesting. The unknown contact's course would take it directly toward the battle group. Thor's adrenaline kicked in with a little tingle.

It still *could* be a commercial airliner, headed across the South China Sea to Brunei or Malaysia, but most of the commercial routes curved slightly to the north, following a great circle route as the shortest distance between two points. He glanced at his radar and noted that the E-2C's contact was now entered into LINK, the electronic data-sharing and targeting system that let the battle group elements share radar information.

"Break, break, Jigsaw One, Homeplate," the Operations Specialist said, indicating a change of callups.

"Jigsaw One," Thor answered.

"Roger, come to new course 325. Request you close and VID contact in question. Jigsaw 2, maintain current station."

"Roger." Thor pulled out of his gentle CAP turn and headed northwest to intercept the contact and visually identify it.

"You get all the fun," he heard his wingman mutter over the tactical circuit.

1145 local (Zulu -7)
Combat Direction Center
USS Jefferson

"You got any modes and codes on that contact at all?" the carrier TAO asked the operations specialist.

"Negative, ma'am. It's off the normal COMMAIR corridor by at least a hundred miles. No modes at all."

The TAO felt vaguely uneasy. A senior lieutenant commander, an E-2C Naval Flight Officer herself, she'd heard the slight change in pitch in her airborne counterpart's voice. So far, there was no real cause for alarm, but experience born from thousands of hours in the back of an E-2C kept setting off alarms in her mind. Better safe than sorry, she finally decided.

"Get the alert five Tomcats in the air," she said to her assistant. He nodded and reached for the 1MC microphone to broadcast the order. Seconds later, she heard scurrying feet pounding down the passageway as the Air Boss and his crew headed for Pri-Fly.

She picked up the telephone and punched the button for the TFCC TAO. If the world was about to go to shit, she wanted to make sure the admiral's watch team was awake.

1150 local
TFCC

"Okay, what've we got?" Tombstone asked as he stepped into TFCC.

"Nothing solid yet, Admiral. The E-2 picked up an unidentified air contact, and a Hornet's vectoring to intercept. Alert five Tomcats are on the cat—excuse me, sir, airborne," the Flag TAO corrected himself as the distinctive grumble of the forward catapult launching aircraft interrupted his summary. The TAO rolled his trackball and positioned the pointer near the symbol for the contact.

Tombstone studied the screen, watching the symbol representing the Hornet track slowly across it. If it was a military aircraft, then it was probably Vietnamese. Its speed leader pointed directly back to the Vietnamese coast, near a major military airfield. Vietnamese fighters had every right to be in international airspace, and were probably just flying out toward the battle group to exercise their right to do so.

The Vietnamese air force flew a collection of Russian-built fighters. Until recently, the most advanced airframe in their inventory was the MiG-23F Flogger, a smaller and less capable version of the airframe reserved for Russia's own use. The single-pilot fighter had limited-range "Jay Bird" radars, with little or no capability beyond fifteen nautical miles. With no infrared or Doppler tracking capabilities, and carrying only the ancient Soviet Atoll and Aphid air-to-air missiles, the export version of the fighter was considerably less threatening than the original model. Russia stopped building Floggers in 1980, although Tombstone recalled that India still built some versions of the airframe under license from Russia. The MiG-29 Fulcrum and the SU-27 Flanker had replaced most of the Floggers in the Soviet inventory.

However, Vietnam had upped the ante in mid-1994, when it had taken delivery of a squadron of SU-27 Flankers. The Flanker was a Russian-built multipurpose fighter aircraft used for air intercept by the former Soviet Union's ground defense forces. There were six versions of the advanced fighter, all produced at Komsomolsk in the Khabarovsk Territory. While the basic airframe had entered service in the Soviet Union in

1984, new versions of the Flanker were reportedly under development. Interestingly enough, in 1991 the fighter had been observed undertaking ground attack roles as well.

The Flanker was also the first Soviet aircraft to make a non-VSTOL landing on a ship. That particular development had caused immense concern in the U.S. military establishment, since the Soviet Union had relied on its land-launched aircraft as the mainstay of its air power until then. Being tied to land bases naturally limited Soviet strategic options in pursuing domination of large areas of the world, and had helped to limit efforts at expansionism. But with a potent carrier air wing and fighters in its inventory, the Soviet Union could dramatically expand its theater of influence—and combat. Fortunately, the Evil Empire had collapsed under its own corruption before developing a truly workable carrier aviation program. Engineering details, such as developing a reliable catapult steam system, had stymied them long enough.

Equipped with afterburners and a relatively traditional airframe containing titanium components but no advanced stealth composite materials, the Flanker was a tough, versatile fighter. It would have been a deadly adversary flying from a carrier, and was no less potent as a land-based fighter in the relatively constrained waters of the South China Sea.

Still, Tombstone reminded himself, this was Vietnam's backyard. There was no good reason for the country not to conduct surveillance on an American battle group in their pond. Given Seventh Fleet's orders to exercise FON *peacefully*, it would not be appropriate to provoke a confrontation unless the battle group's safety was at stake.

"VID and watch him. Unless his wings are dirty, I'm not opposed to a flyover look-see," Tombstone said finally.

"Yes, Admiral. The Hornet should be in position any minute now." The two aircraft were closing in on each other at a thousand knots.

"Tomcat 201, airborne," Tombstone heard a woman's voice drawl. Tomboy, flying as RIO in the alert five. He felt a momentary irritation that he hadn't known she was launching, and then realized his feeling was ridiculous. Why would they have told him who the alert five crew was? And, to be honest, if it had been anyone else, he wouldn't have cared.

"Homeplate, Jigsaw One." Another RIO's voice cut in on the circuit, a hard edge of excitement in the tone. "This ain't no MiG! It's an Su-27—a Flanker, two-seater version. Wings are clean—no weapons on this boy—and Chinese insignia on the fuselage and tail. I'm moving off to his right, about five hundred yards away. Looks like he's headed your way," the Hornet conducting the intercept said.

"Roger, Jigsaw One. Escort him on in," the calm voice of the carrier TAO answered.

"Chinese!" Tombstone said thoughtfully. "I'd heard there were some Chinese aircraft down there with a detachment conducting training, but what are they doing flying operational missions with Flankers out of Vietnam?"

In 1991, Tombstone recalled, China'd taken delivery of the first eight Flankers. Since then, the remainder of the first order of twenty-two had been delivered. Intell sources believed that China might buy up to twenty-eight more of the agile, fast fighters before Russia closed the door on foreign sales. Other sources reported that China was developing her own prototype advanced fighter, code-named the F-10.

It's supposed to be years away from being fully operational, Tombstone thought. *But that's what I thought about the JAST program, too, and I've got two of them sitting on my deck right now. No sure bets on anything these days.*

"This would be the Flanker-C or -IB—those are the two-seater versions," an intelligence officer chimed in. "The C version was primarily a trainer, but it was fully combat capable. The IB was the fighter-bomber that was supposed to deploy from their carriers. And Admiral, while the Flanker is equipped for in-flight refueling, the Chinese have had notoriously little training in it. If they wanted to come out and take a look-see at us, they'd probably rather be launching from Vietnam than China's southern coast. It's a hell of a lot closer, and they can get out and take some pictures with their onboard stores."

"Let's not get completely convinced by the tail artwork. A Flanker is a Flanker, be it Chinese or Vietnamese," Tombstone said. "Okay, ladies and gentlemen, let's play this one like pros. The Flanker—whoever he belongs to—gets a look as long as he plays nice. But keep that Hornet on him every second. Something starts looking hinky, I don't want us scrambling for cover."

A whiff of light, clean perfume floated through the air. Tombstone turned to find the source.

"Good morning, Admiral," Pamela said, stepping over the knee-knocker threshold to TFCC. "The Chief of Staff told me I'd find you in here."

"We're a little busy right now, Miss Drake," he said, momentarily grateful for the subdued red lighting in the operational center. Damn it, he couldn't afford to be distracted right now!

"I'll stay out of the way," she answered, moving over to an unoccupied corner of the tiny space.

While his nose quickly became accustomed to the scent of her perfume, and Pamela was now out of his direct line of sight, Tombstone could feel her in TFCC. Apart from the normal physical sensations and memories just thinking of her generated, her presence was doubly uncomfortable with Tomboy flying CAP on the unknown contact.

As much as he tried to deny it, there was something about the female aviator that inevitably drew his eyes to her. Tomboy had been his RIO when *Jefferson* had faced down the Russians on the Kola Peninsula, and during their mission over the

Polyarnyy submarine base. Their Tomcat had taken a hit, and they'd punched out. Tomboy had come out of it with a broken leg and an extended hospital stay.

She'd been lucky. Not every female pilot had been, he thought. Lieutenant Chris "Lobo" Hansen had been shot down on the same mission. The militia that'd captured her had gang-raped her and left her naked and shivering, displayed in a wire cage. When the Marines rescued her a few hours later, she was already deep into psychological and physical shock.

Tombstone had heard from Tomboy that Lobo had completely recovered and been sent to an instructor's billet at Top Gun school. There'd been some talk of barring her from further combat duties, but in the end the Navy did the right thing. Lobo had finished her tour as an instructor, and had received orders to VF-95 as the Safety Officer. Whatever else the Navy had learned from the integration of women into combat squadrons, it was that there was only one personnel policy that worked— treating each and every aviator as a professional. Tombstone approved.

He wondered if he'd feel the same if it had been Tomboy who'd undergone the same experience. Involuntarily, he remembered how her head barely came up to his wings on his chest, and how her voice sounded over the ICS. A pilot and regular RIO were always close. During combat, the RIO's voice merged with the pilot's thoughts, until every comment from the backseat sounded like his own mind. Was that what he was feeling? The traditional psychic bond between two aviators that depended on each other in the air? Or was it something else?

He turned his attention back to the screen and forced himself to depersonalize the aircraft on the screen. It wasn't Tomboy and Snoopy—it was Tomcat 201. If the Navy had the intestinal fortitude to insist on equal standards for its male and female pilots, the least its admirals could do was the same. Anything else would have been a slap in the face to the aviators, both male and female, that had worked so hard to make the policy succeed.

Finally, since there was nothing else that really required his attention, he turned and faced Pamela. It felt odd to be facing his old lover while listening to Tomboy's voice on the net. But when you got right down to it, why should it be difficult? What was Tomboy to him? She certainly wasn't his lover—couldn't be, not while she worked for him and they were assigned to the same ship. But whatever she was to Tombstone, he could feel her presence behind him as the arcane symbology representing her aircraft crept across the screen.

"That was her, wasn't it?" Pamela said softly.

"Who?" he managed to say. Damn her, she always *could* seem to read his thoughts.

Pamela shot him a wry grin. "Don't worry, Tombstone, nobody noticed it but me. She was your RIO last cruise, wasn't she?"

"She was a lieutenant then," he said, and then swore at himself for sounding like a blithering idiot.

"Ah," Pamela said, as though he'd just made sense.

1210 local (Zulu -7)
Hornet 401

Thor eased back on the throttle and slid behind the other aircraft. Its slipstream buffeted the light Hornet. Although the Flanker looked like it was about the same size as the Hornet, the slipstream of the Chinese fighter carried a punch.

Something about the aircraft bothered him, although he couldn't have said exactly what it was. He slid the Hornet over to the Flanker's other side and studied it carefully. Nothing unusual caught his attention.

It was, he decided, just the other pilot's attitude that seemed strange. During peacetime, most military pilots would at least wave to each other, acknowledging the bond that all airmen felt. Weeks later, if hostilities broke out, they'd do their damnedest to kill each other.

The Flanker pilot had not even glanced his way, much less proffered a friendly, universally obscene gesture. Thor shrugged. At least being able to move around a little eased the cramp in his lower back.

1220 local (Zulu -7)
Combat Direction Center
USS Jefferson

"TAO! I'm picking up communications downlink from the Flanker!" the Electronics Warfare Specialist, or EW, said over the CDC net.

"You sure?"

"Positive! Frequency, everything's right on."

"Make sure the Hornets know," the TAO snapped to the OS monitoring the two fighters, picking up the TFCC telephone again. "And get the alert 5S-3B up. That bogey is talking to somebody we don't hold contact on. That means one thing."

A submarine. Had to be. The tactical picture was really starting to stink.

Minutes later, the distinctive sounds of an S-3B engine spooling up overhead vibrated through CDC. She watched the two symbols on the large-screen display, the Hornet and the Flanker flying so close together that their symbols occasionally merged. The carrier SPS-49 radar alone couldn't have broken the two contacts apart. Only the powerful SPY-1A radar on the Aegis cruiser could positively distinguish between the two. She glanced at the information display screen to the right of her desk and confirmed her suspicion. The radar symbol displayed on the screen came from the Aegis's radar, relayed to the carrier over LINK 11.

Four minutes after the video downlink was detected, she heard the Hoover go to full military power, the roller-coaster rattle of the steam catapult, and the final surprisingly soft thud as the catapult piston reached the end of its run and tossed the S-3 into the air. Seconds later, the Operations Specialist controlling the ASW aircraft reported radar contact on Hunter 701. The S-3B vectored toward the bogey, scanning the ocean's surface with radar and FLIR, trying to find the bogey's playmate.

It could be anywhere, she thought. The bogey's altitude gave him enough horizon to cover at least a thousand square miles of ocean. Somewhere out there, the nondirectional video downlink was giving someone accurate targeting positions on the battle group. A brief shiver ran up her spine. Irrational as it might seem, she would have given anything to be airborne herself right then instead of trapped inside steel bulkheads on the 03 level of the carrier.

1222 local (Zulu -7)
Hunter 701

"We got the last one—let's get the next," Rabies said grimly.

"And he almost got us," Harness muttered from the back-seat.

"We'll stay a little further away this time," the pilot acknowledged. "One nice thing about torpedoes—don't have to get all that close to drop them."

The S-3B Viking carried two Mk-46 torpedoes on its inboard weapons stations. The high-speed torpedo was the most widely deployed lightweight torpedo in the Fleet, although its five-hundred-pound weight made the classification "lightweight" seem like a misnomer. Capable of speeds up to forty-five knots, the torpedo had a maximum range of approximately six nautical miles. Its ninety-five-pound warhead was composed of PBXN-103 high explosives.

Two Harpoons graced the outer weapons stations. At Mach 0.85, the missile could deliver a five-hundred-pound conventional high-explosive warhead against a surface ship or a surfaced submarine target seventy-five miles away. The 1,172-pound Harpoon was a massive drag on the aircraft, but each one carried enough destructive power to make the weight trade-off well worth the cost in additional gas and loss of speed.

"How far is far enough?" Harness asked.

"Max range on that surface-to-air missile is probably around six miles," the TACCO replied. "We can stand off and safely drop the torpedoes."

"We're going to get attack criteria without a MAD run?" the AW persisted. Getting accurate positioning data from the MAD book extended out the back of the S-3 required being virtually overhead the submarine.

Neither the pilot nor the TACCO replied.

Great. Just great, Harness thought, fuming. *We can shoot from outside the missile's range, but we can't get attack criteria unless we get in close and personal.*

Still, the possibility of actually firing a shot in anger was an attractive one. He let that thought console him, and pushed away the thoughts of the very real danger they were standing in.

"Got something," the TACCO announced. "Possible periscope, bearing 120, range seven thousand yards. He punched a "fly-to" point into his computer, and the location was transmitted to the pilot's screen. The aircraft heeled to the right as Rabies stomped on the rudder controls.

"Let's take a look, shall we?" the pilot said calmly.

"Bingo," the TACCO said softly a few minutes later. "You see anything?"

The copilot squinted out the window. "Yeah, I think so. Still at communications depth—it looks like nothing but a snorkel mast and a couple of antennas. The sail's still submerged. Call it positive visual identification, though."

"She doesn't have to surface to be dangerous," the TACCO warned. "Intell says they can still fire those Grails from shallow depth."

"I'm watching her," the copilot answered. "Hold on, let me get some guidance from Homeplate." He switched circuits and updated the carrier on the tactical situation.

1228 local (Zulu -7)
CDC
USS Jefferson

The TAO listened to Hunter 701's report with a sinking feeling. The situation stunk, outright stunk. There was no clear-cut answer as to whether the battle group could attack the submarine immediately, or whether it had to wait for some indication of hostile intent. Moments later, the bitch box that connected her with TFCC buzzed angrily.

International rules of engagement contained so many vague requirements that deciding when it was legal to shoot was a matter for a court rather than naval officers. While there was no requirement that U.S. forces take the first hit before they could open fire, they did have to determine that the submarine had committed a hostile act, or demonstrated hostile intent.

The communications downlink was certainly evidence of something. The most probable explanation was that the aircraft was passing targeting information to another platform, either a surface ship or a submarine. Rule out surface ship, she thought, studying the display. Any combatant of significant size would have been detected and reported immediately. And the fact that a submarine—perhaps even this one—had fired on an S-3 only days before added strength to her inclination to have the S-3 blow the bastard out of the water.

Still, there was no evidence that this was the same submarine. So many nations now owned production models of the Russian-built Kilo diesel sub that there was no way to be certain.

Additionally, they all knew that tensions in the area were at the highest level they'd been at since World War II. Killing the submarine now could be that final element that pushed China and the other nations over the brink into open warfare. And, more likely than not, all the nations clamoring for ownership of the Spratly Islands would put aside their differences long enough to unite against the American forces. While she was confident that the battle group could take care of itself, the purpose of a presence mission was to deter wars—not to start them.

She toggled the lever on the bitch box, hoping that the Flag watch officer would give her permission to follow the most ancient adage of warriors.

Kill them all, and let God sort them out.

CHAPTER 9
Saturday, 29 June

"Permission to attack with torpedo denied, Hunter 701. If you see some indication that she's preparing to launch or taking some other hostile action, you're weapons free on her. Until then, maintain contact and keep us posted." The TAO on the carrier sounded reluctant to give the order.

Rabies shot a look of disgust at his copilot.

"Fucking rules of engagement," the copilot obligingly said.

"Ask them just what the hell they want—a declaration of war? This SOB took a *shot* at one of our aircraft yesterday, and they want us to just let him go?"

"You know what they're going to say," the TACCO joined in. "Can't prove it's the same sub, and retaliation's not authorized by ROE. You know the drill."

"Doesn't mean I have to like it," Rabies muttered. "Ask them. Make them tell me I have to wait to take the first shot."

"They won't do it," the copilot said. "They'll say you can shoot in self-defense the second you see the sail start to break away from the missile launcher, or if the sub starts any preparation for firing."

"And just how the hell are we supposed to see that with that pigboat still half-submerged?"

"Get lucky, I guess. Come on, Rabies, don't make me look like an idiot on the circuit."

"Okay, okay. But the second I see anything—*anything*—that bitch is toast. And you pussies damned well better back me up on it!"

Silence on the ICS. Rabies felt a pang of guilt, but smothered it in the overwhelming frustration he felt. Every member of the crew wanted to take the sub out—he knew that. They all had been debriefed on the previous attack, and had seethed with the righteous indignation that he'd just voiced. Not a man—or woman, he added reflexively—in the S-3B squadron wouldn't have shot instantly, given the slightest justification.

"It sucks," he said finally. "It just really sucks."

1230
Hornet 401

Thor dropped back behind the Flanker, opening the distance enough to shoot if it became necessary. Although he'd never tried it, he was quite certain that being five hundred feet behind another aircraft when it exploded was not good for him. Even if his Hornet blasted through the fireball, the odds of sucking a piece of metal into his engines was just too great.

"Hornet, say state," he heard the OS query from the carrier.

State of fucking frustration, he thought. *Maybe state of idiocy, too.* He glanced at his fuel gauge, resisted the temptation to be a smart-ass, and settled for telling the OS how much fuel he had left.

The Flanker was now sixty miles from the battle group and showed no signs of changing course or even acknowledging his escort. Thor could hear Aegis trying to contact the Flanker, requesting intentions and explanations on the unencrypted IAD—International Air Distress frequency.

Suddenly, the Flanker nosed down and headed for the deck. It traded speed for altitude, accelerating past five hundred knots. Thor followed it down, wondering what the hell the other pilot was thinking. The adrenaline that had subsided into a muted throb roared back through his body like a freight train.

The Flanker leveled off five hundred feet above the waves, its shadow racing like a pace car below it.

"Hornet! What the hell's he doing?" the E-2C RIO demanded. "Aegis is demanding some answers—the contact's dropped off their screens."

"Tell them to figure it out for themselves! Their radar horizon can't be more than forty miles, the altitude he's at! Still getting video downlink. That ought to narrow the search area."

"Unnecessary," the E-2 RIO answered tartly. "Hunter 701 is sitting on top of his playmate, about fifty miles to your west. If you were paying attention, you'd have heard his reports."

"I'm a little bit busy myself, buddy. This bastard moves a lot faster than some sewer pipe taking up water space." Come to think of it, he *had* heard the S-3's reports, he reflected. He'd been too focused on the Flanker to make the correlation.

Thor glanced at his altimeter, then took the Hornet up another hundred feet and selected an IR heat-seeking Sidewinder. If the time came for it, he wanted to be in the best position for a killing shot from behind. The fastest way to eliminate the missile threat from the submarine would be to take out the platform providing targeting data to it. And for that little job, there wasn't anything better than a Marine and a Hornet.

"Let me see the missile profiles for whatever that Flanker's likely to be carrying," Captain Killington demanded. "Are they sea-skimmers?"

"Here, sir," his TAO said, handing him the tactical handbook. "Left-hand side."

Killington studied it carefully. "Just because the Hornet didn't see missiles doesn't mean the Flanker's not carrying any. Look at how they misidentified those U.S. helicopters as Hinds. Killed our own people with two war shots."

"It seems a little different scenario," his operations officer, now standing watch as the TAO, offered tentatively. The TAO tried to decide whether he'd heard a note of regret in his CO's voice. "Circling around a helicopter doesn't give you as good a view as pacing another jet. I don't think they ever got closer than five miles to those helos. But Hornet was right up on this bogey."

Killington glared at him. "You're missing the point. Aircrews make mistakes. They *do*—everyone knows it! I'm not staking the safety of this ship and crew on what some airdale thinks he saw while playing grab-ass with another jet at five hundred knots. Besides, there's another possibility, one you haven't considered."

"What's that, sir?" the TAO asked quietly.

"That he's on a suicide mission—a kamikaze, just like they did in the last war! Ever think of *that*? Huh?"

"A kami—Sir, that was Japan, I believe. Not China."

"I know that! Do you think I don't? Listen, mister, don't try to smart off at me! There's a reason they put me out here

instead of giving command to a lieutenant commander. The
Pentagon knows that a knowledge of history is absolutely
essential to effective, aggressive command. That's why over
one-third of the curriculum at the Naval War College is
military history—strategy and policy!"

"But, sir—"

"Don't argue with me! It'll make you feel like a fool later
when I save your ass. Get those birds on the rail. That bastard's
not getting inside *this* air defense perimeter!"

The TAO glanced around for the XO, wondering if anyone
else was listening to the irrational arguments. Of course they
were—even with their radio headsets on, the OSs on Aegis had
an almost telepathic ability to hear every conversation in CDC.
He saw it in their studiously blank faces, their eyes carefully
glued to their scopes. It wasn't the first time that the CO had
worried them all.

"Aye, aye, sir," the TAO said. He spoke quietly into his
headset microphone, then looked up. "Birds on the rails, sir."

"Good. Now let's hope we have a chance to use them," the
captain said sternly.

The TAO stared at his screen grimly. Captain Killington was
known as an aggressive player, but his refusal to acknowledge
the possibility—and danger—of a blue-on-blue engagement
had been the subject of countless quiet discussions among the
more junior officers on the cruiser. Every one of them knew the
ship's history, and few had any desire to repeat the tragic
mistake committed by the previous crew in the Persian Gulf.

Captain Killington had done little to make them feel any
easier about the possibility. Their CO repeatedly quoted
extensive passages from the former CO's book and steadfastly
maintained that the shoot-down had been justified. According
to him, there had been fighters tucked under the wings of the
airbus, attempting to hide from radar by using the larger

aircraft as a shield. Captain Killington believed that shooting down the airbus had prevented serious loss of American life.

Better to be judged by one than carried by six, the TAO thought, pondering the equally unattractive alternatives of facing a court of inquiry or a funeral. *If it comes down to it, I'm shooting first and asking questions later. I'd rather be branded with* Vincennes's *mistakes and history than the* USS Stark's *record.* The *Stark* had exercised restraint—out and out negligence, many claimed—in failing to fire on an inbound aircraft. That decision had cost her lives when she'd taken a missile amidships.

Not on my watch, buddy, the TAO thought, staring at the symbols tracking across the screen.

1240 local (Zulu -7)
Hornet 401

"Low level's no trick, buddy," Thor said out loud. "Just what the hell are you up to?" He watched the Flanker make a minute change in course and tapped the flight controls to follow it.

He glanced at the clock. In another ten minutes, it would all be over anyway. The Flanker would transit the battle group, and then either turn to make another pass or continue on to wherever it was bound. He could follow until the aircraft left the battle group's airspace, take a quick drink from the tanker, and then head home.

Suddenly, the Hornet's ALR-67 radar warning receiver buzzer went off. A radar was sweeping him, radiating a fire control signature. He felt a sudden chill.

"Hawkeye, I'm getting—what the hell is going on?" he said on the tactical net. "That's a damned Aegis radar!"

"Roger, Hornet, we're getting it. Aegis is locked on to the incoming bogey," the E-2 replied.

"Oh, shit. Hawkeye, talk to me! They're not thinking of shooting, are they?" Thor's hand itched to push the throttles forward of its own accord. To be this close to a bad guy—or even a potential bad guy—with missiles in the air, wasn't healthy. He fought down the impulse to get the hell out of Dodge. If the Aegis was planning on launching one of its SM-2 antiair missiles in their direction, Thor had a burning desire to be very gone. The SM-2 was the same missile that *Vincennes* had used to shoot down an Iranian airbus in 1988, believing that the contact was an Iranian F-14 fighter. If their electronics emanations were any clue, the *Vincennes* was still confused about who the good guys and who the bad guys were.

The SM-2 was a long-range, high-speed missile, capable of attaining velocities exceeding Mach 2. Its 1,556 pounds of massed destruction carried a high-velocity controlled fragmentation conventional high explosive atop a single-stage dual-thrust Aerojet Mark 56 solid-fuel rocket. It had an inertial navigation system with two-way communications link for midcourse corrections from the Aegis ship, along with monopulse semiactive radar homing and a proximity/contact fusing system. It was the standard missile (SM) used by surface ships against any airborne target, aircraft or missile. A potent, lethal missile, and one that Thor was not interested in trying to outsmart and outmaneuver.

The Flag TAO's voice came onto the circuit. Thor listened as the Admiral's staff berated the Aegis cruiser and ordered them to cease targeting the Flanker. The signal blipped off his ESM warning receiver.

The Flanker kicked in its afterburners, and the twin Saturn/Lyulka AL-31F turbofans spat bright fire out the twin tailpipes. Thor felt the increase in its wake buffet the Hornet as the Flanker ascended. Reflexively, he followed the Flanker, maintaining a good firing solution on it from behind.

The Flanker twisted and turned, behaving for all the world

like a fighter suddenly engaged in air-to-air combat. Since he was carrying no missiles, the pilot would be solely concerned with allowing Thor to get a decent shot off.

The Flanker veered suddenly and raced back along its original course, heading for the coast of Vietnam, still twisting and dodging. It must have taken being illuminated by fire control radar seriously, and the pilot must be thinking he was in immediate danger. Thor let the pilot open the distance between then, wishing there was some way to convey that despite his air-to-air armament, he had no intention of taking a shot at the other pilot.

He followed the Flanker, still conducting evasive maneuvers, to the edge of the air protection envelope, and then broke off. *Paranoid little bastard,* he thought, and felt a moment of sympathy for the other pilot. If Thor's experience was any guide at all, the Flanker driver was going to need a clean pair of skivvies as soon as he got back to his base.

1245 local (Zulu -7)
Hunter 701

"Any activity?" the TACCO asked again.

"Nothing." Rabies took his eyes off the window and turned in his seat so he could see the TACCO. "You're pretty antsy about this one. Quit worrying—we're far enough off that we can outrun anything a Flanker's likely to shoot at us."

"This isn't feeling right," the TACCO answered over the ICS. "That Flanker hauling ass out of here after passing targeting information down to the sub—why?"

"You don't know for sure it was talking to the sub. Maybe it was just some sort of exercise. And she went buster because idiot Aegis lit her up. How'd *you* feel if an unfriendly carrying long-range surface-to-air missiles lit you up with fire control radar?"

"About like I do right now, Rabies." The TACCO leaned forward, trying to see out of the cockpit. The sub was out of sight, lost to view by being head-on into the setting sun.

"Getting machinery noise, flow tones. Hull popping—she's changing depth!" the AW said suddenly. "Sir, where is she?"

The TACCO felt a cold chill. "Rabies, get us out of the damned sun," he said urgently.

"Ready one," the copilot announced as the S-3B moved— now painfully slowly, it seemed to the TACCO—out of line of sight with the sun.

"Sir!!" the AW insisted.

The TACCO strained forward to see out the canopy.

Below them, he saw disturbed water, dark shadows moving below the warm murk of the South China Sea. Was there movement? He couldn't tell for sure. Illogically, he wondered whether the submarine could see him through the canopy, looking up at the aircraft through the periscope. Could it see his pale white face peering forward between the two pilots' seats? He rubbed his hand over his chin, feeling the rough afternoon growth.

Suddenly, the water below them exploded into white froth and foam, boiling up from below like an undersea geyser reaching higher and higher into the sky. Twenty feet above the water, the sea peeled back like a banana skin, revealing the slender white form inside it.

"SHIT!" Rabies screamed, throwing the S-3B into a hard right turn. The copilot lurched in his seat as he completed the remaining sequences to drop the torpedo, coldly reporting his actions to the carrier. The TACCO felt the Viking buck, as 506 pounds of Mk-46 torpedo dropped away from the wing.

"It wasn't a fucking Grail," he shouted over the ICS. "That wasn't aimed as us!"

"What the hell was that?" the E-2C was screaming at the same time over the tactical net. "Hunter, what the fuck?"

Rabies knew the rest of his crew had seen the missile, but they hadn't really *seen* it. They'd seen what they expected to see—another SAM launched at their aircraft.

"It's a cruise missile!" Rabies screamed over the net. It wouldn't be bothering with the Viking circling overhead. No, the ships in the battle group provided a much more inviting target.

1246 local (Zulu -7)
Combat Direction Center
USS Vincennes

"Missile inbound, sir!" the EW yelled on the net, as his SLQ-32 ESM gear detected the missile seeker head and started blaring warnings. Seconds later, the air tracker jumped in, reporting the radar contact.

The TAO reacted instantly. The Aegis combat systems were fully capable of handling an entire air engagement on full automatic, doing everything from identifying threat targets to assigning weapons based on priorities and firing the air-to-air missiles. When it was on automatic. Under the current threat condition, though, it still required operator intervention.

The TAO acknowledged the contact on his screen, his fingers flashing over the keys. He was aware of the CO standing behind him, asking questions and demanding answers. Reflex and training paid off—within seconds, the SM-2MR streaked off the rails, another missile sliding into firing position immediately behind it.

The TAO, his eyes fixed on the radar screen, said, "One away, Captain." Now that the actual missile was launched, he had a few seconds to wait before he would decide whether to launch a second salvo. There was still time.

It looked good. The attack geometry was perfect, and they'd had enough warning and data to get a good fix on the incoming missile. There were too many friendly ships and aircraft in the area to indiscriminately launch a spate of long-range missiles, especially when the geometry for a single-shot kill looked good.

Even if the missile missed, the cruiser had one last-ditch chance against it, as did the carrier. Both ships, as well as all the other ones in the battle group, were equipped with CIWS. The TAO prayed it wouldn't be necessary. While CIWS could fire like a gatling-gun and nail a missile up to two miles away, even a destroyed missile would probably shower the ship with burning fragments of fuel and flak. The debris could knock out either the SPS-49 air radar or the super-sensitive SPY-1 that made the Aegis such a formidable platform.

Ten miles from the carrier, the SM2-MR caught up with the intruder. On the radar, the two blips merged, then disappeared. From the bridge it would have been a spectacular sight, the fireball of missile-on-missile lighting up the sky and reflecting off the water. Here in combat, in the bowels of the Aegis cruiser, only a faint dull thud provided outside confirmation of what their radars told them.

"I guess next time you'll listen up," the CO snarled. A look of unholy jubilation lit the older man's face. "I knew those bastards would try something! If I hadn't had those birds on the rails, we would all be toast! Think about that next time, before you start running off at the mouth."

"Yes, sir." The TAO leaned forward over his screen, staring at it as though it held some secret. Whatever doubts he'd had about the CO before seemed grossly unprofessional. No matter that Captain Killington had been prepared for air-launched missiles and a submarine had actually taken the shot. The launch platform was irrelevant because the captain's instincts had been right. The TAO's best judgment might have gotten the ship sunk.

He glanced over at his coffee cup. He'd drained down the last bitter dregs just before the missile shot. With the ship at General Quarters, he was unlikely to get a refill anytime soon. Not until they stood down to Condition Two, at any rate. It didn't matter right now, while the adrenaline from the missile shot still pounded in his veins. Four hours from now, however, he knew he'd be aching for a caffeine fix.

Just as well that he couldn't get a refill on the coffee right now. The other thing that was secured during General Quarters was the head.

He wondered whether caffeine deprivation and full bladders played much part in the course of war at sea. Probably so, he concluded, as he remembered that the Captain of the *USS Stark* had been in the head when his ship had taken a near-fatal missile shot in the Persian Gulf. That hadn't been a declared war, either, although a lot of sailors had died.

From down here in the sandbox, he concluded, it didn't matter that there was no declared war or prior warning. They could be just as dead, and just as short on head calls and coffee, as any force had been in a declared war.

At least with Captain Killington in command, it looked like *Vincennes* would never take a hit. And that was of more comfort to the TAO than caffeine right now.

CHAPTER 10
Saturday, 29 June

1245 local (Zulu -7)
TFCC
USS Jefferson

"Now just how the hell do we explain this to Seventh Fleet!" Tombstone shouted into the receiver. "This was supposed to be routine FON ops—how many times do I have to explain that to you? Do you think that includes lighting up a foreign national's aircraft? With fire control radar? Do you suppose he and his government might take the slightest bit of offense at that? Damn it, Killington, that's a violation of every known rule of peacetime engagement!"

"And because my ship was ready, I'm talking to you now, Admiral! With all due respect, if you are ordering me to compromise the safety of the *Vincennes*, I decline." Captain Killington's voice was coldly self-righteous.

Tombstone glanced across the desk at the JAG officer, a lawyer with extensive expertise in international maritime. The JAG shrugged and nodded.

No help from that corner, Tombstone thought. *I know as well as he does that no Board of Inquiry will ever blame him. That SOB is damned lucky he got shot at! The end justifies the means, in this case. But it's entirely probable that he provoked the whole incident.*

"I better not see a single action that can possibly be interpreted as aggressive out of you," he warned Killington. "You've damned near gone over the line this time."

"If I had, you'd have already relieved me," Killington snapped. "And if you're certain I have and you don't, then stand by to join me at that long green table, shipmate. Because if I go down, you're going with me!"

Tombstone slammed the receiver down and flung himself back away from the desk. The bitch of it was that Killington was right. If he relieved the man of command now, Killington would claim that he'd energized his fire control radar in self-defense. And if he didn't, he would appear to condone any subsequent actions by the Aegis cruiser CO.

"You're taking notes," Tombstone said finally to the JAG officer sitting quietly across from him.

"Yes, Admiral. For what it's worth, I don't envy your position." The JAG officer shook his head. "Either way, we've got problems. Can you afford to take the chance that he was right?"

"At this point, I'm going to. My gut tells me not to do it, but I'm going to leave him in command. Maybe the Navy knew what it was doing when it gave him command, maybe it didn't. For now, I'll trust the selection boards—if not Captain Killington himself."

Tombstone leaned forward and punched the intercom button for CAG. Captain Cervantes answered up immediately.

"CAG, get me some airpower up there. I don't want any repeats of the *Stark* business."

As the JAG left the office, Tombstone glanced at the Western history book still open on his coffee table. As surely as Wyatt Earp had known what awaited him at the OK Corral, Tombstone knew that the battle group was standing into danger. If the Chinese wanted a shoot-out in the South China Sea, he'd be damned if he'd show up unarmed.

Onboard *Jefferson*, life suddenly became simultaneously much simpler and more complicated. Most of the more restrictive rules of engagement had just gone out the window on the trail of the submarine's cruise missile, uncomplicating the maze of determinations a commander needed to make before launching weapons. However, the logistics of getting enough metal into the air to protect the carrier battle group more than made up for any simplification of the battle group's engagement status.

The flight deck boiled with technicians. Red-shirted ordnance technicians hauled yellow gear to waiting S-3B and ASW helicopters, manhandling the torpedoes up to the weapons stations on the wings. Other ordies restocked the sonobuoy slots along the underbelly of the aircraft. Purple Shirts, the enlisted men and women who handled refueling, waited impatiently. Refueling and rearming an aircraft simultaneously was too dangerous.

The helos were ready to go first. They carried smaller weapons loads than the fixed-wing ASW aircraft, only two torpedoes each. The SAR helo, always airborne during flight operations, circled the carrier, waiting for the carrier to declare a green deck.

Up in Pri-Fly, the Air Boss swore to himself. He'd left two S-3's on alert ten. As he watched, the stubby ASW hunter-killers taxied to the bow. The first, Hunter 702, lined up on the waist catapult. Hunter 710 went straight ahead to the port bow cat, its jets throbbing with the low, mesmerizing sound that gave it its nickname of Hoover.

The bow cat was ready first.

"Green deck!" the Air Boss snapped, scanning the flight deck for any lingering technicians within the lines that delineated the operating area.

"Green deck, aye," the Air Traffic Controller, or AC, echoed. He repeated the Air Boss's order into the sound-powered microphone that hung around his neck, and it was relayed to the Yellow Shirts and catapult officers on the deck.

The Air Boss saw the handler motion, and two technicians scampered out from under the forward Viking. The shuttle was now attached to the S-3's forward wheel strut. The Viking's engine ramped up, crescendoing into the full-throated roar of military power. The handler snapped off a salute, then ran to safety. The Air Boss could almost feel the catapult officer pause, take one last look around, and then press the pickle switch that would unleash the steam piston.

The Viking shot forward, reaching over 120 knots of ground speed in four seconds. With thirty knots of wind across the deck, that equated to 150 knots over the wings, enough to keep the aircraft airborne until its own engines could get it moving faster.

Fifteen seconds later, the same intricate ballet was complete on the waist cat, and the second Viking was airborne. The ASW helicopters followed in short order, three of them.

The Air Boss looked grimly satisfied. With a total of six ASW aircraft, along with the towed arrays of the surface ships and the cruiser's own ASW helos airborne, being a submariner just got a lot less fulfilling.

1305 local (Zulu -7)
Admiral's Cabin

"Admiral, how about a JAST Tomcat?" Batman asked quietly. "That look-down capability might come in real handy about now."

Tombstone shot his former wingman a thoughtful look. "Are they configured to handle a sub-launched missile?"

"Don't see why not. The best parts of the new avionics and radar are designed to handle sea-skimmers. Can't come much closer to the sea than getting shot from a submarine, now, can you?"

"TAO—all the ASW birds launched?"

"Yes, Admiral." The TAO pointed at the plat camera display on the closed-circuit TV monitor. "Last Viking just took off. Air Boss called Red Deck a few seconds ago."

Tombstone turned back to Batman. "Go see CAG. It sounds to me like a good time to try out one of your toys in the air, but he may have some other plans. It's going to take a while to get one fueled and armed, anyway."

"They're *Tomcats*, Admiral. Hardly toys."

"Don't forget who you're talking to, Captain."

"Sir?" Batman stiffened, wondering if he'd overstepped the bounds of their long friendship. Surely Stoney hadn't let his stars turn him into a pompous asshole!

He studied his old friend carefully. One corner of Tombstone's mouth twitched. "They're all toys, Batman. Until they start shooting, that's what they are."

1310 local (Zulu -7)
Hunter 701

"Get those active buoys in the water *now*!" Rabies snapped.

"What the hell do you think I'm doing back here, playing with myself?" the TACCO snarled. "Here!" He punched the button that fed fly-to points to the pilot's display.

"Got it!" the copilot said, the report rendered superfluous by the hard banking turn of the S-3.

Sixteen minutes later, Hunter 701 had ringed the last

position of the submarine with DICASS buoys, which were pouring electromagnetic energy into the water, alternately pinging and listening for a sonar return.

DICASS buoys operated like a shipboard sonar. They provided highly accurate range and bearing information to the AW. The disadvantage was that the submarine could hear the sonar pings, trace back to locate the sonobuoys, and maneuver to evade the pattern. Additionally, using DICASS buoys gave away the fact that someone knew that there was a submarine in the area—and was trying to find it. The submarine, alerted, could exploit every advantage the ocean offered, including anomalous acoustic conditions, to evade contact.

Don't matter if she knows we know, Rabies thought, banking the S-3B sharply to get into position for the next drop. *She already knows about us!*

"All buoys sweet and cold," Harness reported, telling the rest of the flight crew that each buoy was operating properly and that none of the buoys had gained contact on the submarine.

"She can't have gotten far," the TACCO muttered. "She only dived ten minutes ago. She's *got* to be in the area!"

"Acoustic conditions aren't the best," the AW said. Both of his hands were on his head, pressing the earphones tightly over his ears. He took one hand off, reached for his water bottle, and took a swig. "Warm, shallow water. Couple of deep trenches nearby. I'm betting she heads for one of those."

Sound energy, the TACCO knew, was essentially lazy. Or at least that's how it had been explained to him in his earliest days as a student naval flight officer. It always seeks out the path that lets it travel the slowest. The actual mechanics of sonar detection and layers in the ocean were explained in a mathematical formula known as Snell's Law. For the TACCO's purposes, the "lazy" analogy was sufficient.

Three factors made sound travel faster: heat, pressure, and

salinity. Increase any one of those elements in a layer of water, and sound energy would bend away from that layer.

The South China Sea had a hard, rocky bottom. This near the equator, the water on the surface of the ocean was continually warmed by the sun. Wave action mixed the surface water with the layer below it, creating an isothermal layer of warmer water approximately fifty feet deep. The depth varied, depending on time of day and the sea state. At night, the surface of the ocean cooled down slightly. During heavy weather, rougher seas mixed the warm water even deeper into the ocean.

If the DICASS buoys were dropped in the shallow surface layer, the returning pings would be trapped below the warmer area of water and would not return to the DICASS receiver. The AW, knowing the characteristics of this part of the world's waters, had set his buoys at a depth of two hundred feet, well below the layer.

"Could be anything," the AW continued. "There're enough pinnacles and rocks down there to block the return. Or, if she headed in toward the coastline, the water might be too shallow to get a good return. I don't know if—Wait!" he said suddenly. He pressed the headphones more tightly against his ears.

"Buoy fifteen hot!" he said. "Bearing 310, range four thousand yards!"

The TACCO glanced at his display. "Westernmost buoy. Makes sense—she's running for the shoreline and shallow water. And for Vietnamese territorial waters. She knows we're going to be reluctant to follow her in there, regardless of her nationality. I can damn near guarantee that if we shoot a torpedo into territorial waters, we're going to hit something that's going to get us in trouble. Murphy's Law."

"Lost it," Harness announced. "She was there, though. I'm sure of it."

"How the hell did she get that far without us hearing her? She'd have to have been making better than twelve knots—we *had* to have heard something, at that speed. Let's lay another pattern," the TACCO said. His fingers flew over the display, calculating the spacing between buoys, and then punched the information up to the pilot's display.

"Sir, you're right," the AW said thoughtfully, staring at his display. "She makes that speed, I'm going to get her, layer or no layer."

"But the DICASS contact was solid, right?"

"No doubt. Too hard and sharp to be a biologic," the AW answered, referring to the possibility that the DICASS buoy could have pinged on a whale or pod of dolphins. Even clouds of shrimp composed of millions of the tiny creatures could reflect back the sound energy from a DICASS buoy.

"And I didn't hear any biologics. No, I had a sniff of a sub, sir. No doubt." The AW's voice was firm.

"Okay, so we chase her down and sink her," Rabies broke in. "Come on, however she got there, she's there. Give me the fly-to points."

"Coming atcha," the TACCO answered. "But watch it— we're getting close to the twelve-mile limit."

"You point, I'll drive," Rabies said.

At this point, the TACCO thought ruefully, that was about the best he could manage. He puzzled over the question of how the sub could have slipped through their net of DICASS buoys.

1336 local (Zulu -7)
Pri-Fly
USS Jefferson

"Come on, it's just a Tomcat to us," the Air Boss snapped. "Same weight, same steam settings. What's taking so long?"

"Uh, sir—that new Captain is down there," the phone talker

said. "He's giving the flight deck crew a hand. Guess he wants to make sure everything's copacetic for those birds."

The Air Boss groaned. "Does he want those JAST birds of his launched or bronzed? Jesus, that's all we need—a 0-6 'helping' the flight deck crew. Is he on the circuit?"

"Yes, Boss. He's calling the JAST birds 'Spook.'"

The Air Boss slipped his headphones on and listened. Sure enough, Batman's voice was there, talking to the catapult officer on the flight deck frequency.

"Captain Wayne," the Air Boss said, a note of urgency in his voice. "I think we need you up here in Pri-Fly overseeing this."

"Roger, Air Boss," Batman's voice said, recognizable even through the background howl of the JAST Tomcat engines. "I'm just checking on a couple of—"

"*Now*, Captain," the Air Boss heard another voice chime in. He grinned. The Admiral had undoubtedly wondered what was taking so long to launch the JAST birds. He must have turned on the CCTV, seen his former wingman on the flight deck, and extrapolated the reason for the delay.

"Aye, aye, Admiral," the Air Boss heard Batman say. "On my way up." The Air Boss watched the captain walk back to the Line Shack, handing his headset to a junior brown-shirted Plane Captain.

"Thank you, Admiral," he heard a high voice say a few seconds after Batman had removed his headset, thus severing his link with the flight deck radio circuit. The Air Boss suppressed a chortle. He wasn't the only one who'd been watching Batman leave the circuit.

While he doubted that the Admiral could put a face to the voice, the Air Boss recognized it as belonging to Aviation Boatswain's Mate First Class Winkler, the yellow-shirted handler supervising the launch.

Then "You're welcome, AB1," the same voice said gruffly. "And stand by to launch another one of those birds. I have a feeling that the only way I'm going to be able to keep Captain Wayne out of your hair is to get his other bird airborne. With the Captain in it."

The Air Boss blinked. If he hadn't already known it, he'd just learned a valuable lesson.

Never underestimate what Admiral Magruder knew.

CHAPTER 11
Saturday, 29 June

"What the hell is that?" Bouncer muttered. The carrier was vectoring the JAST Tomcat to the last position of the submarine to provide air cover for the helicopters and Vikings sowing the ocean with sonobuoys.

"You got something?" Mouse demanded.

"Wait a second—let me tweak and peak a little. Come on, come on," the RIO coaxed, practicing his expert knobology on the radar.

"There," he said a few seconds later. "Things just got shook up a little on the launch, that's all. I'm picking up some air contacts to the west. Low fliers, about five hundred feet off the deck. Flight of four, it looks like."

"Anybody else got them?"

"Nope. *Vincennes* is checking right now, but they're not holding anything along that bearing."

"But you've got video there?" Mouse persisted.

"Sure do. Four solid blips, speed 450 knots, on a bearing that will take them just north of the carrier."

"Let's go take a look, then," the pilot said, tilting the nose of the modified Tomcat down. "We might as well find out if this PFM gear works."

"Might want to have some backup. You got people firing missiles around here, Mouse," Bouncer said uneasily. At that airspeed, and heading for the carrier, the contacts weren't likely to be commercial airliners.

"One Tomcat is enough for a look-see," Mouse argued. "We need help, the carrier will get it to us ASAP."

"I don't think they're going to wait for that," the RIO said, listening to the tactical circuit chattering in his right ear. "They're getting ready to launch the other bird right now."

"Let me guess," Mouse said. "Batman's driving."

"You got it. I never thought that flight rotation schedule would last for much longer than it took to get here. It surprised the hell out me when he let *us* launch."

"*Me* launch, you mean! It's not like he'd steal your hop, Bouncer. He likes to sit up front with the adults."

"No accounting for taste," Bouncer mused. "Me, I'm kinda happy back here. My ejection seat fires three-tenths of a second before yours does, don't forget. And I've got a handle for it!"

1415 local (Zulu -7)
Pri-Fly
USS Jefferson

"Launching four more Tomcats," the Air Boss said over the flight deck circuit. With the alert five Tomcats already launched, as well as one JAST bird and Thor's Hornet, that put seven American fighters up to intercept four Flankers. The JAST air contacts, fed to all the ships' radar displays through the LINK, had initiated a flurry of action. Even though the SPY-1 radar on the Aegis had not detected the contacts, the carrier TAO was making the safety play—get help and gas in the air before it was needed. The Air Boss thought that Batman had probably had some input into that decision, said input resulting in said

Captain grinning like a possum in the front seat of the other JAST bird.

The Air Boss picked up the mike for the flight deck circuit. "Shoot that queer Turkey now," he ordered. The Yellow Shirt on the deck whirled around, stared up at the tower, and flashed a big smile and a thumbs-up. With Batman airborne, there'd be less chance that he'd be able to kibitz anything else that happened on the flight deck.

1416 local (Zulu -7)
Spook Two (JAST Tomcat)

"Damn!" Tomboy gasped, as the acceleration off the catapult slammed her back hard. "Sir, you sure about those settings?" she asked, referring to the weight figures the Cat Officer had displayed on the grease pencil board. The weight was used to determine the pressure settings on the piston that drove the catapult shuttle forward.

There was no answer for a few moments as Batman concentrated on getting the JAST bird airborne and gaining altitude. "It's Batman up here, Tomboy," he said finally. "And yeah, I'm sure the weight was right. You're just used to flying with that old lady, Tombstone. Got to get you used to a *tactical* launch again!"

"There's tactical and then there's *tactical*, sir. Batman, I mean. You talking about the latter *tactical*?"

"You betcha. Speaking of tactical, how's your gear?"

"Up and sweet. Need to screw with it for a while to figure out the finer points. Bouncer gave me a real solid rundown on it, but it's one thing to talk about it, another altogether to get *tactical*."

"That's what we're up here for. Play with it until you're comfortable, but learn it fast. And don't worry—we've got plenty of company up here. If things get hot and you don't feel one hundred percent yet, we'll buster out. Not that we're expecting any trouble. Most likely this is just a routine flyover."

"Routine—right," she said, letting her hands wander over the dials, feeling the familiar shapes and watching the display change in response to her tweaking. "Nothing's ever routine when you're *tactical*, sir!"

"Who'd you learn that from, Tomboy? Tombstone? And it's Batman, damn it!"

"Not Tombstone," she said. Batman glanced in his small rearview mirror as the low chuckle in her voice caught his attention, but her head was still buried in the scope. "Better teacher than that."

"And just who might that have been?" he said, his curiosity piqued by both her tone of voice and her answer.

"Best teacher of all, for a Tomcat RIO. A MiG driver was kind enough to continue my education, back when we were over Norway," she said, referring to the combat she'd seen on her first cruise. "And when a MiG teaches you a lesson, you don't forget it. Not for a long, long time."

1425 local (Zulu -7)
Flight Deck
USS Jefferson

"About time!" Bird Dog muttered. He might be the last bird off the cat, but at least he wasn't sitting alert five. He eased forward on the throttle, feeling the vibration from the jets transmitted to his seat. The Tomcat, as clumsy on land as it was agile in the air, rolled forward. Bird Dog let it pick up a little speed, steering it toward the Yellow Shirt, and then eased back on the throttle. He tapped the brakes gently, chafing at the slowness of the flight deck ballet, as it became apparent from the Yellow Shirt's frantic waving that the Tomcat was bearing down on him just a little too fast.

Airman Alvarez scanned the flight deck, got his bearings, and then started across the hot tarmac. Although the sun was already dipping below the horizon, the rough nonskid still held the heat of the day. He could feel it through the soles of his boots, the prickle of the heat making his feet sweat and aggravating the athlete's foot he'd picked up last week. It had to be from the showers, he thought, desperately wishing he could rip his boots off and scratch.

The tie-down chains slung across his right shoulder bit into his flesh, the weight making him list slightly. He shrugged, trying to hitch the chains up closer to his neck as he felt one trying to slide off his shoulder. Carrying them on one shoulder had been a mistake, since he was now unevenly balanced, but putting one over each shoulder increased the probability that he'd step on the trailing ends and stumble.

He squinted at the sun, which was merging with the horizon off the carrier's port side. The flight deck throbbed faintly under his soles as the carrier accelerated. He saw the sun shift relative positions slowly as the carrier turned into the wind. He'd better get moving, or the Air Boss would have his ass for fouling the flight deck.

Alvarez started across the flight deck. The yellow-shirted handler, forty feet away and slightly to his right, was lost in the setting sun. If he hurried he could get the tie-down chains over to Groucho before the Air Boss caught sight of him.

Only two more years of this shit, he reminded himself. Then his enlistment would be up and he'd be back to cruising the beaches of sunny San Diego, feeling the heat beating down on his back from the sun instead of radiating up through his flight deck boots from the baking nonskid and steel decks.

The way he felt right now, he'd have to spend the first month of his new civilian freedom sleeping, just to catch up. But he wouldn't have to sleep alone, he mused, and certainly not with eighty other men, the way he did now, in the packed berthing compartment six levels below the flight deck. His thoughts drifted away from the flight deck and into a series of explicit daydreams that lacked just faces on the girls to make them come true.

Bird Dog felt the brakes slip and stamped down harder on the pedal. He swore, feeling the mush beneath his feet. Hydraulics, it had to be! Suddenly, the problem was not how fast he could get to the catapult, but how much deck space he had in which to stop. The time-distance calculations flashed through his mind intuitively. Not enough distance heading toward the catapult, he was sure. He stamped down, slewed the taxiing Tomcat into a hard left-hand turn, and dropped the tailhook. If he could get it headed back down the flight deck toward the stern, the drag produced by the tailhook and the extra time might let the marginal brakes act. As a last resort, he could snag one of the arresting wires with his tailhook and get the jet stopped before it rolled off the stern into the ocean.

Ten knots had never felt so damned dangerous before.

1426 local (Zulu -7)
Spook One

"Nothing here," Mouse said.

"Still showing contacts on the scope. Hell, according to this, we ought to be right in the middle of them!" Bouncer muttered, disgusted.

"Can't help what isn't here. Maybe the avionics took a hit from the cat shot."

"Or maybe it's ghosts. The way conditions are out here, all that warm, unstable air, it could be something else. A reflection off a contact miles away, multipathing through the atmosphere, an air burble, anything."

"Wouldn't be unheard of in the South China Sea. Well, whatever it was, it's not here now. I guess the Aegis guys were right—if they don't see it, it's not here."

"Shit," Bouncer said, disgusted. "Better let the carrier know before they get all spun up about nothing."

1426 local (Zulu -7)
Flight Deck
USS Jefferson

Alvarez felt as much as heard the jet wash from the F-14 dissipate. One moment he was leaning into the blast to stay upright. As it disappeared abruptly, he fell to his right, the heavy tie-down chains unbalancing him. He hit the deck hard and felt the nonskid scrape the skin off the back of his hand. One chain bounced off the deck and landed across his legs, curling between his ankles. He swore and struggled to his knees, wrapping the tie-down chain even more tightly around his ankles. He reached back to loosen the knot and looked forward toward the catapults for the first time.

"Jesus, Bird Dog!" Gator shouted. "Wrong end!"

The Tomcat was now nearly halfway through its 180-degree turn. Bird Dog was staring at the side of the carrier, trying to increase the rate of turn through sheer willpower. Two E-2C's were parked directly in front of him. It looked like his wingtip would just barely clear them. For a second, he wondered if he could fold his wings, decreasing the amount of room the massive aircraft took up. No, it wouldn't be necessary, he

decided, estimating that his wing would clear the E-2C's by at
least three feet. He shifted his gaze down to the end of the
flight deck, focusing on the arresting gear, and caught his first
glimpse—and last—of Airman Alvarez.

The F-14 that had been headed for the catapult was now staring
straight at him. Alvarez felt the wind scream by his head, first
tugging, then jerking him off his knees. He screamed and
grabbed for a pad-eye inset on the deck, desperate for something to hold on to to stop his roll toward the catapults and the
F-14. His fingers slid into the pad-eye loop and caught. The
tendons in his wrist and the muscles in his arm flashed into
instant agony. The F-14, now only ten feet away, was generating typhoon-strength winds, the hungry jets sucking up
everything in their path. Alvarez screamed again as the bones
in his first three fingers snapped, and he began rolling back
down the nonskid toward the jet engine intakes.

Bird Dog jerked the throttle back, killing the twin jet engines.
He felt them immediately start to spool down. But for the
airman on the deck, it wasn't soon enough.

Alvarez's body lost contact with the ground when the jet was
five feet away. His head hit the edge of the nacelle and was
crushed just seconds before the screaming turbines inside
pulverized his body.
   The Yellow Shirt who'd been directing Bird Dog onto the
catapult was behind the Tomcat, flat on the deck to avoid the
jet wash from the engines. He caught a glimpse of the airman
on the deck in front of the aircraft and had just enough time to
scream a warning out on the flight deck circuit before a hot red
wash of liquid and flesh spat out of the back of the engine
nacelle. The spooling-down whine of the engine changed to a
gritty clatter.

CHAPTER 12
Saturday, 29 June

The Sikorsky SH-60F Ocean Hawk helicopter hovered forty feet above the ocean. From beneath its belly, it lowered a large reflective metal ball toward the surface, the wet end of its Allied Signals (Bendix Oceanics) AQS-13F dipping sonar. A wire cable connected the ball to the avionics equipment in the helo, making it appear as though it were tethered to the ocean. Its auto-hover capabilities enhanced the illusion by making it an exceptionally stable hovering platform, even with two Mark 46 acoustic homing torpedoes slung under an external weapons station on the port side. First deployed to the Fleet in 1991, it was the replacement airframe for the SH-3 LAMPS Mark III helicopter. ASW experts bragged about its impressive passive and active tracking capabilities. Submariners from every nation hated it for the same reasons. The Ocean Hawk was the pit bull of ASW helicopters.

"Going down to one hundred feet," the AW announced.

"What's the surface layer?" the other enlisted technician asked.

"Sixty feet today. That ought to put us well below it," the first AW answered.

"We'll see. There's nothing I like about this contact at all, not a thing. Surface-to-air missiles on a submarine! God! It's unnatural, and unsportsmanlike!"

"You better get something *here*," the pilot announced, his hands and feet moving in coordination to keep the helo hovering. "We're too near to the twelve-mile limit to go in any further."

"You watch the surface, sir. Any sign of her coming shallow, you're going to want to be skedaddling out of here." With a max speed of 150 knots, the SH-60F needed a good lead on any SAM the sub would fire to survive.

"Speak of the devil—Sir, probable periscope, bearing 285, range three thousand yards!"

"That's it, boys!" the pilot snapped. "We're getting the hell out of here! Reel that sucker in!"

The winch sang, heaving the sonar transducer out of the water. As soon as it was clear of the sea, the pilot kicked it in the ass.

"Hunter 710, she's all yours!" the pilot said.

"Thanks a lot. We'll sneak in a little closer, see if we can get a VID from outside of missile range," Rabies answered. "Want to stick around in case we drive her back under?"

"Roger, we'll be around—just outside of the SAM envelope."

1431 local (Zulu -7)
Hunter 701

"Can't say that I blame them," Rabies said. "Now let's see if we can get a visual."

He circled the datum the helo had passed to him, watching the black stovepipe sticking up. A small wake, a feather, curled behind it, showing the direction of travel.

"Surfacing!" the copilot said. Slowly, a black sail emerged from the sea, water streaming off its sides. "Oh, shit," he said after a second. "It's not possible."

The AW craned his head around, looked through the cockpit windscreen, and whistled. "Sure as hell is, boss," he said softly.

"A Kilo submarine fired on Hunter 701," the TACCO said slowly. "And that—"

"Is definitely *not* a Kilo. It's a Han-class diesel boat, one of China's own production models. We've been chasing the wrong boat," Rabies said.

1900 local (Zulu -7)
Admiral's Cabin
USS Jefferson

Tombstone studied the young pilot sitting across from him. Of all the mistakes of the day, this was the most painful to deal with. Amidst the confusion of the sub-launched missile from the Kilo, the Han submarine, the Flanker incursions, and the ghost contacts, they'd lost an airman. While the tactical errors would be debriefed endlessly, no amount of analysis could change the result for Airman Alvarez.

He'd already talked to the squadron CO about Bird Dog, and he had a fairly good idea of what the pilot was like. Now that all the aircraft were back on deck, and the pilot had been debriefed by both the Safety Officer and the JAG Officer, it was Tombstone's turn to try to determine exactly what had happened.

Not so different from any of us at that age. First cruise, still psyched about flying Tomcats. By now, it's feeling normal to strap on a jet after breakfast and launch screaming into the wind, but that hasn't cut through the sheer excitement of it all. He knows about fear, just a little, from trying to get back onboard at night, but he hasn't faced the reality of it yet. Not how bad the fear can really get.

He thought back to his own earlier days on the carrier. With far more experience than this pilot had, Tombstone himself had had to face the fear that was a daily part of their lives. Two bad passes at the carrier, at night in foul weather, and Lieutenant Commander Magruder, hotshot F-14 pilot, had been ready to call it quits and settle into civilian life with Pamela. In the process of helping Batman fight his own personal demons, Tombstone had come to terms with his own. Flying F-14's wasn't a guarantee of immortality—every student pilot knew that—but it took time and age to assimilate that fear.

"You know there'll be a formal JAG investigation," he said. He kept his eyes fixed on the pilot's face. Deep in the blue eyes, he saw his own image reflected back at him.

The pilot nodded and looked down at the floor. "I couldn't think of anything else to do. It all happened so fast. One second I was taxiing, the next second the brakes are blown and I'm heading for the side. I remember thinking about the E-2's, wondering if I'd clear them. That Plane Captain—he just appeared out of nowhere. I'd just taxied through that part of the flight deck, and he wasn't there then. Then all at once . . ." The pilot's voice trailed off.

"That's the way it happens," Tombstone said. "Even in the air. Four hundred knots, ten knots—makes no difference. You train to react without thinking, because there's never enough time. You either do the right thing, or you're dead. Sometimes you do the right thing and you're still dead."

"I keep seeing him—just those last couple of seconds." The younger pilot's voice was a low monotone. "He'd snagged a pad-eye. I cut the engines as soon as I saw him, but it wasn't fast enough. He was looking at me, and I could see him screaming. I don't think it was words, not from the way his mouth was moving, just screaming. I keep wondering what I could have done to prevent it, why I didn't just ram into the JBD or one of the E-2's and save the kid's life. Then I realize there wasn't time; I couldn't have gotten turned fast enough by the time I saw him. Maybe if I'd looked before I turned, maybe—"

"Maybe you could have," Tombstone said, interrupting the emotionless recital of the facts. Bird Dog's voice suggested that he was still in shock. The sooner Tombstone could cut through the cocoon that was isolating the pilot from reality, the sooner he'd start to deal with what had happened. "It's not probable, but it is possible."

Bird Dog flinched as though Tombstone had struck him. "You're saying it was my fault."

"It doesn't matter right now. It might have hours ago, when either you or a plane captain might have noticed the hydraulics leak that caused your brakes to fail. But nothing you can do will change what happened. You either learn to live with it, or you'll be tossing your wings on CAG's desk before the cruise is over."

"Maybe I should just do that now," Bird Dog said. He shut his eyes for a moment and tried to imagine taxiing an F-14 on the flight deck again. All he could see was the screaming face, eyes hidden by the goggles and cranial helmet, one arm stretched out against the baking black non-skid, the fingers slipping, the horrifying rumble of the Tomcat's right engine, the wet sucking grinding, metal clashing on metal as the body and the tie-down chains were ingested. Two turbine blades tore through the fuselage, barely missing Gator, ripping narrow bloody gashes in the cockpit.

It had been as sudden and unexpected as the destruction of the Spratly rock. Once minute the tank crew had been alive, staring up at his aircraft. If he'd been closer to the island during those last moments, he might have seen the same expression on their faces as he'd seen on Alvarez's—a stark realization that cut to the heart of each man, the inevitable truth that no man was immortal.

He shuddered and tried to block the vivid details out of his mind, as well as the logical conclusion to that train of thought. If he'd been close enough to see the tank crew's faces, to look into their eyes in the split second before they'd died, he would have been close enough to die himself. Even if the missile had not sought out the Tomcat as preferred prey in the deadly long-range game of strike warfare, fragments of debris thrown aloft by the explosion would have surely been sucked into the Tomcat's jet engine.

FOD. A silly-sounding acronym for Foreign Object Damage, FOD was a long-standing nightmare for some pilots. It was odd the things they came to fear, it occurred to him. Each pilot had his or her own peculiar fixation. Some obsessed about cold cats, the failure of steam pressure during the flight stroke. Others worried about hydraulics leaks, or the wiring harnesses that carried the complex electronic connections between the pilot's instruments and the avionics black boxes.

Unlike most of his peers, Bird Dog had never had a particular item he worried about. Coalescing in his gut, however, was a conviction that it was not any one *thing* so much as a particular accidental sequence of events that would finally get him. Something meaningless, like a hydraulics leak.

He shut his eyes and shook his head, trying to clear his thoughts. It kept coming back to him, one persistent thought. Had Alvarez been conscious long enough to feel the jet mince his legs, to know that the deadly blades would work their way up his body to his torso, then his head? Had he had those milliseconds to know that he was dying in one of the most horrible ways possible on an aircraft carrier? To Bird Dog, that was the most horrendous thing he could think of—to see death coming, and to know there was no way to avoid it.

"Stop," Tombstone ordered. "Look at me."

Bird Dog opened his eyes and stared at the admiral.

"There are two things you're going to do. First, you're going to Sick Bay. Second, you're going to get some sleep. If you're going to make it through this, it's better that we find out immediately. Commander," Tombstone said, turning to the squadron CO.

"Understood, Admiral," the commander said. "He's back on the flight schedule tomorrow."

Bird Dog stared at them dully. Back on the flight schedule, back on the flight deck. Strapped inside a jet with no way out, other than ejecting, which was as likely to kill him as anything else. Just like Alvarez . . . a little faster if he hit the canopy and snapped his neck, a little slower if his seat launched too soon and flung him into the flaming exhaust of his RIO's seat.

How easy it was to die on an aircraft carrier! Somehow, that wasn't something that had ever really sunk in, despite numerous hours of safety lectures and briefings. He shuddered, wondering if anyone else in the squadron knew how dangerous it was on the flight deck.

Of course they did, he reminded himself. They'd been doing this for years. Hell, Bird Dog had lost classmates all the way through the training pipeline. Aircraft broke, pilots did stupid things, and aviators died.

But somehow it'd never been brought home quite as dramatically. It was one thing to launch with another aircraft and never see the aviator again. It was another experience altogether to have a young sailor shredded by the blades of your jet engine. And to know that you were partially responsible.

A picture flashed in his mind, something he'd seen as he'd staggered out of the Tomcat after the accident. What was it? It was important, he was sure. Suddenly it came to him.

Across the flight deck from him, perched on the top of a Tomcat, had been Airman Shaughnessy. He could almost see the jet blast and wind ruffling her short hair, tossing it over in front of her eyes. Her hair! That was it! Shaughnessy had been on top of the Tomcat without her cranial on, a clear violation of every flight deck safety regulation.

Hot anger flooded him. People ignored safety rules at their own peril. Look where it'd gotten Airman Alvarez. He'd forgotten the first rule of flight deck survival and hadn't kept his eyes continually scanning the area around him.

Bird Dog might not be able to do anything about Alvarez's death—not now—but he might be able to keep another airman from dying through her own stupidity. He stopped abruptly and reversed his direction. He'd put a stop to her dangerous attitude right now.

He finally tracked Chief Franklin down in the Chiefs' Mess. The Mess was a combination galley and lounge that provided some privacy for the more senior enlisted members on the ship. Its door was decorated with an intricately woven display of "fancy work," a collection of specialized knots and braided line that enclosed the anchor insignia of a chief petty officer's collar insignia.

Bird Dog knocked on the door and then pushed it open without waiting for a response. Twenty chiefs, both male and female, were clustered around the room, drinking coffee, playing cards, and just generally trying to unwind. A few glanced up as he entered the compartment. It wasn't unheard of for an officer to look for a Chief in the Mess, but it was considered bad form to discuss business in the Mess. Common courtesy and tradition dictated that the officer merely ascertain the presence of the Chief, and then take care of business outside in the passageway or in their work center spaces.

Chief Franklin stood up as Bird Dog stormed into the Mess.

"Evening, Lieutenant. Something I can help you with?"

"Shaughnessy was up on the aircraft without a cranial on,"

Bird Dog said abruptly. A slight chill seemed to settle over the Chiefs' Mess. "You know the rules, Chief," he continued doggedly, ignoring a few pointed glances from the master chiefs.

The older man rubbed his face thoughtfully. "She's bad about that," he admitted. "But I gotta tell you, Lieutenant, she's a damned fine technician. Got a real feel for those Tomcats, and takes her job real serious. Good sailor, right attitude. She's gonna do real well."

"She's no good to the Navy if she falls off an aircraft and cracks her skull open. And if she can't follow safety rules herself, how competent does that make her as a supervisor? Damn it, Chief, a good sailor in my book follows orders!"

"I see your point, Lieutenant. I'll have a word with her. And no disrespect, sir, but which would you rather have? An up aircraft or all the nitpicky little rules followed?"

"I don't consider safety rules to be nit-picking. My Branch follows *all* the rules, Chief. It's not up to Shaughnessy—or you or me—to decide which ones we're going to obey and which ones we aren't. I don't expect to have to talk to you again about this. Put her on extra duty—two hours a day for two weeks. Maybe that'll teach her a lesson."

"Sir, I don't think—we've got shit hitting the fan out there, Lieutenant. As tough as the flight schedule's going to be, those techs are going to be dragging ass. And Lieutenant," the chief continued, his voice unexpectedly gentle, "no disrespect, sir, but you've just been through a pretty nasty experience. It'd shake anybody up. Those guys on the flight deck saw everything, too, and I guarantee you even the old timers are being super cautious up there. It hits you real hard, the first time. Every time, maybe. Now, don't get me wrong, I agree with you about Shaughnessy. We got to do something—that's why they pay us the big bucks, to make sure these kids don't get hurt. But why don't we think about this overnight, give things a chance to settle down. Might be that there's a better way to accomplish what you want. This extra duty—I don't know that I'd recommend it."

The sympathy in the older man's voice infuriated him—insinuating that he was making decisions based on emotion, that he couldn't handle what he'd seen on the flight deck! For a moment, Bird Dog wanted to punch the Chief, to make him take back the words that Bird Dog somehow knew were true.

"Extra duty, Chief. I want a report from you every morning about what she's been assigned to do. That clear?"

The Chief uncurled from his chair and stood rigidly at attention. The other chief petty officers in the mess looked studiously away.

"Sir, yes, sir!" the Chief snapped. His normally good-natured expression had faded into an impassive mask.

Bird Dog stalked out of the Chiefs' Mess, slamming the door behind him. From the passageway outside, Bird Dog heard the murmur of voices increase in volume.

CHAPTER 13
Sunday, 30 June

Shih Tan glanced up at the sun. Even though it was already midday, the hazy morning fog still hung in the air. Hot, humid, and dull—how much worse could military duty get?

A lot worse, he recalled, if the reports of his friends were to be believed. Last summer, a typhoon had swept into the South China Sea, and his friend's cadre had been evacuated with only hours to spare before the pounding winds became too strong for the helicopters to operate.

Despite the heat, Shih Tan shivered at the thought of being marooned in the bamboo structure during one of the vicious storms. He glanced up at the Mischief Reef base camp. While strong enough to survive the normal vicissitudes of summer storms, no bamboo structure could possibly survive a typhoon out here.

He wondered why it had taken the authorities so long to decide to evacuate the base camp for the typhoon. Certainly, there was classified material at the site, and that would have to have been destroyed. The equipment, too. Years of occupying the tiny rock had led to the accumulation of radio gear, spare parts for the tanks, and the numerous bits of jetsam and flotsam that human beings accumulate whenever they inhabit confined quarters.

Despite the comforts of Buddhism as a religion, Shih Tan had no illusions about his own equanimity in facing death. Back on the mainland, he had a wife and two children. Given any chance at all, he'd fight to see them again. While human life might have been less valuable than tactical advantage to his politico-military superiors, Shih Tan valued his own skin.

1246 local (Zulu -7)
Spook Two

"Doesn't look so special from up here, does it?" Batman asked over the ICS.

Spook Two was on its second special surveillance mission. After the ship-based radars had proved that the ripple-skinned Tomcat was almost impossible to track or target, Batman had convinced Tombstone to let the two Spooks fly CAP above the Mischief Reef area.

"Not to me. But then, we're not politicians," Tomboy replied.

Maybe you aren't yet, youngster, Batman thought, glancing back at her. *I wasn't at your age, either. But, oh, if you ever put that fourth full stripe on, the world changes. Yes, indeedy, it does.*

After six months in the Pentagon, Batman was just starting to get a feel for the place. It was a massive readjustment, going from being a captain in the Fleet, with all the courtesies and privileges that went with it, to being a Captain in the Pentagon. Hot and cold running admirals, the joke went. An aviator captain, qualified to command a Carrier Air Wing at sea, was barely senior enough to make coffee in the Pentagon.

Not until the Captain learned the ropes, anyway. Batman had figured that out fairly quickly.

He'd never been entirely sure exactly what his first billet there entailed. He remembered going to a lot of meetings, reading countless white papers, and reviewing tech manuals. Some of the material seemed to bear some relationship to the F-14 program, but much of it didn't. That last puzzling study, for instance, on military health care and Navy Exchange operations. He still had no idea how that'd ended up in his In box, much less in the urgent stack.

Finally, he'd run into Admiral Dunflere, another proud member of the F-14 community, in the cafeteria. The Admiral had been a Commander when Batman was a senior Lieutenant, and remembered him.

More importantly, the Admiral had a vacancy on his staff and wanted him. Batman had jumped at the chance to transfer out of whatever it was he was doing into the JAST shop.

It was only later that he learned how to manipulate the system sufficiently to be forced to conduct frequent field inspections on the JAST birds, and to wangle himself into the training pipeline. Admiral Dunflere seemed perfectly content to receive his weekly field reports via the laptop computer and modem, and Batman took full advantage of his newfound freedom.

And this was what it'd gotten him. An extended trip away from the five-sided office building and back in the cockpit. He glanced down at the Chinese camp perched on top of Mischief Reef and wondered if Tombstone really had any idea of what he was in for on his next tour to DC.

Well, at least Batman's politician days were on hold for a while.

"See anything unusual?" Tomboy asked, breaking his train of thought.

"Nope. You?"

"Not a thing. As long as we're out here, though, maybe we can take another swing around it. After that incident last week, it wouldn't hurt."

"You got it. Let's do a little more op testing on this Tomcat on the way back, though." Batman stood the Tomcat on its tail, reveling in the feel of gravity cementing him back into the ejection seat. God, how he'd missed that! He punched in the afterburners and let the full-throated roar wash over him.

At ten thousand feet, he rolled the Tomcat out into level flight, completing the Immelmann. The Mischief Reef camp was now almost two miles below them. He eased back on the throttle and put the Tomcat into a gentle descent, bleeding off altitude and speed at the same time. Experimentally, he flicked off the auto-angle control and swept the wings forward. He felt the increase in drag and speed and let the aircraft slow almost to stall speed before reengaging the auto-control.

"Looks like everything works as advertised," he advised Tomboy.

"Roger." Had his RIO not been so much junior, Batman might have been tempted to hear the slightly grumpy note in her voice. He smiled. Backseaters never appreciated aerobatics.

1247 local (Zulu -7)
Mischief Reef

Shih Tan glared at the aircraft circling so far away in the sky. Out of range of the Stinger missiles, no doubt. Despite the destruction of the neighboring rock camp, his superiors had taken no steps to upgrade the offensive capabilities of the island. The missile emplacements that were barely masked by bamboo screens and the Stingers were their only protection.

He'd heard the blast from Island 203 and rushed outside in

time to see the rain of litter and rock fall back into the ocean. One sentry said he'd seen the American aircraft dip low over the island and release a bomb, but two other lookouts couldn't confirm the report. Still, there was no doubt in anyone's mind where the bomb had come from. The American aircraft had been the only possible source of it.

The lack of defenses on his tiny island bothered him. While it was well within China's span of control, and should have been sacrosanct in the South China Sea, there was no telling what drove the Americans to do anything. Attacking an undefended, tactically unimportant island was just the latest in a series of American actions that made little sense to the rest of the world. That China should have to tolerate that sort of aggression in her own seas bothered him more than he could say.

Had Shih Tan been in charge, he would have armed the tiny islands to the teeth and ringed them with every capability in the Chinese navy. Not that there were really so many ships, but it was critical to maintaining China's face in the region to put a stop to the American intervention.

A slight breeze rose up, ruffling the damp hair on the back of his neck. He heard the distant whine of insects, but dismissed it. In the next second, his head snapped up, and he gazed frantically around.

Insects? This far out at sea? It wasn't—

The vast bamboo structure behind him erupted in a fiery explosion. He barely had time to process the information in his brain before the shock wave reached him, blasting him off his feet and into the warm waters of the South China Sea just seconds in front of the fireball.

Shih Tan hit the water hard and plummeted fifteen feet beneath it. He retained just enough consciousness to try to struggle to the surface. He heard a muted series of thuds as debris hit the water around him, flames instantly extinguished and steam churning the water. As he stroked for the surface, he saw a film of flames spreading out above him, broken only by debris crashing through it to the water.

1248 local (Zulu -7)
Spook Two

"Shit!" Batman yelled, instinctively putting the Tomcat into a sharp climb. "What the hell was that?"

Tomboy craned her head around and looked back at the surface of the ocean. Thick black smoke flecked with flames covered the surface of the ocean, obscuring Spratly Three.

"I don't know, Batman," she said finally. "But it looks like whatever happened to the other camp just happened again."

"Where're those goddamn Flankers!" he demanded. Over tactical, the other three Tomcats were buzzing about the explosion, each RIO denying that they'd seen anything out of the ordinary, and double-checking each other visually to ensure that all the weapons they'd left with were still on the rails.

"Fifty miles to the west." She gave him a bearing to fly, then added, "Thor's on his now, and I still don't know if the other three were ghosts or real contacts. The one Thor intercepted didn't have anything on his rails, and there was no indication of any communications downlink. Whatever happened to that camp, I don't think Thor's Flanker had anything to do with it."

"It's a damned strange coincidence that he just happened to be out here, don't you think?" he asked sarcastically. "I mean, a nasty, suspicious mind might just be tempted to think that there's some connection between a Chinese Flanker cruising toward an American battle group and a Chinese outpost smearing itself across five square miles of ocean."

"Don't have to tell me that," she answered. "But you have

any idea about what could have done it? It wasn't us, and it wasn't them. So who?"

"I don't know, Tomboy. But if I had to bet between us being responsible and the Chinese, I know where my money'd be."

"You and me both. Wait, Homeplate's talking."

"Flankers have turned and are headed back toward Vietnam," she heard the *Jefferson* TAO say. The TAO then reeled off orders and directions recalling the five Tomcats and the Marine Hornet to the boat.

"And that ought to clinch it," Tomboy said. "Soon as he saw the explosion, he turned and ran for home base."

"Not exactly. He ran for Vietnam. And for a Chinese Flanker, that's a little bit different than home," Batman said.

1300 local (Zulu -8)
Operations Center
Hanoi, Vietnam

"At some time," Mein Low said, "we will have another conversation on this matter. You must know that we have only the best intentions for our southern brothers. In the interest of regional security, we must stand united. Would you have either of our countries become slaves to the American culture, as the Japanese have become? I think not. For too many years, we have both fought to avoid that."

Bien nodded politely. "Naturally, the differences in culture are too extreme to permit that to happen. The Chinese have always been supportive of our independence." *While they have simultaneously fought to prevent us from assuming control of our own destiny. Throughout the Vietnam wars, first with the French and then with the Americans, you have sought to control events in our country.*

"Our joint operations have been the beginning of even more

cooperation," the Chinese Commander continued. "You are wise to understand that we must present a united front to the world on this issue."

"My pilots have gained a great deal of useful experience operating with your forces," Bien added politely. *Experience in being the victims of your aggression! In every exercise, we are forced to play the hapless victims patrolling the skies, while your Flankers pounce on them. It is just good joss, as you would say, that no one has been killed thus far.*

The Chinese Commander permitted himself a small smile. "We have tried to share our experience with you," he agreed. "Your forces have shown much progress. Together, I believe we can repel this American battle group. With one stunning sweep, we will ensure that they will never meddle in our affairs again!"

"Our wish as well," Bien murmured. At least that much was true. Vietnam needed neither Chinese hegemony nor American imperialism any longer.

"Then we are of one mind. As I said, we will talk more about these matters when we approach a final solution."

Bien executed a tiny bow, one that almost verged on insolent. *Pig.*

The Chinese Commander stared after him as he left. *Scum.*

CHAPTER 14
Sunday, 30 June

Amidst the noise and the lights of the Swedish ambassador's reception, the delegates to the United Nations still found time to conduct business.

"And again," T'ing said, barely raising his voice above an icy whisper, "once was not enough."

"Sir, the United States had no part in the attack on your—on Mischief Reef Island," Ambassador Wexler said, catching herself just in time. She was under instructions to avoid any positive acknowledgment of China's ownership of the South China Sea rocks. She saw Ngyugen, the ambassador from Vietnam, nod ever so slightly at her correction.

T'ing sighed. "No other military forces were in the area, madam. As it was last time—an American jet circles an isolated Chinese oceanographic research station, and then the island mysteriously explodes. Perhaps a fishing boat attacked the scientific camp?"

"An oceanographic research station? With tanks and fighter aircraft? And Stingers and submarines on patrol? Forgive me, but I doubt that the ambassador from China is being entirely candid."

"With unprovoked attacks by the United States on our land, what nation would not make some self-defense preparations?" T'ing replied. He knew it would be impossible to hide the presence of military forces on the islands from the circling satellites.

"The United States has attacked no one," the ambassador insisted, struggling to keep her temper under control. "It was China who attacked us! Your submarine, sir, fired on one of our aircraft operating in international airspace."

"Following," T'ing said, "the American destruction of an undefended research station, an attempt to provide a radar lock-up on one of our patrol aircraft for firing an Aegis cruiser missile, and the continued presence of American forces in a legally declared exclusion zone. Only the United States could have the audacity to claim status as a victim while simultaneously attacking our forces herself!"

"We are prepared to make our tactical logs and crews available to an impartial investigating committee. Whatever is causing these incidents in the South China Sea, I believe that the ambassador from China knows more about it than we do."

"A very generous offer," T'ing broke in. "Very generous indeed—if the United States had not had sufficient time already to completely fabricate records pertaining to that time. The gentle art of manipulating electrons—who better than the Americans at it?" T'ing shrugged. "Fortunately, we will not need to rely on electronic memories and fabrications. We have something far more reliable."

"What, a confession?" Sarah Wexler asked sarcastically, immediately regretting her words.

T'ing locked her with a cold stare and let the seconds tick by while all eyes in the room turned to him.

"Something better than that, I believe. And far more reliable. Late this morning, a Chinese naval vessel initiated a search for survivors. Three members of the Spratly base camp survived.

One, Shih Tan, was standing outside when the attack occurred and observed the overflight of an American military aircraft, followed minutes later by the explosion. The force of the blast tossed him off the island and into the sea. Shih Tan almost drowned trying to avoid the rain of fiery debris. Only his will to live and superb training, plus his determination to tell of American perfidy, enabled him to survive."

"And a very interesting story it will be, I'm sure," she said tartly. "Excuse me, but I believe I need to greet our hostess."

Battle-ax! How well that suits you, madam, T'ing thought. *But no matter how skilled you are in this arena, too many preparations have already been made in other theaters for your words to make the slightest bit of difference in the outcome. You've missed the battle, and the war is almost over. For without the cooperation of the sniveling mongrels' countries that yap at your heels, you have no future in our seas—and you lack the will to make it otherwise!*

"She seems quite annoyed," Ngyugen said, slipping smoothly into the gap in the conversation. "Defensive, almost. They are behind these incidents—you are sure?"

"We have our sources," T'ing snapped. "As you well should know. And should you be the least bit confused about this, let me remind you of the landing rights we assert within your own country. Do you really wish to enter into this political discourse? Oh, yes, we're aware that normalization of relations is the watchword in your country now. But remember who you will have to live with when the Americans are gone!"

"And you believe that they will leave this theater of operations? Still, with all the increases in trade and travel?" Ngyugen pressed.

"I have no doubt about it! And it will be sooner than you ever dreamed!" T'ing turned and stalked away. It was one thing to tolerate the arrogance of the American ambassador. While that might be required in the short term, it would eventually

come to an end. Impudence from Vietnamese politicians was
another matter entirely.

Lab Rat swore silently and shivered as a particularly cold gust
from the overhead air conditioning vent blasted down his neck.
Only when the carrier was deployed to the brutally hot Persian
Gulf did the temperature in CVIC ever approach habitable. In
the South China Sea, the temperature in the room packed with
electronics gear hovered between fifty and sixty degrees. No
amount of pleading with the ship's engineers could get it
stabilized at an almost livable sixty-five degrees. It was an
article of faith with every engineer he'd ever met that electrons
worked better when frozen.

He looked up from the debriefing form and stared at the pilot
and RIO across the table. To them, just coming off the hot
flight deck, the temperature must seem refreshing. In a few
minutes, when the sweat dried and their damp flight suits
chilled, they'd change their minds. Lab Rat hoped he could
keep them from dashing back to their staterooms for flight
jackets or warmer clothes. Once they were out of CVIC, the
details of their flight, along with their willingness to cooperate
in the debrief, would evaporate just as quickly as the sweat.

He tried again. "It just blew up? That's all? No I&W—
indications and warnings? What about those four contacts you
were tracking?" he asked.

"Sir, you saw the same picture we did. We were up in the
LINK the entire time, except when we got too low and lost the
signal. According to the Aegis, those contacts were ghosts.
Something strange about the atmospheric conditions, maybe.

You know how it is out there. I wish I could give you a better answer, but I just don't know whether there was one Flanker or four," Tomboy replied wearily.

"What about when you were down on the deck and dropped out of the LINK? Anything then?" Lab Rat pressed.

"She said she didn't see anything, *Commander*," Batman said sharply.

Lab Rat leaned back in his chair and stared thoughtfully at the aviator captain. It was a good thing, he decided, that he'd taken on debriefing the flight crew himself. While mission debriefs were normally done by lieutenants or more junior officers, the rank and importance of this particular crew seemed to warrant his personal attention, even apart from the strange events that had occurred.

Captain Wayne, he reflected, was just as impressively intimidating as he'd been led to believe. At the same time, he was certain that Batman understood the reason for the repeated questions, the cross-examination that he and his RIO were undergoing. It wasn't that anyone doubted their account, but lives were at stake. The simplest detail overlooked in the initial debrief that surfaced in more intensive sessions might save another aviator's life. And the captain's protective attitude toward his RIO was hindering that investigation.

"I understand what she said, Captain," Lab Rat said politely, but firmly. "Sometimes new details surface when we go over something several times."

"There *are no* details to surface! Look, we've spent the last six hours in these flight suits, and I for one could use food and coffee. I don't know what the hell made that island explode, and neither does she," Batman said, pointing at his RIO. "We can't come up with explanations for everything. Now, if you need anything else, we'll be forward in the dirty shirt mess, grabbing a couple of sliders." Batman motioned to Tomboy, who followed him out of the CVIC.

And that's the difference between your job and mine, Lab Rat thought. *You didn't see it, you don't have to explain it.* Intell officers, on the other hand, are expected to have an answer for everything that happens, and an accurate prediction of everything that *will* happen. Doesn't matter whether or not there's good data, bad data, or even no data at all. This admiral's going to want some explanations, and he's damned sure not going to be demanding that the pilots come up with them.

And I wonder just how much of your protectiveness toward your RIO is based on the fact that she's a very attractive woman, he thought. *I know pilot-RIO teams are tight, but this goes a little bit beyond that, I believe.*

This cruise had been filled with too many firsts. First cruise in PacFleet, first exposure to unraveling the strange intricacies of Pacific Rim politics, and his first cruise with a coed crew. After five months on board the *Jefferson*, he was finally getting accustomed to seeing women—lots of women!—in the passageways of the ship while it was underway.

From an intelligence standpoint, his previous cruises to the Mediterranean and North Atlantic had been a piece of cake. Europe and the Soviet Union were at least known quantities— strange, querulous, and liable to break into myriad warring factions on the slightest pretense, but at least semipredictable. Here in the Far East, Lab Rat was not only short on answers, he wasn't entirely sure he understood the questions.

He glanced at the books packed into the narrow shelf over his desk and reached for one slim volume. He had to lift it straight up to clear the metal strut that ran the length of the shelf, parallel to the edge of the shelf and midspine to the books. Without the strut, or a set of bungee cords, the first heavy roll at sea would have dumped every book onto the deck.

He sat back down, leaned back, and put his feet up on a corner of his desk. He'd bought the book as soon as he'd heard he was going to a West Coast carrier, hoping for some insights into the areas he'd be deploying to.

So far, it hadn't paid off. The small book was a translation of one of China's most famous military strategists, Sun Tzu. His book, *The Art of War*, had been studied by centuries of military leaders, both in China and in the Western world.

Lab Rat leafed through the book, looking for inspiration and wondering idly if whoever was responsible for the attacks had a copy of the book over his desk, too. It gave him an eerie feeling, thinking about his adversary reading the same book at the same time.

A sentence caught his attention. Like so much of the book, it seemed to be either a trite adage or a profound statement. He read the sentence again slowly, wondering how it applied to his situation.

All warfare is deception, Sun Tzu had written. Well, that certainly applied to the current tactical scenario. To the nations rimming the South China Sea, it appeared that the United States was committing acts of war against their powerful northern neighbor. Unable to offer evidence to dispute China's claims, the United States faced an increasingly hostile United Nations.

As Lab Rat saw it, there were two distinct problems. First, whatever munitions were responsible for the destruction— maybe the mythical stealth sea-skimming cruise missiles— were proving damned difficult to detect. Second, even if the United States *could* detect and track the missiles, how could they convince the other nations that the United States hadn't fired the missiles themselves? After all, what other nation had both the stealth technology and the platforms to be able to conduct such attacks?

Malaysia and Brunei? Not likely.

Vietnam? A definite possibility. But was it likely that Vietnam would openly challenge the massive giant to their north just when both countries were engaged in reopening diplomatic ties with the United States? Again, not likely. But not impossible.

Finally, China herself. Technologically, she had the means and ability to fire long-range stealth cruise missiles, either from land or from a submarine. Certainly the Kilo armed with SAMs had proved that China had made major advances in weapons technology, and had little hesitation about using it. And what about the F-10 program? Was it further along than anyone suspected, and so stealthy that it could trick a combat-tested RIO into believing it was a ghost contact?

And the most intriguing question of all still remained unanswered. If China were behind the incidents, why was she destroying her own bases? Maintaining a presence on the tiny rocks was the keystone to China's continued claims of ownership.

While ownership of the Spratly Islands was a sore point among the South China Sea nations, *would* China go so far as to kill her own troops to try to frame another nation? And why the United States? The U.S. had no designs on ownership of the Spratly Islands, just a desire to make sure that there were still some constraints on China's influence in the area.

Lab Rat slammed the book shut and tossed it up on the shelf. Geopolitical machinations were way out of his league. He hungered for some intell, just one or two hard data points to hang some sort of theory on for the admiral.

Deception as a theory made a damned boring slide show.

1930 local (Zulu -7)
Flag Briefing Room

"So what do we do now? Blanket the area with assets until we find something? Throw everything we've got at the submarine? The floor's open for suggestions," Tombstone said. CAG,

COS, OPS, and *Jefferson*'s CO all looked at each other glumly. They were gathered around the briefing table outside of TFCC, looking at a small-scale chart of the South China Sea.

"It's a catch-22," COS said. "We know *we're* not responsible, but nobody believes us. To get proof, we need to have the air saturated with assets during the next attack. But under the circumstances, putting that many aircraft up continuously is going to look ominous. It'll just look like we were behind the attacks all along."

"Not to mention the ops tempo you're talking about," CAG interjected. "How long can we keep up a complete umbrella of good look-down assets? Tankers, escorts, everything that goes along with it."

"*And* provide protection for the rest of the battle group," *Jefferson*'s CO added. "Sooner or later, someone's going to run out of islands and come looking for the next best thing."

"*Jefferson*'s bigger than either of those rocks," Tombstone said. "And a lot better protected. We're going to have to rely on the surface ships, particularly the Aegis, if we siphon off that much CAP to do surface surveillance."

"Aegis can handle it," COS said. A former Aegis skipper himself, he had a comprehensive familiarity with the platform's capabilities.

"Not sure her CO can, though," CAG said. "Got a little *too* proactive last week with that fire control radar."

"Get your pilots to quit fucking with him, then. Turned out to be a good thing he *was* so trigger happy, didn't it?" Tombstone snapped.

"Except that he may have provoked the whole thing by lighting up that Flanker," CAG responded, not backing down an inch. "Admiral, I don't want to rehash last week's problems. It's *this* situation I'm worried about."

"How about this?" OPS asked. "We figure out where and when the next attack is going to be and make sure we track the missile or whatever in from its point of origin. Then we've got evidence."

"Great. Just great," CAG sneered. "And just how do you propose that we do that? Ask the bad guys—once we figure out who they are, that is!—to fax us their battle plans?"

"Admiral," Lab Rat said suddenly. The sentence from Sun Tzu's book kept repeating in his brain, insisting that there was an answer in it. "I think I might have a couple of ideas on this. We don't exactly need to predict the next attack. We just need to use it."

Tombstone stared at the most junior member of the group. "I think maybe I'm going to want you to explain that a little bit more."

"The Chinese believe that deception is the basis of all warfare. It's fairly obvious to all of us that these events are supposed to make the world believe that we're responsible for the bombings—whatever causes them. Nothing happens unless American aircraft are in the area," Busby said.

"What about satellite coverage?" OPS asked.

"Not conclusive. The Chinese will simply claim we doctored the pictures, which would be well within anyone's capabilities with a reasonably good graphics program. And don't rule out the fog of war. Things go wrong, sir, at the damnedest times. We may just miss the picture we need."

"Don't we know it," CAG murmured. "Interesting line of reasoning, Lab Rat."

"But what's the *point* of it all?" OPS persisted. "If they're so damned subtle and inscrutable, then how are we supposed to use these incidents to our advantage?"

"I think we probably can assume that the point is to make us look bad in this theater of operations," Tombstone said. "That part of their plan is working damned well. So what are you suggesting, Commander?"

"I think," Busby said slowly, trying to collect the cascade of ideas into some semblance of order, "that if they want us to be around when explosions occur in the Spratly area, our first priority should be to *not* be there. We need to *not cooperate* with whatever it is they're trying to achieve. And we need to look very closely at the sequence of events and determine exactly how they are using our own forces and assets against us. The Flankers, the sorties from Vietnam—those are distractions, Admiral, intended to draw us away from what is really happening. Same thing with the submarines. Look at the assumptions we're already starting to make. I've heard anything from guesses about advance stealth technology on their aircraft to land-launched Tomahawk-style strike missiles to particle beams from satellites. All of those things are well outside of what we believe the Chinese are capable of. And they're all intended to make China look a good deal more potent militarily than they are."

"But why the flights out of Vietnam?" Tombstone asked. "Follow your train of thought on that."

"If I may, Admiral—what does the fact that China is flying out of Vietnam suggest to *you*?"

"Makes me wonder how close the Chinese and the Vietnamese are on this thing," Tombstone responded. "I'm thinking it may set back normalization of relations with Vietnam for quite a while."

"And who would *know* if the Chinese are launching any sort of strike from Vietnam?" Busby pressed.

"The Vietnamese," CAG said suddenly. "They'd know. They have to see the aircraft going out and coming back in. If they leave with weapons on the wings and return clean, Vietnam would know that China was behind the attacks."

"And yet, just the opposite seems to be happening, doesn't it?" Busby answered. "We see the Flankers come out *without* weapons, right? So the Vietnamese—"

"Know that the Chinese *aren't* responsible," Tombstone

finished. "And we end up with Vietnam appearing to us to be supporting China just when we're normalizing relations."

"And as a corollary, Vietnam's gotta be convinced that we're responsible, because they know China's not," CAG concluded. "So far, it makes sense to me. And the final objective is what?"

"To make sure the South China Sea remains China's lake. To completely eliminate any political support from any littoral nation. You know what that means." Busby glanced around the room. Yes, they did know—he could see it in their faces.

"No land bases, no logistics support. We've already lost the Philippines. If China's plan works, we might lose support in Singapore. And with China assuming control over Hong Kong, the primary money center for the Far East, she suddenly becomes a lot more important to these nations than the United States," Tombstone said.

"And there you go," Busby concluded. "To gain regional dominance, all it costs them is some of their own troops. At last count, China's population was almost two billion. If there's one thing that China *does* have, it's people."

"So where does that leave us?" Tombstone asked. "What do you see as the primary threat axis?"

"If I could speculate, Admiral?"

"Go ahead."

"It seems at least possible," Lab Rat said, "that China has some form of long-range strike platform. It's not the aircraft it has deployed to Vietnam—we've seen too much evidence that they're coming out clean. That leaves a ship, a submarine, or a land-launched platform. I doubt it's a ship. We'd have detected her on SUCAP. A submarine is a strong candidate, given the stealthy nature of the attacks, and the fact that we've seen one sub launch a cruise missile against us already."

"Oh, great. Submarines," CAG said, disgusted.

"Probably at least one. But just because we've found *one* answer doesn't mean that we've found all the answers. There are problems with the submarine answer, too. Subs are hard to talk to on a regular schedule. I don't think that they'd be the choice for coordinating attacks with our patrols around the area. Too much uncertainty, too difficult to make sure the attack happened when we were around. I think we have to at least consider—and plan for—the possibility that China has a long-range land attack missile. If they do, it's got to be launched from their mainland. No way that they'd take that technology to Vietnam and run the risk of losing it. Besides, that would blow their plan as far as Vietnam is concerned. Then their neighbors would *know* that China is behind all the attacks, and they'd have no reason to be suspicious of us."

"So we end up with a missile threat from the north, from China's mainland. And an air threat to the east, from the Chinese aircraft stationed in Vietnam. As well as a submarine cruise missile threat to the ships from just about anywhere."

"I think so," Lab Rat agreed. "And we may have some information leaks as well, although I'm not certain about that. But the safe thing to do is to keep any plans as tightly compartmented as possible, to minimize the risks."

"I can just hear Killington now," COS said thoughtfully. "Based on these assumptions, you're probably going to want to send him north. He's going to want to know why, and you're not going to be able to tell him."

"He'll live with it," Tombstone said shortly. "Be good practice for him, obeying orders for a while."

"I'll rough out an air plan for you immediately, Admiral," CAG said. "We'll be putting some extra fighters on alert, as well as some ASW assets. Your flight crews are going to be pulling some long hours sitting alert."

"It builds character," Tombstone said. "At least that's what my first CO told me when I bitched about it."

CAG chuckled. "I can think of at least one young aviator who could use some of that, sir."

"Gentlemen," Tombstone said, standing up and picking up his notepad, "thank you for your time. Commander Busby, I think we have some insight into the operational scenario. Good work. Now let's see what we can do to turn the tables on these bastards!"

CHAPTER 15
Monday, 1 July

0518 local (Zulu -7)
On board Vietnamese patrol boat, vicinity of Island 508
Spratly Islands, South China Sea

The Vietnamese lieutenant stared out at the still-dark horizon, trying to see through the early morning fog. Timing was critical to this mission. It was still twenty minutes until sunrise, enough time to maneuver into position near the tiny rock in the middle of the ocean. Ideally, the sun would just be rising as the occupation team deployed.

He looked back toward the fantail, at the small group of men and equipment standing around in the predawn gloom. He pitied them. While life aboard the Soviet Zhuk-class patrol boat was certainly not luxurious, it beat the hell out of where those men were headed.

The Vietnamese naval force was an odd mixture of discarded Soviet and American small vessels. The lieutenant's Zhuk was one of the most modern additions, transferred to Vietnam in 1989 from the Soviet Union. The twelve-man crew was one of the more motivated crews he'd served with. The boat was twenty-four feet long, and could cruise through the seas at thirty-four knots. While it certainly wasn't the largest naval vessel to ply the South China Sea, it was more than large enough for this mission.

He wished he could say the same about the occupation team. The stack of boxes and survival equipment that would be placed on the rock with them looked pitifully small. He'd been told that there were enough concentrated rations in one box to feed the five men for two weeks, long enough for the resupply crew to get to them. Beside that box, a tarpaulin to provide shelter from the sun was rolled into a compact cylinder. A few blankets, some rudimentary radio equipment, and a water-distilling pump completed the loadout. And the Stingers—the all-important Stingers. It was the last item that completely blew the team's cover story of establishing a fishing camp.

Better you than me, he thought. The battle for ownership of the Spratly Islands, according to his superiors, required establishing a presence on the desolate rocks that composed the South China Sea chain. This outpost would be left on a patch of barren igneous rock that was barely bigger than his Zhuk. For not the first time, the Vietnamese navy lieutenant gave thanks that he'd joined the right branch of the military. While navy units might ferry the occupation teams to the rocks, standing presence duty in the South China Sea was solely the province of the Vietnamese army.

"All is ready, Captain," his phone talker said, relaying the words he received from the other talker on the fantail.

"Very well. Just a little more light, and we will make our approach." Getting close enough to unload the men and equipment into the small boat that would take them to the rock would be tricky. While the waters were well charted, and his GPS equipment gave him an accurate fix on his own location, too much could always go wrong. Navigating around rocks and shoals in his thin-hulled patrol craft would be safer when his lookouts could see what some lazy cartographer might have overlooked.

Ten minutes later, his forward lookout reported that visibility was clearing. The lieutenant moved back inside the pilot house.

"Take us in, Ensign," he ordered. The younger officer nodded.

"Engine ahead one-third," he said firmly.

The lee helmsman echoed the command, and the steel deck began thrumming as the powerful diesel engines that drove the two propellers increased speed.

"Come right, steer course 005," the ensign ordered. The small craft heeled slightly to the right.

A few minutes later, the ensign said, "There it is, sir." He pointed to a barely visible rock projecting from the sea.

"Very well. Let's get on with it."

In response to the ensign's orders, the men on the fantail moved over the side into the Rigid-Hull Inflatable boat tethered to the ship. The RHIB, pronounced "rib," was a mainstay of many naval services. Since it could be deflated, it saved on precious storage space. The outboard motor could drive it through the ocean at far greater speeds than the hull could withstand, so it took careful handling to avoid overturning it.

The young captain of the patrol boat, preoccupied with off-loading his passengers and their equipment, had even less warning than the tank commander had. He saw motion on the horizon and reached for his binoculars. Seconds later, the missile slammed into the patrol boat, impacting amidships at the waterline after cutting through the RHIB and her crew.

The missile penetrated completely through the patrol boat before it exploded. The blast disintegrated the entire midsection of the boat, driving a rain of steel fragments through every other part of the interior. Metal shredded flesh, killing most of the crew instantly. The explosion cracked the hull in half, broke the keel, and peeled the weather decks away from the supporting framework of stanchions and strakes. The warm sea poured in.

The fire had just enough time to ignite the small arms

ammunition and the Stinger missiles before the sea claimed the
boat and crew.

Monday, 1 July
0900 local (Zulu -8)
Operations Center
Hanoi, Vietnam

The two men were alone in the conference room, as alone as
possible in the former Communist country. "What are the
Americans thinking?" Ngyugen hissed. "To invade our waters,
destroy our islands—it is war!" The Vietnamese ambassador
to the United Nations seemed to swell up with indignation,
which was part of his standard repertoire when talking about
the Americans.

"Be calm for a moment and let me think," Bien ordered.
"There are matters that must be decided, and anger will not
help us."

"You would see them ashore in our country again? Burning,
raping, destroying in the name of their democracy?"

"Come now. They have hardly landed on our shores. There
is not even an amphibious vessel with the ships. No marines,
no army."

"Guns and aircraft alone can do enough damage," Ngyugen
muttered darkly.

"So can foolish talk!" Bien snapped. "Think for a minute!
Do you really believe that the Americans have destroyed both
of those islands?"

Ngyugen shot him an uncertain look that gradually solidified
into outrage. For a general to talk so to him—it was unacceptable. But to have said those words, Bien undoubtedly pos-
sessed some key bit of information that he believed exempted
him from the respect due to the older man. Still, the facts were

obvious. "Of course. Their aircraft were above both locations as the explosions took place. What other purpose could there be for the ships being in our waters? And Colonel Mein Low assures me that the Chinese intelligence and satellite reports—"

"—say exactly what the army wants them to," Bien finished.

"Are you implying that I have been misled?" Ngyugen's face darkened as he considered the possibility. If it were so, then Bien indeed *did* have knowledge that would prove exceedingly useful. Perhaps it would be better to overlook the earlier disrespect, at least until Ngyugen could determine what secrets the general held.

"I imply nothing. Ambassador, you must remember that you are a prime target for Chinese manipulation and deceit. They understand how important you are to your country, and have chosen to try out their scheme first on you," Bien said soothingly. "Luckily, I can tell from your comments that their plan will not succeed."

Ngyugen recognized the attempt to placate him and allowed himself to be calmed. Bien might think him a fool, but Ngyugen was a critical part of Bien's source of power, and the military commander knew better than to alienate his political connections. At least not until Bien could replace Ngyugen with someone more useful. Ngyugen watched Bien smile ingratiatingly at him.

"They do know of my army career," Ngyugen said meaningfully, as the possibility that Bien might be right began to make sense.

"Of course they do. How could anyone overlook your two years of military service? Undoubtedly why they chose you as the key test of how believable their story is," Bien said calmly. "Their foolishness is our gain. Very few members of the delegation could have hidden their insights so well. I am pleased that you chose me as the test of your facade. You must remember, I know you far better than most, yet I was deceived by your reaction for almost five minutes." Bien forced a chuckle. "I almost believed that you believed their story. My apologies."

"Accepted," said Ngyugen, since nothing else in Bien's entire conversation made sense to him.

"So you see the truth to this, of course. It is *not* the Americans who are behind this, if for no other reason than because the Chinese claim that they are. There are other facts, certainly. The fact that the Americans rarely intervene anywhere anymore without a United Nations resolution to validate their meddling. That they were here for a month before the bombings began, and have followed a routine pattern of operations and deployments for the South China Sea." Bien shook his head. "Clearly the Chinese will have a difficult time convincing anyone of their deception, much less the more astute political observers such as yourself."

"We must expose this sham to the world!" Ngyugen declared.

"Perhaps—in time," Bien said musingly. "But I think there are other ways that it can be used to our advantage at this time."

"What are you suggesting?"

"That regardless of which country is behind the destruction— or even if it is a renegade group of terrorists acting alone—the Americans are taking entirely too much for granted in our area of the world. Withholding normalization of relations with our country, dictating trade terms to our neighbors—no, it would be extremely useful to all of us if the Americans perceived a united Pacific Rim standing against them. Then they would be desperate to gain a toehold in this area, which could only help us gain valuable trade concessions."

"So we unite the region against both the Americans *and* China!"

"Not just yet. Remember, even after the Americans leave, we will still have to live with China. Better, perhaps, to pretend to believe China's story for now. Place them in debt to us for our cooperation, assist them in persuading the others. That could be more useful to us in the long run."

"But the Spratly Islands! The oil! That is our property, Bien! You suggest we just sit idly by while America and China apportion out our rights?"

"No, of course not. But another approach might work just as well."

Bien talked for another fifteen minutes, explaining a plan that his eight-year-old son would have understood in five minutes. Finally, Ngyugen started nodding.

CHAPTER 16
Monday, 1 July

"You're certain this will work?" Tombstone asked the Intelligence Officer.

"If it were certain, it wouldn't be intelligence," Lab Rat replied wryly. "High probability, Admiral, based on the patterns we've observed, but no guarantees."

Tombstone sighed. "No guarantees if we *don't* do something, either."

"Exactly. At least this plan takes advantage of what we do know about the Chinese."

"It sounds too simple."

"Simple doesn't mean easy. Timing is everything on this." Lab Rat held up his hand, ticking the points off on his fingers. "We know that the attacks are occurring while we have aircraft in the area. Coincidental? Probably not. Presumably, someone intends to make it look like the U.S. is responsible, especially since it's happened more than once. That leads me to the second point." Lab Rat held up the next finger.

"*How* do they know when we're in the area? Couple of possibilities, offhand. First, satellites. A possibility, especially if they have long-range Tomahawks on alert the entire time, but not a high probability, since the reaction time is so fast. Remember, though, that *our* satellite coverage may be of intense interest to them. This would be important to them because a satellite might catch the missile in the process of launching, which would completely blow their cover. So I'm looking at our satellite coverage, not theirs.

"The second possibility is surveillance of some sort. But we haven't detected surface ships or aircraft at the time of every incident. Maybe the submarine, but I doubt it. It's too slow and has too low a horizon. Third—and my favorite possibility— reports by the sites themselves of visuals on American aircraft. Now *that* makes sense!"

"I'm not sure I agree completely," Tombstone said reflectively. "There's always the possibility that they just understand how carrier flight ops work, and are taking their chances that we'll fly by to look at their rocks during cycle times."

"A possibility, of course, but one that leaves too much open to chance. First, what if we'd changed flight cycle time, for whatever reason? Fouled deck, you name it—a thousand things can throw a flight schedule off. Second, even if they know *when* we're launching aircraft, they can't know exactly *where* the fighters are headed. *We* don't even know that, other than they're headed for CAP stations with a few surveillance checkpoints along the way. No, too much to chance. Remember, there are three reported incidents. Every one took place when our assets were in the area. More importantly, *none* took place when we weren't there."

"Sounds like the best way to avoid more incidents is to pack up and go home," Tombstone said wearily. "That's not an option, by the way."

"But there's more to this problem, Admiral. Remember, we're just up to the second step—the timing. The next factor to consider is the attacking platform."

"I thought we'd agreed that it was long-range cruise missiles," Batman said. "That's the pretext I used for getting the JAST birds out here, anyway."

"That's one possibility. Remember, there's nothing that says all three attacks were done by the same means. Additionally, you know how unpredictable atmospheric conditions are out here. Could be we just *thought* we saw low-fliers, just like the E-2 picked up those ghosts the other day. Some unexplained circumstances, a few radar ghosts—hell, we're letting the fog of war do all the Chinese's work for them, inventing explanations and causes."

"I personally think it's *possible* that the Chinese have developed their own version of the Tomahawk," Lab Rat continued. "Except, perhaps, in one instance."

"Which one?" Batman asked.

"The attack on Mischief Reef. That was too short notice. Building a Tomahawk package takes time."

"Could have done it with something like a Harpoon and fly-to points," COS said reflectively.

"Of course. But now we're back to a mobile platform. Except for the submarine, no evidence that a platform that could carry something like a Harpoon was even around."

"Okay, so what do *you* think it was?" Batman asked, exasperated.

"If I can, Captain, I'd like to hold that thought for just one more moment. I think you'll see why shortly," Lab Rat said boldly.

Tombstone waved at Lab Rat to continue with the briefing.

"Finally, the last attack on the Mischief Reef base camp," Lab Rat continued. "Again, executed just as our aircraft were overhead. No indications of anything inbound, no surface platforms in the area, and a massive detonation. One survivor, who reports that he'd seen our aircraft executing a flyover. Surely he wasn't the only one to see it. Picture the sequence, gentlemen. An aircraft flies over, ten seconds later the camp explodes." Lab Rat fell silent and watched their faces.

"Oh, my god," Tombstone said softly. "They did it themselves, didn't they?"

Lab Rat nodded. "I think so."

"The Chinese blew up their own bases to make us look bad?" Batman asked. "What's so radical about that—I thought that's just what we've been discussing."

"It's more than that, Batman," Tombstone said, his voice taking on a grim note. "More than just intentionally attacking your own people. Think about the timing. There was nothing in the area and no sign of a submarine-launched weapon. I think La—the commander has the right idea."

"Deception is the key to all Asian warfare planning," Lab Rat said. "It's fundamental to the way they make war, and they plan for it in ways that we can't even begin to imagine. There's only one way for that base camp to have been destroyed so quickly. *It was command-destructed.* Somewhere ashore—or maybe on the sub, I don't know for sure—someone has a transmitter that can send a signal to each Spratly Island. Somewhere in the foundation for the larger camps is a self-destruct package. It's not under the on-scene commander's control—he may not even know it's there. But when the mainland gets word from the base camp that American fighters are overhead, there's a way to make it look like we're the cause of the destruction."

"Assuming that's how they're doing it, how do we use the information?" Tombstone asked, looking at the intelligence officer with new respect. He would make it a point, he thought, to make sure that the man got a better call sign. Whatever the reason for earning the name Lab Rat, he'd just outgrown it.

"That part's a little tricky," Lab Rat admitted. "The first option is trying to expose what China's done. Unfortunately, we're lacking a little technicality called proof."

"Sure would be nice, though. At least the other nations would start listening to some sense instead of blindly following China's lead," CAG said.

"Not necessarily," Lab Rat disagreed. "The concept of losing face is of enormous importance here. The other nations probably already *know* that China's behind this. They may not know the details, but they'll suspect something. If we simply call China's bluff, we put them in a difficult position. Remember, after we leave the South China Sea, they're still going to have to deal with the giant to their north. And an unhappy, embarrassed China is going to be a more difficult neighbor. Second, we'll lose face with the smaller nations—not for having been tricked initially, but for not arriving at a solution that turns the situation to our advantage and allows China to save some degree of face."

"Who the hell *cares* whether China's embarrassed!" Batman exploded.

"*We* have to," Tombstone said grimly. "Different answers to problems at this level, Batman. Things were a lot simpler when it was simply a matter of ordnance on target and time on top. You'll see, the first time you're sitting in this chair instead of behind a desk."

"Understood, Admiral," Batman said formally.

"As the commander has explained, we lose face if we can't play by the rules of this game. So what we need to do is turn this situation to our own advantage, without getting our people killed and without forcing the issues. That about it, Commander?"

"Yes, Admiral, I'd say that's an accurate summation."

"How?" Tombstone said simply.

Lab Rat smiled a little. "I was hoping you might ask that."

"This better work," COS said grimly. He stared at the TFCC big-screen display, watching the small symbol representing the Aegis track to the west. "Otherwise, we're in serious trouble if China decides to launch an alpha strike against us."

"*Vincennes* is fifteen miles off the coast of Vietnam, sir," the TAO reported. "Sufficient to be outside of territorial waters."

"She was supposed to move further north," Tombstone said, eyeballing the distances. "He can probably surveil the northern approach from where he is, but I'd like to give her the additional sensitivity that being closer will give her. I need those famous Aegis eyes and spies giving me more warning. Flankers coming off the coast of Vietnam aren't the only threat we have to worry about out here—not if Commander Busby's intelligence estimate is correct."

"I suggested that, Admiral, but her CO mentioned that he'd prefer the additional reaction time to the additional coverage," the TAO answered.

Tombstone sighed. "Get him on the horn for me. Private circuit, encrypted—and piped to my cabin alone."

"Aye, aye, Admiral," the TAO said, suppressing a grin. He picked up the carrier telephone line to call the communications officer and arrange the patch-through. For just a second, he was tempted to ask for the circuit to be patched to his dialer as well, and then he thought better of it. Aegis had been a pain in the ass all day, ever since the new OPORD had gone into effect. Judging from the admiral's expression, a full two-way duplex circuit wasn't going to be necessary. This was one conversation that looked like it was going to be strictly one-way.

• • •

Within five minutes, the private circuit was patched through to Tombstone's cabin. The Communications Officer, or COMMO, had gotten quite adept at arranging that particular configuration, since Tombstone found reason to have to speak privately with the Aegis CO on a regular basis.

Tombstone held the receiver to his ear and listened to the hum of encrypted static as he waited for the Aegis TAO to locate his commanding officer. A few moments later, he heard Captain Killington's distinctive voice.

"You got a problem with your orders, Captain?" Tombstone said frostily.

"No problem, Admiral. Just a couple of questions about our position that I was discussing with your TAO. I wasn't sure how familiar he was with the nuances of Aegis antiair capabilities. Moving up north is going to decrease our—"

"*I'm* aware of everything I need to know about an element of *my* battle group, Captain. There are reasons for your orders—they were not invented out of thin air simply to make your life more difficult."

"I wonder if the Admiral is free to share some of those reasons with me," the Aegis CO said. Even over the encrypted net, the stiff, formally polite tone of his voice was evident. Tombstone could almost understand it. From *Vincennes* point of view, there were too many submarines in the vicinity of the carrier. Additionally, since the size of battle groups had declined drastically in the last several years, *Vincennes* was the only truly capable antiair platform around, doing double duty filling a role that previously would have been supported by at least two cruisers. The only questionable air contacts they'd seen in the last month had come from the coast of Vietnam. Additionally, given the Chinese's questionable air refueling capabilities, any strike would most likely *not* come from China's mainland, but from a detachment deployed to Vietnam.

The sensible AAW coordinating position was off the coast of Vietnam, and quite definitely not so close to land. From the position Tombstone had ordered the Aegis to, Killington would be forced to try for a tail shot against a missile fired at the battle group if a raid did come off the coast.

Unfortunately, Tombstone could not possibly explain his rationale to the Aegis CO, even if he had been inclined to. The real reasoning behind the operational plan was on a strictly limited need-to-know basis, and Killington didn't need to know. All he had to do was execute a normal Aegis role in the battle group.

"It's not necessary that you know why. Just that you know where. You do—so get your ass on station," Tombstone said impassively.

"Aye, aye, Admiral. We're heading north at flank speed," Killington said finally, a note of suppressed anger in his voice.

"*Not* flank speed! Your orders are to use normal transit speeds. Thirty-plus knots is an aggressive posture, and you're supposed to be assuming a normal patrol station. Listen to me very carefully, Captain. My chief of staff had command of one of your precious Aegis cruisers before he was assigned here. Given any provocation at all from you, I'll give him a second command. Yours. Got that?"

"Yes, Admiral."

Tombstone slammed the receiver down and then switched the dialer off the private frequency. He stared gloomily at the CCTV, focused on the now-quiet flight deck. So much depended on the Aegis fulfilling her delicate role in the maneuvers! Killington's request hadn't been unreasonable—to be filled in on the big picture, and to know how his ship's orders contributed to it. Still, coming from Aegis, he'd been predisposed to deny the request out of hand. And now, with the Aegis headed north smartly, every hour simply increased the logistic problems associated with flying the CO over to the carrier.

Damn, hadn't he learned this lesson as a lieutenant commander? The problems associated with managing the highly competent men and women who made up the modern Navy? Wasn't there some point at which he'd feel certain he was capable of doing his job and leading his people?

Tombstone sighed. Too much depended on this plan coming off exactly as planned.

CHAPTER 17
Tuesday, 2 July

"You set?" Bird Dog asked as he tucked his kneeboard in over the preloading button on his G-suit. Sudden acceleration would depress the button and activate the suit before it could react automatically. One more thing that could go wrong, something in the back of his mind noted, another little mechanism for killing pilots: gray out and unconsciousness brought on by high G-forces.

I might not even know, if it was bad enough. Be in the drink in seconds if I passed out. Cold seawater, hot jet engines, big explosion. It'd be fast, anyway. God, at least don't let me stay conscious. Don't let me have to watch it.

An involuntary tremor shook him, and he pushed the thoughts away. This was no time to be thinking about the dangers he faced every day, not while sitting on the cat. *Keep your mind in the cockpit, idiot. That's what kills more pilots than anything else—getting distracted at just the wrong minute and forgetting to fly the aircraft. Look at Gator. He's done this a million more times than you have, and you don't see him sweating the load.*

Bird Dog glanced in the mirror and saw the RIO give one

191

last tug on his harness. Ice-blue eyes, framed by the flight helmet and the face mask, met his. Gator gave him a thumbs-up.

"Ready now," Gator answered.

Bird Dog snapped off a salute at the handler and pressed his head and back hard against the back of the seat. Seconds later, he felt the first slight motion of the Tomcat. The steam piston rammed forward to the bow of the ship, accelerating the F-14 to 145 knots in six seconds. Catapulted off the carrier at just above stall speeds, the Tomcat clawed for airspeed and altitude, but settled for just staying airborne.

"Always a miracle," Gator said, taking a deep breath.

"I haven't let you down yet, have I?" Bird Dog asked, trying for a light note in his voice.

"First time's the last time. So you know where we're heading?" Gator asked, abruptly changing the subject.

"You think I wasn't paying attention at the brief? South."

"South is the right answer, my man. You get the nose pointed that way, I'll give you a vector."

Bird Dog winced as he thought back to the one time he hadn't managed to keep the aircraft pointed in the right direction. Then he forced the thought away and resolved to keep his head in the cockpit. His RIO hadn't taken a slam at him. It was Bird Dog's mind that was the problem.

"Sure you trust me that much?" Bird Dog replied lightly. "Awful tough task for a pilot, figuring out which way's south."

"I think you're up to that part of it. Okay, come left to 187. That ought to put us dead on course for it. No, it's the other part that bothers me. The part about why."

"Now who was nodding off during the brief?" Bird Dog ribbed. "I thought they covered that fairly well. With all these islands going boom, we're supposed to go watch and see if this one does. A real challenge for a multimillion-dollar aircraft."

Bird Dog heard the RIO fidgeting in his seat and glanced in

the small rearview mirror. "Hey! You hear me?" Bird Dog asked.

"I heard you. I heard the brief, too."

"And?"

"And what?"

"Aw, come on, Gator! Don't make me play Twenty Questions with you!"

"It's nothing, Bird Dog. Nothing firm, anyway. It's just that I don't entirely believe that that's why we're going out to circle a bunch of rocks. Think about it. We're headed directly away from everything that's happened in the last couple of days. Seems strange, that's all."

"Well, why else *would* we be going out there?"

"I'm not entirely sure. And that's what bothers me. If it were really pictures of rocks blowing up, you'd send a TARPS bird to take pictures. Or an S-3. Or a helo. Or something that could go low and slow and get evidence. Not an F-14 with a combat load. And not on this type of cyclic ops. You notice that, Bird Dog? We're on flex deck ops, massive alert five birds, and no CAP in the one area we ought to be interested in. Now why do you suppose that is?"

"Hadn't thought about it, really. I didn't see my name posted for alert, and that's all that I looked for."

"Well, doesn't it strike you as unusual? For the next four days, we're going to be operating at very specific hours on very specific missions. And this in the middle of some weird shit going on out here. I don't know, Bird Dog, it's just not making sense to me."

"Me, neither, now that you mention it." *And I'm not sure I really care, except for the alert part of it. Sitting on the flight deck for hours, all I see is Alvarez. Every time the engine turns over, every time some idiot plane captain gets near me, I see it again.*

"At least we're getting one of the flights today," Gator said. "Better than sitting on the deck."

Bird Dog looked in the mirror again and saw the RIO looking back, a speculative gleam in his eyes.

"Yeah. Gotta love that," Bird Dog said finally.

0830 local (Zulu -7)
TFCC
USS Jefferson

"There goes the first flight," Tombstone said, watching the plat camera.

"Think it will work?" Batman asked.

"It should. Lab Rat came up with a damned fine plan. Shit, remind me not to call him that anymore."

"Noted."

"The way this op is planned," Tombstone continued, "it's the Chinese that are going to be running the maze, not us. They're going to see a lot of American air activity to the south, around the furthest away rocks that are part of this island chain. We're hoping it's going to get their curiosity up. At the very least, we're acting exactly the opposite of what they probably expect. One way or another, that ought to provoke some sort of response from them."

"With an unarmed E-2 up overhead, I hope it's not an armed response," Batman said.

"Me, too," Tombstone said soberly. "We're taking a chance, I know. But look at the facts. They haven't fired at our aircraft up to now—"

"—just our ships, and an occasional shot at an S-3—" Batman interrupted.

"—and the shot at the *Vincennes* might have been kicked off by the *Vincennes* playing grab-ass with her fire control radar.

We have some strong indications that they're doing targeting exercises, data links between the fighters and the submarines, but no real indications that they're prepared to forcibly eject us from the South China Sea."

"Not that they could," Batman added.

"The fastest way to get us out of here is going to be to apply political pressure on the United States. And you're right about the force part of it. Even if they wanted to, I doubt that they could do much more than make life uncomfortable for us for a few days. Not much matches the firepower we carry with us."

"So we try to avoid cooperating with their plan and force them to tip their hand to their neighbors?" Batman asked. "Shit, Stoney, doesn't sound like much fun to me!"

"It's not. Particularly for the E-2. But if you've got any other ideas, speak up." Tombstone regarded his old wingman fondly. "Didn't think so."

0930 local (Zulu -7)
Tomcat 205

How long had he been staring at the horizon? Bird Dog shook his head and resumed his scan. Complacency about routine CAP missions killed aviators.

"You still awake up there?" Gator asked. "We're only thirty minutes into this mission."

"Who do you think's flying? Santa Claus?" Bird Dog snapped.

"Just asking, buddy, that's all. You looked rough during the brief."

"I'm fine. Just a little tired, that's all."

More than just a little, if he were truthful with himself. He'd tossed in his rack for four hours, succeeding in doing nothing except getting the sheets tangled and sweaty.

When he'd finally fallen asleep, it hadn't been much better than being awake. Alvarez haunted his dreams, a silent, screaming phantom swirling around his cockpit. He'd been on a mission, some sort of bombing run, and every time he turned onto the final vector for the drop, Alvarez appeared. In the dream, somehow the airman had been blown onto the front of the aircraft instead of being chewed up by the engines. He clung there like a June bug on a car, plastered to the canopy by the force of the catapult shot and the wind. Those eyes, pleading, tears filling them without ever spilling over onto his cheeks, the mouth open in a silent entreaty.

Bird Dog had startled awake, still shaking from the vision. For a few minutes, he'd been filled with incredible rage at the dead airman. He hadn't meant for his brakes to fail, or for Alvarez to ignore normal flight deck safety precautions. It hadn't been his fault, it *hadn't*!

"Let's just get through this mission, Gator," Bird Dog said quietly. Arguing with his RIO suddenly seemed like the last thing he wanted to do today.

"Okay. But when we get back on deck, I think we're going to have a long talk," Gator said finally. Bird Dog recognized the tone. Gator would let it slide for now, but back on deck he'd assert his seniority and his privileged status as Bird Dog's backseater to pry into his pilot's head. While Gator had been in the aircraft when the accident had occurred, he hadn't been the pilot, and both men knew it. No amount of reassurance that it'd been an accident would bring the dead airman back. Or, Bird Dog suspected, prevent the nightmares from returning. He wondered if he'd be seeing Airman Alvarez in his dreams for the rest of his life.

"Strangers, bearing 245, range 120 miles," the OS on the carrier said suddenly. "Tomcat 205, intercept and VID."

"Roger. We'll want to tank in about an hour, though," Gator

said. It was unlikely that the OS would forget to check their fuel state, but it never hurt to remind them. "Any IFF?"

"Negative IFF. Speed five hundred knots, rapid rate of climb. Based on the egress point, could be Flankers coming out off the coast again. Or MiGs, for a change of pace."

"Any other info?" Bird Dog asked.

"Negative. I'll let you know if there's anything else," the OS said calmly.

Bird Dog turned southwest, following the OS's intercept vector. Moments later, Gator reported gaining the contact on his radar.

Ten minutes later, the unknown contact was a black blip on the horizon. "MiG-23," Gator reported matter-of-factly, "based on the radar he's using."

"You called it," Bird Dog said, as the contact grew larger. "Definitely a MiG. They're sending their front-line units out."

"What's he look like?" Gator asked.

"Clean wings—no weapons on any station."

"Good news for Homeplate."

"Depends on whether there's a submarine in the area. Clean-winged didn't mean anything last time."

The MiG suddenly tipped its nose down and headed for the deck, not actively evading the approaching Tomcat, but clearly not in the mood to cooperate with an American inspection.

"Catch the Vietnamese markings on the tail?" Bird Dog asked.

"Yep. I'll let Mother know."

Bird Dog glanced at the fuel gauge. "We've got time to play follow the leader. Let's see what he's up to." He turned the Tomcat and followed the MiG down.

"Surface contacts," Gator announced.

"I see them." A huge RO-RO, a roll-on, roll-off container ship, came into view. "Whose is it?"

"Can't see the flag," Gator muttered.

"E-2 got anything on it?"

"Hawkeye's calling a U.S.-flagged ship," Gator reported, after querying the circling E-2. "It's on a normal commercial route."

"So what's the MiG want with our merchant ship? Don't tell me he wants to play kamikaze!"

"Not likely. The Vietnamese don't have so many that they'd be willing to waste them. Probably doing just what we're doing—going down for a look-see and a photo op."

"Hard as hell to take pictures at 450 knots," Bird Dog said.

"Hey, I didn't say they'd be good pictures."

"Jeez, he's low and fast. Gonna scare the hell out of that merchant!" Bird Dog said.

"Sometimes they've only got one person on the bridge during a long haul, and there's no guarantee that he's awake."

"Maybe we ought to loan them you," Bird Dog said snidely.

0950 local (Zulu -7)
On board *Kawashi Maru*
Vicinity Spratly Islands, South China Sea

Third Mate Gringes settled back in the chair and glanced at the engineering status display for the hundredth time in the last two hours. Two more days at sea before liberty! While the weather had been relatively good on this voyage, even the most favorable conditions—and the generous amounts of overtime—couldn't completely make up for the monotony of being at sea.

For want of anything better to do, he checked the surface radar display again. Still no contacts, although he wouldn't be surprised to start seeing more ships soon. While the South China Sea was a large body of water, the trade routes were heavily traveled.

With the automatic pilot functions engaged, there was little to do on the bridge. He strolled out to the bridge wing and took a cursory glance at the horizon. Radar picture confirmed—not another ship within fifteen miles or so, at least.

A strange thrumming sound caught his attention, and he glanced up, looking for the aircraft that was causing it. After two years of making voyages on the *Kawashi Maru*, he knew every sound his ship was capable of making. This was clearly external to his ship.

He saw the movement first and went back inside the pilot house to retrieve his binoculars. By the time he'd found them and lifted them to examine the aircraft, the contact was gone. He dropped the binoculars and let them dangle around his neck from the strap.

The sound returned, coming now from the other side of the ship. Thankful for anything that broke up the sheer monotony of his four hours at the conn, he strolled across the pilot house to the other side of the ship.

The aircraft was much lower now—lower and closer. It didn't take binoculars to identify the sharp angles of a MiG-23 slicing through the humid South China Sea air. He watched the aircraft come from astern, draw abreast of the ship, and then cut quickly to the right.

Within seconds, the aircraft was above him, so close and so low that Gringes felt as much as heard the thunder of the engines. His hands went to his ears automatically, trying to block the sound waves assaulting him. As the MiG raced in over him, he felt his eyes shut involuntarily. The noise consumed him, vibrating through his bones and rattling his guts.

As the sound dropped lower in frequency, down-dopplering from the relative motion of the aircraft and the ship, he opened his eyes again. The MiG raced off toward the horizon, turning as it reached a point near the horizon and heading back in toward the ship.

The intership telephone buzzed, sounding faint and fuzzy after the assault on his ears by the aircraft's passage. The captain, he suspected, wondering what idiotic aircraft was finding amusement in buzzing the heavily laden RO-RO. He raced back into the pilot house and watched the aircraft approach as he lifted the receiver.

As the captain testily demanded an explanation, the thunder of the MiG's engines filled the pilot house again. Gringes covered the mouthpiece with his hand for a moment and then opted for protecting his own ears rather than those of his captain. As the aircraft passed over again, he craned his head to look at its underbelly. No weapons, as far as he could tell.

Third Mate Gringes waited for his ears to stop ringing and then started drafting a radio message to the home office. They'd do the right makee-talkie to ensure that those damned Vietnamese quit disrupting his quiet watches.

0930 local (Zulu -8)
Operations Center
Hanoi, Vietnam

The operations analyst burst into Mein Low's office, tension evident in his plain face. "A Flanker just picked up some interesting changes in the Americans' operating pattern. They've stationed an unarmed surveillance aircraft, an E-2C, over the islands. It's alone."

"Where are the fighters?" Mein Low demanded.

"South of Mischief Reef."

"And our assets near the fighters?"

"None."

"This presents a problem, I believe."

"Not an insoluble one."

Mein Low stared at the chart. The blip representing the American aircraft cut lazy circles over a piece of empty ocean to the south. Almost empty. His overlaid projection showed that the tip of one small rock protruded from the ocean at times. Hardly large enough to support an asset, much less any firepower.

Still, it couldn't be helped. Obviously, the Americans had decided that that piece of ocean warranted their attention. The schedule called for another incident in three days. Unless the Americans changed their patrol patterns, it would be a problem.

Perhaps they could be lured in toward Mischief Reef again. Rebuilding of the extensive camp there had already begun. Surely that warranted more American attention! What would catch their interest the most, ensure that they resumed flights over the new camp?

A new structure resembling a rocket launcher of some sort or a new radar signature might get their attention. The Americans were compulsive about collecting intell photos and new electromagnetic signatures for their threat libraries. It need not be an actual weapons control system—it merely had to look like one. A high frequency source with a high rotation rate should do it, perhaps a frequency modulated one. He'd ask the engineers—they ought to be able to come up with something.

"Watch them," he said finally. "See if they establish a pattern, how often they schedule their flights, whether they are tanking or doing short cycle operations. We have some time to plan."

The operations analyst nodded.

"And have air ops schedule me for a flight. I want to see their reactions myself."

"Sure don't like being out here by our lonesome," Fingers grumbled. The E-2C RIO tweaked and peaked her radar display for a few moments.

"Help is only a squawk away," her pilot said.

"It'd be better if it were only a TER away."

"Oh, right. Like there's any place on this antiquated airframe to hang a triple ejection rack. You've got jet envy, Fingers. Worse than penis envy, I hear."

"Funny, I'd heard the same thing about you," she said.

"Oh, good one. Fingers, you realize if they ever catch us talking like this on the boat we're both going to get court-martialed?"

"Yeah. But that's on the boat. As long as we're up here, different rules apply."

"Roger, copy," her pilot said. "You know, I was worried about having to fly with you—thought I'd have to be watching my language and learnin' how to be politically correct. But, hell, Fingers—you're worse than I am!"

She sighed and leaned back against the hard cushion. She rubbed the small of her back with both hands. Flying sideways had definite disadvantages to it.

"Listen, Rabbit, you think I would want to spend eight hours a day with people who were always watching their damned language? Flying with somebody paranoid? Hell, we can't be a crew like that! You have to be able to talk to me. I have to know that you're going to listen to me when I tell you to get the hell out of Dodge, and you have to be able to talk to me to stay away. It's not like you've got anything else to do up there."

"Aw, fuck you, Fingers. If you'd had the eyesight, you'd have been a pilot, too!"

"You've made that offer before, Rabbit. Someday I'm going to take you up on it."

He heard the enlisted technician snicker. "She'll call your bluff someday, Rabbit," he said. "Or maybe not—maybe she's *heard* how you got that call sign!"

"Hey, you too? What the hell happened to male bonding?" the pilot whined

"Replaced by RIO bonding," he said. "I'll take smart-wearing-glasses over stupid-with-good-eyesight any day!"

"How about taking new contacts over blank screens instead?" Fingers said, suddenly all business. "In your sector, Jamie."

"Got him," the technician replied. "Classify it as a Flanker, based on the radar and speed. Loitering in area, it appears. He's doing the same thing we're doing, hanging around watching."

"So we watch him while he watches us," she said softly. "And we wait to see who blinks first. I'd sure as *hell* feel a lot better with a TER right now."

"We don't need no stinking weapons," the pilot grumbled. "At least that's what they told us in the brief. We've got the Aegis to protect us, right?"

"Yeah, the Aegis and a satellite. I'm feeling real secure," Jamie said.

"You and me both, brother," Fingers said softly. "You and me both."

"Keep a close eye on that Flanker," the captain ordered. "If the balloon goes up, I want to be ready."

"Aye, aye, sir," the TAO said. A week ago, he might have been tempted to dismiss the captain's order as more of the reflexive paranoia he'd come to associate with the man. Now, since the missile shot last week, the CO's premonitions didn't seem nearly as unreasonable. Sure, the Chinese were claiming they'd been provoked into firing after the Aegis had locked up their MiG. But with the new cool-down policy, that E-2 had to be feeling awful lonely up there without CAP. No matter that the Admiral thought it'd ease the tensions in the area to stand down the number of flights. He wasn't the one on the front line.

The TAO was. And he didn't like the feeling one little bit.

"We'll be ready, Captain," he said, keying the Combat circuit as he spoke. A series of clicks cluttered the circuit for a moment, acknowledgment from the other operators. "We *are* ready," he amended.

"Phase One," Tombstone said to Ops. "They know we're there."

"Now let's get them thinking the way we want them to," Ops said, glancing at CAG.

"Already scheduled. They're going to see the Hawkeye

relieved every six hours. No tanking, no CAP, just the little ol'
Hawkeye up there all by himself."

"You've got the alert package ready to go?" Ops asked.

"Starting next cycle. We're skipping this one, giving them
some time to look us over and get lulled into the rhythm of it.
Get the crews some rest, too. It's going to be a while before
they get that, once we start the next phase."

"This afternoon," Tombstone said suddenly. "They're not
going to do anything right now—they'll have to talk to their
staff, try to figure out how to use our operations plan to their
own advantage. It's going to take them a while—I doubt
anything is prepositioned on that miserable piece of rock down
there. It's not even above water most of the time, so the
self-destruct scenario isn't going to play."

"But you think there'll be another incident," CAG said.
"Something directed at the rock, not at the Hawkeye?"

"I'm betting on it," Tombstone replied. "Intell agrees with
me on this one. China's not likely to attack us directly, not
without some excuse for provocation. As long as Aegis stays
under control, and nobody screws up, we won't give them that
excuse. No, they don't want to attack us—it's a losing
proposition, this far from their shores, with their lousy air
refueling skills. Unless they get Vietnam to allow them
land-launching permission, China's aircraft don't have the legs
to reach out and touch us hard."

"Now if they'd bought that aircraft carrier from Ukraine like
they were planning last year, it'd be a different story," Ops
mused. "The Soviet Union was just starting to get the hang of
carrier aviation when it collapsed. Those Flankers—I read that
they were getting halfway decent at getting on board the
Admiral Kutnezsov."

"It might be, although I'm not convinced they'd be able to
operate effectively with it that quickly. Certainly not run flight
ops the way we do, not without a sizable contingent of Russian

crew members. And somehow I just don't see Russia getting in the middle of this, not with all the problems they've got at home," Tombstone replied.

"Still don't like sending the Hawkeye out like that," CAG said somberly.

Tombstone glanced at him. In a few years, CAG might have the opportunity to find out for himself how it felt to have to order a Hawkeye out alone. Until then, he wouldn't know if he could do it, wouldn't understand the true burden of command.

Tombstone knew he hadn't.

CHAPTER 18
Wednesday, 3 July

The battle group settled into standard cyclic operations quickly. Spratly Island surveillance missions by the Hawkeyes were launched every five hours, each flight following exactly the same patrol pattern. Every eight hours, one lone fighter left the deck, occasionally accompanied by a tanker. The Hawkeyes went north, the fighters south, and neither intruded on the other's operating area. Alert birds crowded the deck, crews in cockpits and maintenance technicians doing busywork around them, waiting.

Further north, the Aegis prowled, silently watching the unarmed E-2C's. Flankers cut lazy circles in the airspace between the Aegis and the carrier, watching the E-2C that watched them.

To the east, Chinese fighters slipped down the coast from the mainland into Vietnam, occasionally cutting across the South China Sea to the north or south of the battle group to land in one of the other littoral nations. With the Aegis and the Hawkeye tracking them, the battle group kept the world intelligence community updated on the tail count.

By the end of the first full day of the operation, the aircrews were getting edgy. The Hawkeye crews were increasingly uneasy about the Chinese fighters and conducting surveillance without their own fighters nearby for protection. The *Jefferson*'s fighter crews were unhappy about both the alert schedule and the lack of information on exactly *why* they were pulling alert instead of flying. The atmospheric conditions continued to generate ghost contacts that flickered into existence for a few minutes, then evaporated.

Rumors and speculation raged around the carrier, each theory more menacing than the last. RIOs and pilots argued continually in the Officer's Mess about the Chinese's capability for aerial refueling, and whether or not China could reach out and touch the battle group from mainland as well as from Vietnam. The RIOs insisted on drawing out the time-distance problem for the pilots, demonstrating time and again how the fighters could not possibly make it to within weapons range, given their fuel package. The pilots disagreed, fundamentally unconvinced that the Chinese were not fully capable of deploying a long-range antiair weapon on their aircraft, or passing locating data to the submarines. The pilots repeatedly mentioned the possibility that the Chinese F-10 long-range fighter was operational. After all, the pilots argued, intelligence had been wrong before.

The F-10 was something to be concerned about. Modeled on the American F-16 and the Israeli Lavi fighters, it was designed specifically to extend China's reach from the mainland into the Spratly Island region. It combined the powerful Russian jet engine used on the Flanker with an in-flight refueling capability integral to the airframe. With an extended range and both ground attack and air combat capabilities, its speed and maneuverability made it a match for even the MiG-29.

The intelligence officers swore the F-10 was not yet operational. The pilots just pointed to the JAST birds sitting on the deck as proof that it could be.

Other than the routine patrols of the American E-2C's and the Chinese fighters, the South China Sea lapsed into an uneasy silence. The Vietnamese were particularly silent, their MiG-23's and Flankers hugging the long coastline and venturing out into international airspace only to conduct air combat training with the Chinese fighters.

The battle group watched the simulated ACM off the coast, monitoring the communications between the Chinese and the Vietnamese flights for shreds of intelligence data. Linguists announced that the Vietnamese aircraft usually played victim for Chinese attack sorties. The exact details were unclear, since the two countries switched to encrypted circuits for most of their tactical communications. When the first night ACM exercise launched tensions on board *Jefferson* ratcheted a notch higher.

"How many now?" Tombstone asked.

"At least fifty Chinese Flankers in Vietnam, maybe more," Lab Rat said. "Maybe ten each in Brunei and Malaysia. Satellite imagery isn't the complete answer to all our questions— they've moved some of them into underground bunkers."

"As bad as the Koreans are," Tombstone muttered, staring at the small scale map projected up on the wall of the briefing room. "That entire area is probably honeycombed with underground facilities."

"Probably, sir. We have some intelligence reports that confirm that."

"Well. Not entirely our problem, of course, but it's going to be hell for the next army that goes in there. Let's hope it's not us. How are they reacting to our air ops?"

"As far as we can tell, it's going according to plan. China is moving aircraft into Vietnam, Brunei, and Malaysia, and continuing routine patrols in the northern portion of the South

China Sea. Aegis reports that all military aircraft simply ignore any and all communications from them."

"Just keeping an eye on us, then. No unexpected jamming, no incidents?"

"Nothing out of the ordinary. Or so we're supposed to think."

"And as *they're* supposed to think, too," Tombstone added softly.

0900 local (Zulu -8)
Operations Center
Hanoi, Vietnam

"No reaction?" Mein Low asked.

"None that we can identify," his staff officer said.

Strange. He would have expected the Americans to increase their patrols in the area, not decrease them. Still, it was consistent with their actions in the United Nations. Ever since their defeat in Vietnam, the Americans had been increasingly reluctant to try to assert their political will so far from home. Of course, it was foolish of them ever to believe that they would have any real voice in how things went in the South China Sea. It simply was none of their concern.

"I think it's time to consider the final events in this course of action," he said, studying the chart. "Politically, events seem to be moving as we wish. Our South China Sea neighbors understand that their future lies with us, not with the crazed Caucasian aggressors who are attacking unarmed island camps. Thus far, we have been models of restraint, reacting only via diplomatic channels and in the United Nations. And tactically, we have three squadrons on the ground in Vietnam, as well as one squadron in Malaysia and one in Brunei."

"The first lesson," his assistant said. "Attack your enemy's alliances and allies."

"An excellent example here," he replied. "And you see how we have used the same events in two different ways. First, the Americans allies doubt her. Second, the smaller countries draw closer to us, uneasy about the possibility that the Americans will attack them. Yes, this was a beautifully fashioned plan. I am pleased."

"Now that we have created the proper climate, what next?"

The older man gently stroked the map, his fingers lingering on the area of the South China Sea below Mischief Reef. "More of the same, but in a different light," he replied. "China and her neighbors have been quietly tolerating these incredible acts of aggression long enough. It is time to seal the fate of American influence in this part of the world."

"War?"

"Hardly necessary. The Americans have so little tolerance for taking casualties that I doubt they will even go to war again. No, war is not necessary. A brief skirmish, a few deaths, and the American public will be screaming for a withdrawal. With them out of the arena, settling the question of the Spratly Islands becomes a simple matter."

"Vietnam may not think so."

"Ah, a hardy people. Tough, resilient, and good fighters. And smart. They will understand the situation, with two billion potential Chinese soldiers massed to the north, and no American presence. After all, we beat them badly in 1987 in the Spratly Islands, and sank six of their precious patrol boats that intruded into our waters. Now that they no longer have the Soviet Union as their protector and source of equipment, I think we'll find them much more cooperative. They've been remarkably silent about the loss of their patrol boat, which is a good sign."

"The next phase will begin when?"

"Soon. Very soon."

Bird Dog studied the next day's flight schedule with a sinking
feeling. The next day's missions were posted outside the CAG
ops door. A hand-lettered sign on the door itself warned casual
perusers to funnel any corrections or deletions through their
squadron ops officers, and not to bother bringing their sniveling little complaints directly to the CAG ops gurus.

"Lemme see," Gator said, reaching for the sheet.

"Hold on! I just got to us," Bird Dog said, dancing away
from his RIO. "Damn, we're on here again."

"Imagine that. Just because you're a pilot and I'm a RIO,
these dogs think they can just go and assign us to fly any ol'
time they want! I tell you, the nerve!" Gator said sarcastically.

"No, that's not what I mean," Bird Dog said. "Look at the
alert schedule."

"Again? Six Alert Five—*six*? What are we doing with *six*
F-14's from our squadron on alert?" Gator stared at the closed
ops door. "We got to get those guys a urinalysis sometime *real*
soon."

"There's more. Check out the Hornets. And the tankers and
the Hummers. CAG's got a whole alpha strike sitting on the
deck, ready to go. Look at the load-out, though."

"All air-to-air, except for the S-3's, of course."

"So we're not going alpha striking. But we *are* ready for an
air threat."

"And in the meantime, with all this airpower sitting on deck
at alert five, the only aircraft CAG's actually launching is that
one lone Hummer?" Gator asked.

"Not quite. Last page," Bird Dog said, flipping rapidly to the back sheet. There, next to the traditional cartoon that always graced the daily flight schedule, was one final note.

"The JAST birds," Bird Dog said. "Out of all the fighter and attack birds on board, they're the only ones that get to go flying tomorrow."

1300 local (Zulu -7)
Admiral's Cabin

Tombstone watched Batman pace and tried to assess his old wingman's frame of mind. Batman wandered restlessly around Tombstone's cabin, pausing to look at plaques on the wall, to pick up a small model of an F-14 from the coffee table, to riffle through some messages left carelessly on the credenza. Finally, he wandered back over toward the couch, put his hands on his hips, and glared at the admiral.

"If you weren't an admiral, Tombstone, I'd tell you what you could do with this damned fool scheme. But since you are—"

"What, you're going to let that stop you this time? Why? Rank's never been a curb on your temper before, Batman."

"Sometimes it ought to be," Batman muttered. Yet Tombstone was right. Until he'd gotten to the Pentagon, Batman had never been one to balk at setting a senior officer straight. But that'd been before he'd seen how casually and easily anyone wearing the stars could irrevocably ruin a career—often just for the amusement of it—with a few well-placed words. Until then, Batman would have sworn that a blue-on-blue engagement could only happen on the battlefield.

But this was Tombstone, he reminded himself. His lead, the pilot he'd logged thousands of hours with, done four cruises with, the man who'd bailed him out of more tough situations than he wanted to think of. No, if Tombstone wanted to do Batman harm, it'd come in the form of a fist in the gut rather than a knife in the back. Batman took a deep breath and vowed that this was his last DC tour.

"It's not safe, Tombstone. It's not safe, and you know it. Sending those E-2C's out there on their own—hell, what do you even need them up for? The Aegis can give you every bit of air picture you need! Sending those fellows out alone, with no protection at all, under these circumstances, makes no sense at all!" Batman paused midtirade, watching his friend.

His nickname had always suited him too well, Batman thought. Tombstone's gray eyes, brown-black hair, and somber expression would have suited an undertaker better than an aviation admiral. Yet Batman had seen the impenetrable gray pools of his eyes flare with inner fire, and heard the hard excitement too many times in Tombstone's voice to believe that he was really as cold as his subordinates believed.

"You think so, Captain?" Tombstone's icy voice cut through Batman's reflections.

"Naw—hell, no, Admiral," Batman said uncomfortably. He forced himself down onto the couch, suddenly acutely aware of how inappropriate it was to treat an admiral—*any* admiral, damn it!—that way. "Sorry, sir. My mouth—"

"—got the better of you, as it often does," Tombstone finished. "Some things never change," he said, shaking his head sadly.

Batman's head snapped up, and he stared at Tombstone suspiciously. Was that a glint of amusement he saw in the admiral's eyes? "Sir, if I didn't know better, I'd swear you're laughing at me."

"Not *at* you, Batman—with you. Or at least I will be in a couple of seconds. Let me show you," Tombstone continued, reaching across his desk to snatch a message and a chart off his credenza, "exactly what we're up to. Your JAST birds are a part of this plan."

CHAPTER 19
Wednesday, 3 July

As the sun dropped down toward the horizon, the heat rising off the flight deck abated enough to entice runners out onto the decks between flight cycles. Bird Dog jogged aft, feeling the sweat pouring off his back and working out the stiffness that came from sitting cramped in a cockpit for six hours that day. The humid air made any exertion doubly tiring, but the chance to get some exercise was not to be missed. Tucked in various strange compartments within the carrier were three weight rooms and one bicycle alley. In various other stray corners, an occasional exercise bike would be placed. While the carrier went to some length to try to make fitness available at all times, no machine could offer the same sheer joy as being out on the flight deck running.

As he ran past two VF-95 Tomcats, he noticed a familiar figure perched on the step next to the cockpit. Even from fifty feet away, he recognized the slim figure barely concealed by coveralls and the shock of short blond hair. Veering off his track, he headed for the aircraft.

"Shaughnessy! What the hell are you doing?" he snapped, coming to a stop next to her Tomcat.

The young airman flinched and almost lost her balance. "Just checking that the seat is safed, sir," she said, not meeting his eyes. "Parariggers were doing some work in here earlier, and I just wanted to double-check it."

"That's not what I mean, and you know it! You're on extra duty, Shaughnessy. That doesn't mean screwing around with the aircraft, it means under close control of the squadron master at arms. You miss his muster, you're UA, young woman. Now get down there!"

Shaughnessy stared at the deck, unwilling to meet his eyes. "Aye, aye, sir," she said softly, her voice barely audible in the wind across the flight deck.

Bird Dog started off down the flight deck again, not waiting to see if she obeyed. *Damned airman was getting out of hand. I'm going to talk to the chief about her again—for all the good that will do me.*

After his last confrontation with his senior enlisted rating, he'd come away with the sneaking suspicion that he'd made an ass of himself. Despite his best intentions, the chief showed little to no interest in being led by the pilot that was responsible for the work center, although he had briefed Bird Dog religiously every morning on Shaughnessy's extra duty assignments.

Come to think of it, the chief's last suggestions sure wouldn't have done any good either. If Bird Dog hadn't assigned Airman Shaughnessy the extra duty immediately, neither of them would have already known she was a slacker.

An hour later, showered and back in uniform, Bird Dog went looking for the chief. He finally found him by calling the Chiefs' Mess. Mindful of his last performance there, Bird Dog asked the chief to come up to the ready room for a few minutes.

"Evening, Lieutenant," Chief said, when he finally appeared in the VF-95 ready room.

"Thanks for coming up, Chief," Bird Dog forced himself to say. He'd been waiting for almost thirty minutes for the senior enlisted member of his division.

"Just had to take care of a few things first, sir. We'd had something planned for the chiefs' mess, but the squadron comes first, of course."

Bird Dog felt the subtle rebuke in the chief's words. There was some justification for it, he admitted. The matter of Airman Shaughnessy *could* have waited until the morning, when Bird Dog would have seen the chief at quarters. There was no immediate need to interrupt the chief's evening to resolve her disciplinary status.

Still, Bird Dog *was* a lieutenant, and senior to the chief. If he wanted to see his branch chief in the middle of the night, he had the right to wake his ass up and talk to him.

"It's about Shaughnessy," Bird Dog said, and related how he'd seen her up on the flight deck fooling around with one of the aircraft during the time she should have been at her extra duty. After a few sentences, he heard how weak his own argument sounded. The chief listened politely, although his face turned a little red.

"Well, Lieutenant, I can see your point," the chief said after Bird Dog'd petered out. "You tell a sailor to be somewhere, that's where she ought to be."

"I'm glad you agree with me, Chief," Bird Dog said. "Nothing seems to be getting her attention. Quite frankly, I don't think we're going to be able to nip this problem in the bud. If her blatant disrespect and disobedience continue, we're going to have to consider Captain's Mast."

The chief was silent for a few moments, intently examining the worn linoleum on the ready room floor. Finally, he looked back up at the young lieutenant. "You've got it wrong, Lieutenant. I *don't* agree with you—haven't about this whole thing. I made that real clear to you in the beginning. You want me to push this, I will. You're the boss. But let me tell you—you're making a big mistake here, sir. That young airman was up there checking out *our* aircraft, taking some initiative and responsibility. Okay, maybe she was late for this bullshit extra duty you've got her on. But I can tell you, I'd a hell of a lot rather have a safe airplane than a shiny clean deck in the ready room, or an extra coat of paint in the division spaces. You start punishing people for taking the initiative, you're going to end up with more problems than you started with. Sir."

The chief stood up, towering over the young lieutenant. Bird Dog stood hastily, not willing to be intimidated by the older man.

"Lieutenant, you concentrate on flying. Leave the troops to me. It works out better that way—trust me."

1920 local (Zulu -8)
Operations Center
Hanoi, Vietnam

"It is time to give them something else to think about," Mein Low declared. He pulled the delicately annotated chart toward him. "I want the American forces confused and uncertain—but not provoked to action."

"What do you recommend, sir?" his operations planner asked.

Mein Low studied the chart, mentally measuring distances and converting that to reaction time, aircraft range scales, and weapons envelopes. He tapped on the edge of the chart, then picked up a pencil. He paused, studying the other marks on the chart, and nodded with approval. Not only was the chart precisely marked out, complete with current American positions and resupply points, but it was done with a certain style, the script of the drafter in harmony with the printing on the charts. A mark of refinement, he thought, and wondered exactly who'd done it. Not his operations planner. The man had the penmanship of a peasant.

"Here," he said finally, making a light mark on the chart. The planner craned his head across the table to see the point his superior indicated.

"A wise choice," the planner said appreciatively.

"You think so, do you? Explain to me in detail the merits of this point." Mein Low's eyes glinted dangerously.

"It is—the distances are, of course, obvious," the planner began. Mein Low let him flounder for a few more minutes, giving him time to fully appreciate the dangers of appearing to know more than one did. Better if his planner had admitted ignorance—always the beginning of wisdom—and simply asked.

"A small airborne strike force, of course," Mein Low said. "Not too many, certainly nothing that would ever begin to challenge the capabilities of the Aegis cruiser. Four fighters, perhaps. Armed, yes, but flying a highly visible flight profile. Slow and high, no suspicious maneuvering. Now do you begin to see the significance of this one point?"

The planner started to nod, and then thought better of it. He studied the point again, measuring the distance to the American aircraft carrier. Finally, he looked up.

"This point—if our fighters fly to it, then turn around and return to base, they are never within weapons range of the carrier."

"Be more specific!" Mein Low demanded. "It is in the details of planning that wars are won and lost."

"The carrier is never within *our* weapons range, while we are undoubtedly within theirs," the planner said hastily. "I see the degrees of relative vulnerability, but I must confess I do not completely follow your plan."

Mein Low nodded. That the young staffer had admitted his ignorance showed progress. Now that the student was willing, the teacher would appear.

"Think of the impression we wish to convey. The South China Sea is ours, and we need no justification for patrolling any part of it. Particularly the area we have declared as an exclusion zone—the Americans are there at our sufferance, and have assumed the risk. I wish to accustom them to seeing fighters patrolling with impunity in the area. You will instill in each pilot the concept of cool confidence, that they have the right to be in the vicinity without any further explanation to the Americans. They will not respond to any challenges or inquiries from the Americans, nor will they ever venture within range to launch weapons on the American forces. You now see the beauty of this plan?"

"I believe so. If the Americans attack our airplanes, that simply confirms to the world our position—that the Americans are hostile belligerents in a peaceful area of the world, stirring up trouble and attacking all other countries at will. If they kill our pilots and burn our aircraft, they will have done more to unify opinion against them than anything we could do."

"And the alternative result?" Mein Low demanded.

"If they fail to act, then they simply reaffirm our rights to patrol our area at will. But, sir, what if they launch escorts to intercept and escort our small group?"

"Even better. Let me show you what I intend."

Fifteen minutes later, the young operations planner began to understand just how much he had to learn about the art of operational planning.

"All quiet back there?" Rabbit asked. It wasn't really necessary to ask—had anything interesting crossed their screens, the scope dopes would have been screaming bloody murder.

"Why? You got somewhere else to be?" Fingers asked. The ICS evened out her hard, clipped Maine accent, catching every additional consonant without emphasizing the missing ones.

"Nope. Just logging the flight pay up here." The pilot grinned at the copilot. It was sheerly one of the joys of being an aviator. Getting to fly, and getting paid extra to do it.

"Looks like you spoke too soon," Fingers said. "Looky who's coming out to play! Four unidentified bogeys off the commercial routes. Inbound, angels fifteen, 420 knots. I call it Chinese fighters."

"You copy, Homeplate?" Rabbit said over tactical. "I'm going to start feeling a little lonely up here real soon." It was one thing, he thought, to fly missions alone off the coast of southern California. An entirely different level of pucker factor to do it in the South China Sea. The quietly reassuring if occasionally obnoxious presence of a few Tomcats or Hornets would have sounded mighty fine right then.

"Roger, copy," the OS said. "Hang tight, Snoopy. We're going to send some playmates up with you. Spook One and Two are launching as we speak."

Fingers shook her head. Spook was the call sign assigned to the two new JAST birds. She'd gotten a good look at them on the deck, both at the impressive avionics and at the stealth coating. Still, when you got right down to it, neither one had been fully op tested under real-time conditions. What looked like a workable system at Pax River didn't necessarily work as advertised after multiple catapult launches, slamming tailhook recoveries, and the gentle ministrations of flight deck technicians. Had she been given a choice, she'd have opted for one of the regular Hornets or Tomcats—preferably the long-endurance Tomcat.

She clicked her mike in acknowledgment and listened to the tactical chatter from the back of his aircraft over the ICS. Within minutes, the OSs on the carrier were complaining about the radar picture.

"I know they're off the deck. We're picking up IFF responses to interrogation. But I'm not getting skin—just mode four squawk. What the hell are these birds, anyway?" the OS on the *Vincennes* asked the air tracker on the carrier over the private LINK coordination circuit.

"Both Spooks are inbound your position," the OS on the carrier advised. "Don't worry—I can't see them either. Aegis is picking up skin off them, and we're tracking them over LINK. Let me know when they get close enough to paint."

"Hell of a way to run a war," the copilot muttered. "Bad enough when we can't see the bad guys, but now the good guys are invisible too!"

"Be advised the Spooks will be taking high station on you," the OS said, a note of puzzlement in his voice.

"High station? What the heck for? Can't we get someone down here close and personal?" the pilot demanded. "What dope-smoking idiot came up with that one?"

"I think that would be me," a too-familiar voice said. "Any problem with that, son?"

The pilot swallowed hard. "No, sir, Admiral. High station sounds just fine."

"Good contact on the inbound bogeys," Tomboy said tersely.

"Man, those guys have got to be sweating it," Batman answered. "What's the range?"

"Three hundred miles and closing. We going in to take a look at them?"

"I'm going to try. Let me know what you're getting off them when we get closer. I don't want them to know we're there. With any luck at all, they'd have to get a visual on us to know we're here, if intell is right about their radars."

Spook Two was nose-on to the intruders, presenting its least detectable aspect. Batman made a minute adjustment in his course, pointing the JAST bird's oddly configured nose at the Chinese fighters. No point in giving them any better a target than they deserved. While Batman still had a number of tricks up his JAST sleeve, he wanted to keep them in reserve.

"Nothing spectacular, Batman. Low-grade air search radar. Not much chance of them seeing us," the backseater said after a moment. "Don't think we can make it into visual range without being detected, though."

"I kinda figured that," Batman said. "Sure would like to get a look at their wings, though."

"Roger that. I'll yell the second I even smell fire control radar."

"That'll have to do. Don't know that I like it, but it's how we planned it."

And if I don't like it, Batman thought, *it's for damned sure that E-2C Hawkeye doesn't. Nothing like being tied to a stake as a sacrificial lamb to make a pilot feel unwanted and unloved. Damned smart plan of Tombstone's. He knows the*

*Chinese would never expect us to leave the Hawkeye up here
alone. Ergo, they'll come to one of two conclusions. Either
we're not worried because we* know *we're not responsible for
the attacks, and we're proving it by putting the E-2C up
alone—or they're not alone.* And with the JAST low observability characteristics, Batman didn't expect to be detected by
any damn Soviet-built airborne radar!

A cold smile crossed his face, hidden by his oxygen mask.
Now let's just let them try to figure out which it is, he said to
himself.

2230 local (Zulu-7)
Chinese Flanker
Off the coast of Vietnam

"We execute our orders," the pilot commanded. "You see how
this was all planned out? Our advisers knew exactly what we
would encounter near the American battle group."

"I admit that I doubted their assessment. Leaving one of
their six surveillance birds unprotected did not seem reasonable," his backseater admitted.

"Which is why we're just paid to fly. Just ensure that your
fingers stay off the targeting functions. We are to give them no
cause for alarm."

"Understood. How close will you approach?"

"Just to the edge of our weapons envelope."

"But tell me—what would we have done if their fighters
had appeared? Four Flankers against all the aircraft that they
can launch? It would be a difficult tactical position, to say the
least!"

The pilot smiled, a cruel edge to his mouth. "They will not
attack us, that much is clear. They cannot risk starting a war so
close to our homeland. Should their fighters appear, we will do

exactly what we are doing now. Fly straight and level, in a nonthreatening fashion, and proceed toward their Hawkeyes. We would simply fly the same escort pattern on their Hawkeye that they would intend to fly on us."

After all, the pilot thought, it was *their* sea. Not the Americans'.

CHAPTER 20
Wednesday, 3 July

"Homeplate, they're getting mighty damned close!" Batman radioed.

"Roger, Spook Two. No deviation from authorized plan," Tombstone's calm voice replied.

Batman clicked his button in acknowledgment. He'd rather be up here, where he could fight and maneuver as necessary. Whatever they paid a rear admiral—and Batman had a good idea of what that was—it wasn't nearly enough. To have to stand by and watch fighters approach an unprotected aircraft, praying that you'd read their intentions correctly and that you wouldn't lose aviators and an aircraft on a stupid hunch—could he have done it himself? As much as he'd disliked it initially, the political infighting and maneuvering at the Pentagon rarely got anyone killed. A career or two, maybe. It was too easy to forget, trapped in the massive rings of the Pentagon, that men and women were still out here on the front lines.

Did the Navy know somehow? he wondered. *Know which aviators had the guts to make the kind of calls Tombstone was making this very second? Did they test us somehow? And have I got what it takes to risk the lives of men and women on a plan like this? Tombstone does.*

This year, Batman's record would go before the rear admiral promotion board. For years, he'd dreamed of putting on those broad gold stripes and silver stars. Now, for the first time, he wondered whether he was ready for it, and whether he'd accept it if the promotion were offered. Listening to Tombstone's calm voice on the tactical circuit, he tried to convince himself that he would have been able to maintain the same solid presence that brought reassurance to the crew of the carrier and the Air Wing.

"They're joining on us, Homeplate," he heard the E-2C copilot say.

"Straight and level, Snoopy," he heard Tombstone reply. "They're not here to start a war—they just want a good look-see. Too close to use anything except guns where they are, if that helps."

"Roger," the Hawkeye aviator replied, a trace of relief in his voice.

"Watch them," Batman growled at his RIO. "The second they look tactical, we're on them."

"Got them solid, sir. They're going to know we're here, picking up our radar, but they won't know exactly where. We're ready."

For fifteen excruciating minutes, Batman watched as the Chinese fighters flew formation on the E-2C, close enough for the Hawkeye pilot to wave at his Chinese counterpart. Finally, without ever acknowledging the greeting, the Chinese fighters broke off. Batman breathed a sigh of relief and heard a few quiet oaths on the tactical net.

"Keep an eye on them, Spook Two," he heard Tombstone say. Batman marveled at the even tone of the Admiral's voice. The gamble Tombstone had taken with the lives of his aviators had paid off.

Could I have sounded like that? Like everything had worked out exactly as I'd planned?

Somehow, Batman doubted it.

The TAO let out a deep sigh as the Chinese Flankers turned north, and glanced at the captain at the next console. The captain ripped off his headset and tossed it on the narrow desk. "Ghosts, huh? I don't think so! We let those bastards push us around like we were the fucking Vietnamese!" the captain snarled. "What the hell do they think this ship is—a patrol boat?"

"What is all this supposed to accomplish, Captain?" the TAO asked. He had spent the last hour with his finger poised above the button that would assign missiles to the incoming fighters. His people were tense and uneasy, and the adrenaline that the tactical situation had generated was slow to ebb away.

The ghost contacts generated by the warm, humid air didn't help, either. Whatever the previous contacts had been, the ones he'd just been staring at for the last hour were real.

"Hell if I know," the CO snapped. "Prove to the world that we're a bunch of pussies, I guess. Not that we haven't proved that often enough. TAO, first time one of those bastards wanders in within weapons release range, I'm going to plug him. Admiral Magruder can put out all the fancy rules of engagement he wants, but there's nothing he can say or do to compromise my right to defend my ship. The first *hint* of hostile intent, and you're weapons free. You got that?"

The TAO nodded. Down here in the sandbox, the captain's plans made more and more sense. A hell of a lot more sense than the admiral's did, as a matter of fact. He stood and stretched, feeling the bones in his back and neck pop. Politics— the Aegis did antiair warfare a lot better than he did subtle diplomacy. And now the captain had dumped it squarely in his lap by ordering him to shoot if the fighters came within range to release their weapons.

If they *did* close the ship to within weapons release range, there might not be time to get the Captain to Combat. With the captain absent, the entire decision rested with the TAO. He rubbed his neck with one hand and stared bleakly at the large-screen display in the front of the packed compartment.

All the delicate maneuverings by diplomats, politicians, and admirals would come down to the judgment of one thirty-one-year-old lieutenant commander running on too little sleep and too much coffee. Well, they'd told him he'd get lots of responsibility early in the Navy.

There was something to be said for the captain's orders. He'd been right before, when the missiles had been inbound. If the TAO had had to depend on the CARGRU's orders then, the ship would probably be a flaming datum now.

He sat back down and glanced at the time-of-day display in the lower right-hand corner of his screen. Good thing it was in military time. He tried to remember how long it had been since he'd been out on the weather decks—or even on the bridge, for that matter. How many days had it been since he'd seen sunlight? His daily routine took him from his stateroom to the wardroom to Combat, with a prewatch check of the engineering spaces every six hours. Without the time counter on his screen, he would have lost any sense of daily rhythm.

Weapons free if fighters come within weapons release range, he wrote in the pass-down log. Wasn't likely that he'd forget to tell the other TAOs, but it never hurt to write it down. He thought for a moment and then added *per CO's order* and signed his initials with a flourish. It never hurt to cover your ass, either.

How delicate are the lines we walk, Ambassador Wexler thought, studying her counterparts. Around the table, the faces staring back at her were fixed in the same bland expression she held on her own. Ambassador Ngyugen looked particularly impassive, while Ambassador T'ing radiated the same pervasive low-level sense of malevolence she'd come to associate with him in the last year.

"Again, we protest the Chinese exclusionary zone declared in the South China Sea," she said, carefully adding a note of indignation to her voice. "These are international waters, and the warships and aircraft of all nations have the right to peacefully transit and use them."

"And has one of your aircraft or ships been denied access?" the Chinese ambassador said smoothly. "If so, perhaps you could make this committee aware of that incident?"

"Chinese fighters have flown threatening profiles against our assets in the South China Sea," she replied. "As of four hours ago, peaceful American aircraft have been under interception by your nation."

"Ah, but you claim every nation has free access to those areas. You must be consistent—either they are international areas, and we have every right to be there, or one nation has the right to control access to them and limit the use of others. If the latter, then I would suggest that authority would fall to those that border the body of water, not to a nation so many miles distant. Or do some rules apply only to other nations and not to America herself?"

Rules apply to restrain the conduct of nations such as yours, she thought. For a moment, she was tempted to give voice to the unspoken and politically deadly thought. *It's true—and we'll never say it out loud—that when nations such as yours learn to act in a civilized manner by international standards, we'll quite gladly pull back to our own playpen. But until some semblance of respect for human rights and the rights of other nations manages to penetrate your policy, you're going to have to count on seeing us around.*

She heard herself mouthing some bland reassurances automatically, requesting merely that the Council take note of the instances and posturing that a formal protest might be filed. It wouldn't, she knew, and every other nation around the table knew it as well.

For the time being, the American forces were going to have to walk the same narrow line between peace and conflict that she did.

1113 local (Zulu -7)
VF-95 Ready Room
USS Jefferson

Tombstone and Tomboy sat side by side in the high-backed leatherette VF-95 ready room chairs. The chairs formed eight rows, taking up the front part of the ready room. Tombstone, by virtue of his rank, claimed a front row seat, and motioned Tomboy into the seat next to his.

"You ready for this mission? Might be a little boring, a quick qualification flight in a normal Tomcat, after what you've been flying," he said lightly, taking the opportunity to study her face carefully.

"Hell, I'm just glad we're on to fly instead of pulling alert. And those JAST birds aren't all that different from a normal Tomcat, Admiral" she said. "They do the same things, only better. The controls are the same, but the black box configurations give me a hell of a lot more gain on the radar. It's a Tomcat with a few extra fancy toys."

"I take it you're enjoying the opportunity, then?"

"Absolutely! Bouncer gave me a good briefing on it, and Batman's making sure I have plenty of opportunities to practice with it." She smiled, and her whole face lit up.

Tombstone felt a slight twinge of disgruntlement. It felt uncomfortable to hear his old wingman's name roll so easily off his current RIO's lips. It wasn't enough that Batman had to borrow his RIO—not that he got to fly that much anymore, he forced himself to admit—but he also seemed to be striking up a fast friendship with the female NFO. That hadn't been part of the deal, had it? It was one thing to have a close connection with your regular RIO and wingman, a bond that transcended transfers and career changes, and it was an entirely different matter to go poaching on someone else's turf.

Now what the hell? Since when did I start thinking of Tomboy as mine? Even before Batman arrived, she was flying with other pilots. I've heard her talk about her missions a hundred times, and I've never felt—what? What exactly am I feeling?

Jealousy. The word flashed into his mind and insisted on being recognized. It'd never occurred to him to be jealous before, because secretly he'd never viewed any other aviator as possible competition for her attention. He was the admiral, damn it! And a better pilot than 99.5 percent of the aviators on this ship—hell, why be modest? In the whole damned Navy.

But Batman—ah, that was a different matter. Within a year, Tombstone felt certain, his old wingman would be sporting silver stars of his own on his collar. And if any single pilot that he'd ever flown with had ever come close to matching Tombstone's ability, it was Batman. And lately, Tombstone had to admit, Batman was probably better. Flying with the JAST program despite his assignment to the Pentagon, Batman was getting a lot more stick time than Admiral Magruder. Dare he admit it? It was even possible that the eminent Tombstone Magruder, ace aviator and key player in every conflict in the last ten years, was getting rusty.

And maybe not just in his flying skills.

"Admiral?" he heard Tomboy say anxiously. "Are you all right?"

"Fine, fine," he muttered, now unwilling to meet her eyes. He was afraid that if he did, she might see something there that he was not entirely sure he wanted known.

"Okay, so about today's hop," she said, reaching for her briefing checklist.

"Umm, yeah. Listen, Commander," he said, and saw her head snap up in surprise as he addressed her formally, "I just remembered a couple of things that can't wait. Call air ops and scrub me from the mission. We'll try to reschedule it in a couple of days."

"Aren't you going to go out of qual if we wait any longer?" she asked, a note of concern creeping into her voice. "Tombstone," she added, pitching her voice low, "is everything okay?"

"Of course," he said, thinking quickly. "It's just that sitting here doing the briefing, I started realizing that I had something a little off for lunch. It's not sitting too well, and I'd hate to be airborne before I—well, you understand. It's a little embarrassing, Tomboy, that's all." He forced himself to use her call sign, and to look her in the eyes.

"Ah," she said, and her expression lightened. Pilots and RIOs became intimately familiar with each other's gastrointestinal tracts and the workings thereof. "Gotcha. Our secret, Tombstone. Just like that time that I had to—"

"I gotta scat, Tomboy," he interrupted. "We'll pick this up another time, okay?"

"Yes, Admiral," she said. As he walked to the door of the

ready room, he could feel her eyes on his back. While she appeared to have been convinced by his last-minute lie, his deception had only bought him some time. Whatever was going on in his head was his problem, not hers, and it was up to him to solve it before it interfered with their working relationship. As a last resort, he could ask for a different RIO.

Wonderful solution that would be—hurt Tomboy's feelings and get rumors started around the air wing about his relationship with Tomboy or, even worse, about Tomboy's competence. Either alternative was unacceptable.

CHAPTER 21
Wednesday, 3 July

"Damn it, I gave her a direct order!" Bird Dog roared. "Are you listening to me, Chief?"

"I hear you. Sir. So does everyone else on this passageway and two decks up and down."

"Then if you hear me so well, how come this stuff's not getting done?" Bird Dog lowered his voice slightly. "Your muster report shows that Shaughnessy scrubbed and waxed the deck in the ready room. Does that deck look like it's had a mop near it in the last two weeks?"

Chief stared at a spot somewhere on the wall. "It's not always a matter of giving orders, Lieutenant. There're some things you just can't demand. We had some birds down last night, and she thought she could get two of them back up for launch today. It's a matter of priorities."

"These are sailors, damn it! They're supposed to follow orders, not decide which ones they're going to obey!"

Finally, the chief looked at him. Bird Dog was surprised at what he saw in the older man's eyes. Anger, outrage, and something more. A certain weariness, as though the chief had been through this same conversation too many times before.

"Let me tell you something about sailors, sir. These sailors, in particular. Your average Blue Shirt is a hell of a lot smarter and more capable than you're giving them credit for. You know how much an E-3 gets paid?"

Bird Dog shook his head. "I have the feeling you're about to tell me, though."

"Somewhere around a grand a month. Plus somewhere to live and all the chow they can eat. Not a bad deal for an eighteen-year-old, you'd think. You're probably thinking you had a lot less than that to live on when you were that age."

Bird Dog nodded.

"But take another look at what we expect of them. That same eighteen-year-old is the last checkpoint between you and disaster. Your plane captain—think there might be a thousand ways he can keep you from getting killed? And just how old do you think the kid is that makes sure your ejection seat works? How about the one that packs your parachute, and maintains your flight gear? And what about the kid that gives you a final look-over before you get shot off the front end of the ship? Hell, he's probably a lot older—like maybe twenty-two or so. The point is, Lieutenant, these men and women you call kids are carrying a hell of a lot of responsibility on their shoulders, far more than you ever did at that age. They screw up, you're dead before you leave the flight deck."

"I know how much they do, Chief. We all do. So what's your point?"

The chief sighed, looked away, and then pinned Bird Dog to the bulkhead with a steely look. "The point is, sir, that they damned well deserve to be treated with a little more respect. And that goes for me as well. We've all of us been doing this job just a little longer than you have. You think going through AOCS and leadership school makes you better than them? You better think again, Lieutenant. Because it don't. It gets you paid more, and gets you out of a lot of the shitty little work details they do—on top of their main jobs of keeping you alive—but it don't make you a damn bit better as a person. Or as a sailor. And the sooner you realize that, the better you're going to do in this canoe club."

"Captain's Mast, Chief," Bird Dog said. "I'm tired of these excuses. And if you ever falsify another extra duty report, you'd better count on seeing the old man, too!"

The chief turned and walked to the door. He put his hand on the doorknob, paused, and turned back to Bird Dog. "One thing you need to remember, Lieutenant. Sailors don't follow orders—they obey them. They follow *leaders*."

CHAPTER 22
Wednesday, 3 July

By the end of the evening brief, cooler air was already starting to seep into the room through cracks around the windows, finally providing some relief from the stiflingly humid daytime temperatures. Bien sighed, and thought longingly of the feel of the evening breeze on his face. The last three hours had not been pleasant, and it appeared that there was no immediate end in sight to the uneasy forced partnership with their northern neighbors. He saw the Chinese commander motion to him from across the room, and regretfully gave up the immediate prospect of getting away from the Operations Center.

"It is time for that final conversation I mentioned," Mein Low said flatly. "This tactical situation must be exploited immediately."

"How so?" Bien asked, wanting to buy some time and collect himself. He knew all too well what his nemesis was referring to.

At his early-morning brief, Bien had studied the operational positions of all the forces carefully. The American cruiser, *Vincennes*, was still meandering around the northern portion of

241

the South China Sea. While she had not yet come close to the Paracels Islands, she was well within Tomahawk strike range of the ragged collection of islands so close to the Chinese mainland.

The battle group, centered around the *USS Jefferson*, loitered east of the Spratly Islands, slowly patrolling east and west in a corridor that ran from Mischief Reef to twelve miles off the coast of Vietnam. For the last ten days, a lone E-2C Hawkeye had been stationed midway between the *Vincennes* and the *Jefferson*, only sporadically accompanied by a U.S. fighter. The American fighter patrols focused exclusively on the areas to the south, staying always outside of weapon release range of the Spratly Islands. It was a strange tactical dispersion, and the positioning of the fighters made little sense to either the Chinese or the Vietnamese.

"The only explanation," Bien said thoughtfully, "is that they are attempting to avoid the appearance of interest in the Spratly Islands. By staying out of weapons range, they believe that they can convince the rest of the world that they are not behind these horrible attacks on the islands." He carefully avoided referring to the islands as Chinese. That issue would be resolved later, although Vietnam had little chance of opposing China without outside assistance.

"A futile gesture." Mein Low shrugged. "After all, you yourself have investigated the facts behind the attacks. It was not China, and it certainly was not Vietnam. Who else could be responsible?"

And now comes the most delicate part of this strange dance between our countries, Bien thought. *How am I to convince you that we believe your story, when past experience would persuade us to believe the opposite? If you told me the sun had risen this morning, I would be forced to go check for myself before I believed you!*

"As you say—who else could be responsible?" Bien murmured. "Perhaps the stealth technology we have heard about, or a submarine-launched Tomahawk? Or even their special operations forces? The possibilities are too many to fully explore."

The Chinese commander leaned back in his seat, apparently satisfied, Bien noted.

"So far, they have limited their attacks to *our* outposts," he said, apparently broaching a new topic. "However, should your negotiations for normalization of international relations and trade concessions falter, do you truly believe that they would abstain from attacking your forces as well? Let us be frank with one another—while neither of us is willing to acknowledge the other's claim to this territory, we are both certain that the Americans have no justifiable interest here. Correct?"

"Of course," Bien said.

"Then it is to the advantage of both to ensure that the Americans leave this region. Permanently."

"It took us twenty years of war to convince them to go home last time," Bien said softly. "Can we dare hope that it would be easier now?"

The Chinese commander nodded vigorously. "It should be, thanks to that very same tragedy. That is the other reason that cooperation between our countries is so appropriate at this time. It is Vietnam's sacrifices that will make this plan work. The result of your prior disagreement with the Americans is that they have no tolerance for loss of life. It must be very comforting to your people that your losses will finally be revenged."

"And the plan?" Bien pressed.

"At the right time, my friend. At the right time. Now," the Chinese commander continued, rubbing his hands together briskly, "I believe you mentioned inspecting the airfield this afternoon? What better time than now?"

"Good evening, Admiral," Pamela said. She was proud of her voice—calm and professional, despite the rage of emotions flooding her.

"And to you, Miss Drake," he answered gravely. His voice was scratchy, rubbed raw by too many cups of bitter black midwatch coffee and too little sleep.

How long can he keep this up? It's been a week, and there's no sign that the Chinese are any closer to doing anything different! Every face I see looks like death warmed over. If these people don't get some sleep soon, it's not going to matter what happens on some damned rock in the middle of the South China Sea. Not that I care about him in particular, she added hastily to herself.

They'd come full circle in their relationship. From friends to lovers, and then engaged—and now back to merely friends. If it was possible. She wasn't entirely sure it was going to be.

And that pilot—what was her name? Tomboy, she'd heard the others call her. From the way Tombstone looked at her, the younger woman was more than just another aviator in his carrier group. She wondered if anyone else had noticed the sparks that flew between their admiral and the pilot. It was more than just the close bond that grows up between men and women facing mortal danger together.

Not that Stoney would do anything about it, of that she was certain. As long as Tomboy was under his command, she had no permanent claim on his attention. To get involved with a woman on his ship—no, the meticulously proper Rear Admiral Tombstone Magruder would never commit that sin.

She listened to the morning briefing half-attentively. Too little had changed to warrant more than a cursory discussion. Chinese fighters still challenged the edges of the carrier's air envelope, still in small groups and still in unthreatening mission profiles. Despite the apparent lack of progress, Commander Lab Rat—Busby, she corrected herself—still looked as optimistic and determined as ever. Pamela forced herself to start paying attention as the intelligence officer stood to give his portion of the morning brief.

"Situation unchanged, ladies and gentlemen," he said. An incongruously cheerful smile spread across his face. "No news is good news, in this case!"

"How much longer?" CAG grumbled. "I've got people walking around asleep on their feet! We can't keep this many alert aircraft manned and the flight deck in this state of readiness forever."

Busby looked thoughtful. "I know it's a problem, CAG, but it shouldn't be too much longer. We have some reasons to believe that something may happen soon."

"You keep saying that!" Ops burst out. "How about some specifics, Commander?"

Commander Busby drew himself up to his full height and stood his ground. "There are some things I can't brief, sir. No disrespect intended."

"Typical intelligence," Ops snapped. "Too late to do any good. And if you've got something useful for us, it's too classified for the people that need it most to see!"

"Enough," Tombstone said. "Ops, CAG—I appreciate the difficulty of your positions. I see the same faces you do, and I know what you're up against. In this situation, however, Commander Busby has my full support. And my utmost confidence. That good enough for you?"

Ops grunted and CAG nodded. Neither one, Pamela noted, appeared to be reassured by their admiral's statement.

"End of discussion," Tombstone added. "Commander, I believe that is the end of the brief as well."

The intelligence officer shot him a grateful look and began rolling up his charts and overlays. Pamela wondered what arcane bit of intelligence information the two of them shared—and why it was secret from the rest of the staff.

1000 local (Zulu +5)
Ambassador Wexler's Office
United Nations

"Well, I don't see how we could possibly work you into her schedule until next Tuesday. It's just—"

Ambassador Wexler paused at the coffeepot and watched her aide. His normally congenial expression had just faded into something that resembled the look of a shell-shocked POW. She stirred in some creamer, wondering what besides a declaration of war could so disturb her normally unflappable staffer.

"I see," the aide said finally. His voice had taken on a musing note. "And you're sure about this?" She watched him reach for her calendar, then motion to her with the other hand, the telephone jammed between his shoulder and his ear. He pointed to her afternoon appointment with her hairdresser and made sure she was watching as he drew a heavy X through it. To one side, along the margin, he wrote the initials, VN.

She shot a sidewise look at him, puzzled. Why? she mouthed silently at him.

He just shook his head and pointed. "The ambassador can see you at two p.m., then," he said finally. "Yes, of course. I understand the need for speed, as will she. Thanks."

He hung up the telephone and stared at her for a moment, reassembling his expression into calm professionalism but unable to completely repress the glee lurking at the corners of his eyes.

"I take it I've got an urgent appointment with the ambassador from Vietnam," she said, settling into the comfortable chair lodged against one wall. "Would it be too much to ask why this is important enough for me to cancel my appointment with Roberto?"

"Not at all, Madam Ambassador," he replied. "And I think you'll agree with me in a few minutes."

Her eyes grew serious at the use of her formal title. "So it's that important?" she said, worry starting to gnaw at her.

"Our former enemy and current ally, the great republic of Vietnam, is not entirely pleased with their neighbor to the north. I think the events of the last few weeks in the South China Sea and the attractive lure of more trade concessions have made them see the light."

"China, I take it. What are they doing now, persecuting more Vietnamese citizens?"

"Better—or worse, depending on your point of view, " he added hastily. "Seems China has been demanding air overflight rights, as well as landing and refueling privileges. Vietnam has gone along with it for now. Understandable—they have to live with China; we don't."

"And now?" she prompted, wishing he'd get to the point.

"Vietnam is wondering whether or not we might like some additional information on the explosions in the South China Sea. It's one thing to try to placate China, and another thing entirely to let them kill your patrol boats."

"Kill patrol—of course," she breathed. "One of those incidents in the Spratly Islands. They've got proof China was behind it?"

"Proof, and more. They're not so bad at snooping around, you know. After the conflicts between the two countries during the Cold War, Vietnam has developed a fairly extensive intelligence network in the region. And seeing as how it might be to their advantage right now, with the U.S. normalizing relationships with Vietnam—and, potentially, China—they'd like to share a little information with us."

"About what?" she asked.

"He didn't want to go into it over the telephone, but I was fairly sure you'd be interested. That a good enough reason to skip Roberto?"

She smiled and stood. "Remind me not to notice the next time you do something stupid, Armand. You've just earned yourself a real big brownie point."

Ambassador Wexler went back to her office, smiling. In the intricate plotting and scheming that defined the relations between nations in the UN, information was golden. It looked like Vietnam had just decided to make a goodwill deposit in the American bank.

Two hours later, the ambassador from Vietnam arrived.

"An interesting opportunity you offer," Ambassador Wexler said, eyeing the Vietnamese ambassador seated across from her. Ngyugen seemed his usual unflappable self. She could pick up no hint as to the reason for his visit.

"An opportunity for both sides," he acknowledged, taking a sip of tea from the delicate bone-china cup. "One that could work to our mutual benefit."

"Let me make sure I understand this. China has amassed a considerable force of fighters in your country, correct? Ones that they're not willing to move anytime soon. Your government is concerned that the United States understand your opposition to this, while of course you feel somewhat limited in your ability to insist on withdrawal. Is that it?"

He nodded. "I'd feared it would be difficult for you, understanding the delicate position we stand in with regard to China. But, yes, that's the situation exactly."

"And you're sure about this information?" she asked. "Careers are going to fall over this one, you know."

"The source is trustworthy, I assure you. As trustworthy as any spy ever is, at least."

She sighed and leaned back in her chair. "We are, of course, most grateful for the information. It will cause some problems, naturally, but not as many as allowing the situation to continue."

"Yes. We thought as much. As it would for us, should the source of your information be discovered."

"I'll do my best to protect you on this, but you understand the difficulties."

"We have fewer such problems in Vietnam. Perhaps you should consider implementing more control over your press, as we have done."

She laughed. "As much as I'd welcome the idea at times, it really wouldn't work here, you know."

"Of course not. Still, it must be an attractive idea at times."

"On occasion. But there are strengths to every weakness, Ambassador, just as every strength is weak at some point."

He lifted one eyebrow. "Odd. You sound very Asian, Madam Ambassador."

"And in exchange for our understanding, and for the U.S. not insisting on Vietnam taking action, you're prepared to offer us information?"

"More than information. Cooperation, where possible. You know, of course, that we're a bit short on fighters ourselves. The bases they're using in the south were all built by American forces, I believe."

"The one thing you haven't made entirely clear is exactly what this cooperation consists of. Or perhaps you have, and I've just failed to see the subtleties in the situation."

"Perhaps this will assist you," he said as he set his cup and saucer down on the coffee table. He opened his attaché case, pulled out a brown folder, and handed it to her. "All their operational traffic and operations plans for the last week."

She suppressed a sudden intake of breath. A treasure trove of intelligence! "Could I impose on you for the salient points of your analysis?" she asked, not yet wanting to leaf through the messages and bits of paper crammed into the folder.

"Of course. China has been conducting a rather delicate campaign of misinformation and deception. You've deduced, of course, that she herself is behind the explosions on the Spratly Island camps." He paused for a moment. "As well as the attack on our own naval forces," he continued grimly. The change in his expression made him look less the well-groomed and urbane ambassador she'd known for two years and more of a warrior. He had, she recalled, fought with American forces during the Vietnam conflict. He now looked more like the combat-blooded veteran he was.

"There is a source inside your satellite monitoring facilities," he continued. "We haven't been able to determine exactly who it is, but there is no doubt that there is one. It influences their planning immensely, although I cannot say what effect it has on their mainland. They're trying to blame it on you, in an effort to unify Southeast Asia against the United States."

"We'd started to suspect that," she commented, still holding the folder gingerly.

"We know," he replied, and allowed a slight trace of amusement to cross his face. "At any rate, you can expect a major incident sometime very soon, one that China hopes will justify in the eyes of the world their attacking your battle group. They plan to launch their strike from our soil. If that happens, we will lose any chance of continuing the normalization of relationships. This must not occur."

"And the cooperation?" she nudged gently.

"I think you might like that part best of all." For the next five minutes, he laid out a plan that rivaled China's.

She listened for several minutes. Grim amusement crept into her expression. "Oh, yes," she said finally. "I like this very much. And I think that Navy admiral in the South China Sea is going to like it even better."

CHAPTER 23
Thursday, 4 July

Bien ran his hands over his face, trying to erase the tiredness he was sure showed there. Mein Low's comments had kept him tossing half the night. Participating in the Chinese strike on the American battle group was unacceptable, yet the plan he'd presented to the American ambassador was almost as risky. He'd awoken at 0400 and finally decided to go to the Operations Center. It was better than lying in bed worrying.

After two hours of paperwork and staring at charts, he'd heard Mein Low's grating voice in the hallway outside his office. Seconds later, the Chinese commander had entered his office without knocking, and was now helping himself to tea from the hot plate on Bien's credenza. And using Bien's own mug. Now, settled into a chair on the other side of the room, Mein Low fixed his Vietnamese counterpart with a cold glare.

"You have two choices," Mein Low said. His voice carried no inflection to betray the least bit of emotion or weakness. "You may either execute this plan as I have given it to you, or I will have you shot. I will proceed thusly through your subordinates until I find one officer capable of obeying orders.

And should anyone disobey me while we are in the air, my deputy here in the center will execute your men. Is that clear to you?"

Bien stared at the small Chinese general. *So it finally comes to this. Even though I have warned Ngyugen, and set all the necessary plans in place, it is actually happening. Odd that I never really believed it would—that I never understood how eternal and deadly the Chinese drive for dominance is.*

Aware that the man was waiting for an answer, Bien nodded abruptly. "We will follow your plan."

"Eagerly, I hope." The commander's demeanor thawed slightly. "After all, it is to your advantage as well to have the Americans out of the South China Sea. Your country, of all those in this region, should understand how devastating American attempts to intervene in Asian affairs are."

Again, Bien nodded. *And China is a more merciful alternative?*

"As you see from the plans, your Flankers and Foxbats will lead the attack on the carrier. It is our wish to allow Vietnam her rightful place as a leader in the region, and since the battle group is closer to your coast than our islands, we decided it was only appropriate that your aircraft lead the strike. Much glory will accrue to you and your pilots if you succeed in making the first direct strike on the American battle group." Mein Low smiled. "My forces will be immediately behind yours, to provide second strike capability as well as vectoring and surveillance services."

"We are, of course, honored at your trust," Bien said smoothly, masking his feelings behind a bland expression. *Although you have neglected to mention the real reason for placing us in the front—to make sure that we do not waiver in our determination. With the Americans in front of us and the Chinese behind us, we are truly left with no alternatives. As soon as the Americans see the raid inbound, they will use their*

surface-to-air missiles. Undoubtedly our faithful allies hope to use my forces as a missile sponge. Once the American fighters engage, the Americans cannot risk their shipboard weaponry. There will be too much danger of hitting their own aircraft.
"And your Flankers," Bien continued. "What will their weapons load-out be?"

"Not just Flankers," the Chinese commander said deliberately. "In a gesture of friendship, we will be augmenting our normal complement of Flankers with our most advanced aircraft. My own personal aircraft, the F-10, is being flown south as we speak. I have had the responsibility for developing and testing it, and I will now provide its worth in a strike. The details of weapons load-out and fueling will be handled by our crews, as always." He shot a sharp, searching glance at Bien. "We will both fly this mission, of course. There is no other way to lead men except from in front. We launch in twelve hours. Our planes are ready now. Make sure yours are as well."

1730 local (Zulu -7)
CVIC
USS Jefferson

Tombstone studied the satellite picture that had been faxed to the carrier from the NSA over secure, highly encrypted circuits. "Looks like they're getting ready to launch," he said.

The IS, a photo-interpretation specialist, nodded. "That would be my call, Admiral. How long will it take to get all those aircraft in the air?"

Tombstone studied the massed formations of aircraft. "If they space them at thirty seconds apart, almost an hour. Drop it down to ten-second intervals, and you're looking at twenty minutes. They're going to wait until at least half of them are airborne, maybe all of them, mass up into a strike force, and then head our way. We've got a little time—not much, but enough."

"Guess we got pretty lucky, getting them to launch just when we've got satellite coverage in the area," the IS said, smiling. "Makes this job a lot easier when you get good data points."

"It might be luck, son. But it might just be something else as well," Tombstone said gravely. "Sometimes you create your own luck by playing on the other fellow's perceptions, feeding him misinformation."

"Is that what happened today?" the IS asked, surprised.

"I can't tell you. But there's one thing you probably already know. Commander Busby is one hell of a fine intelligence officer."

"We know that, sir," the IS said. "A little paranoid some-times, maybe, but you gotta like that in an intelligence officer."

"I know I do," Tombstone murmured as he reached for the bitch box toggle switch. "TFCC, this is Magruder. Get those JAST birds in the air, and launch the alert EA-6B Prowlers. Make sure everyone down south is tanked to the gills. I want them bustering back up here. Chinese raid is inbound now!"

As Tombstone pulled open the door and strode down that passageway back to TFCC, he could hear the Prowlers' engines spooling up to full military power. Within thirty seconds, the train-rattling sounds of catapults lumbering forward shook the overhead, ending in the gentle thump that signaled another aircraft airborne. Moments later, a second and then a third Prowler took to the skies. It was time for the second phase of the plan to begin.

Eighty aircraft ringed the airfield, their engines turning as the pilots performed preflight checks. The air around the field shimmered as unburned fuel floated through the air. The rain yesterday had left the ground around the strip soggy, and the hot, humid air seemed to concentrate the fumes. Red streaks of dirt crisscrossed the runway, evidence of the maintenance truck's trips out to the waiting aircraft.

Poised at the end of the runway, ten Vietnamese Flankers and sixteen MiG-23's followed a similar routine. The roar of their jet engines igniting was completely drowned out by the larger Chinese force. Even though both countries were flying the same airframes, Bien thought he could tell the difference between the Chinese engines and those of his own country's aircract.

Bien circled his silent aircraft, preflighting the exterior by checking that each panel was dogged down tight, that there were no leaks or unexplained puddles of liquid around the jet, and that the tires and landing gear appeared to be in good repair. He then climbed into the cockpit and began going through the preflight checklist automatically. His earlier confidence had gradually eroded into a numb certainty that this was his last flight. The familiar details of preflight steadied him.

He glanced down to the last aircraft to start its engines. Mein Low had walked out to the airfield with Bien, then broken off to head for his aircraft without even a word of good luck. Now the five F-10's sleek and deadly, shimmered in the heat waves coming up off the tarmac.

At last, Bien started his Flanker's engines. The engines spooled up, slowly at first, then the RPMs rising quickly as the stator gained momentum and overcame initial mechanical friction. The sound slid up octaves in seconds, and had soon picked up enough harmonics and undertones to be the normal full-throated scream of raw power.

His radio popped and crackled for a moment, then began spitting out permission for the Vietnamese fighters to launch. Bien led the two squadrons into the air. He quickly ascended to four thousand feet, and then began orbiting, waiting for the rest of his squadrons to join on him. He heard the voice on the radio change, and the language shift from Vietnamese to Chinese. He could see the Chinese fighters beginning their roll-out, rotation, and initial climb. The Chinese squadrons were joining up to the south of the airfield, the Vietnamese ones to the north. Evidently the spirit of brotherly cooperation did not extend to sharing airspace.

Finally, the signal came, first in Chinese then repeated in Vietnamese. Bien turned east, increasing his speed to 420 knots and climbing to seven thousand feet. His wingman bobbled for a moment and then settled down to his left, and the rest of the circling wolf pack of fighters broke into their respective flights. Behind them, the Chinese were settling into the fighting formation that Bien had seen entirely too many times in the last five months.

Seventy miles to the east, the American battle group waited.

1800 local (Zulu -7)
Spook Two

"Well, will you look at that?" Tomboy said softly.

"Got them?" Batman asked.

"You betcha. Looks like about eighteen—no, make it closer

to twenty-five high-speed contacts leaving the coast. Tight formation. Any other bird, it'd be difficult to break them out in this soup." She twiddled with the radar, tweaking and peaking. "But I got them—oh, yeah, do I got them!"

"Best we wake Mother up, then," Batman said, a tight note creeping into his voice. "I think we might just back up off the front line a little, too. At least until our posse arrives."

"Concur. We just did our job at the OK Corral."

"Homeplate, this is Doc Holliday," Tomboy said into the mike. "Suggest you wake up Wyatt Earp."

1810 local (Zulu -7)
TFCC

Wyatt Earp could have done with snipers, Tombstone thought, staring at the TFCC screen and waiting for the air battle to unfold. Snipers provide a force multiplier that can't be beat. If a year at the Naval War College had taught him nothing else, it had taught him that operational planning was the key to winning an engagement. *Define the desired end state, and plan for that state to exist. We studied enough military history and strategy planning to have a variety of examples, both good and bad.*

The shoot-out at the OK Corral and the Peloponnesian wars. It was a combination that he didn't think had even occurred to his professors.

"Could be another feint," Batman said neutrally.

"Not with that many aircraft," Tombstone said. "It's gone on too long. We've held off long enough to convince them that we're lulled. They'll take advantage of our complacency. They're convinced now."

"You can't be sure."

"Neither can they. But look at it from their point of view. We haven't reacted to the last two probes. In this sea state, they're going to feel a little more confident that their submarine can get in close, and that our radar may be degraded. They've got to know that we're tired, and they're launching so that the sun will be in our eyes when we intercept them."

"I almost hope so, for the aircrew's sake. They can't take much more of this, Tombstone."

Tombstone shot his old wingman a hard look. "You think I don't know what they're going through? It hasn't been that long, Batman, since you and I were pulling alert five."

"We never pulled this many in a row, shipmate—not on top of normal operations."

"I know that. But there was no other way. I know this air wing. They're tired, but they can do it."

"I hope you're right, my friend," Batman said softly to himself. "Because if you're not—the options become unacceptable real fast."

"As long as the Vietnamese do their part," Tombstone said. "Feels really strange, depending on them."

"You're the one who's always telling me that war is more than blowing aircraft out of the sky."

"Let's just hope the politicians understand that part of it. Because if they didn't, that's all this is going to amount to."

"That's it!" the TAO shouted. "Admiral, you were right! Tomcat's reporting numerous fighters inbound!"

"TAO, get a raid count from that Tomcat," Tombstone said quietly, ignoring the jolt of adrenaline flooding his body.

"Gunslinger 101 estimates ninety aircraft, Admiral," the TAO replied. "Feet wet off the coast of Vietnam five minutes ago. Air boss requests permission to set flight quarters."

"Do it," Tombstone ordered. "And tell him I expect to see a new record set on launching the alert CAP."

Ten seconds later, the thunderous roar of a Tomcat at full

military power shook the space. Tombstone glanced at the CCTV and saw the afterburners light the deck in an eerie hell-like fire. Five seconds later, the catapult sang its rattling song, ramming forward to toss the first alert fighter off the deck.

The carrier shook with the differing rhythms, as a forward catapult, followed by the waist cat, then the other forward catapult launched the alert package. For ten minutes, the refrain was Tomcats. The lighter-voiced scream of the Hornets picked up the second verse, followed by the rumble of a KA-6 tanker.

Within twenty minutes, the carrier felt eerily silent, the last of the alert aircraft launched. Overhead, he could hear the odd rattlings and vibrations that came from aircraft being moved around the deck in preparation for normal launch.

Tombstone felt strangely disconnected from the battle. Unlike every other time in his career, this time he'd be following it on the communications net and from the radar screen instead of in the air. His hands curled, missing the feel of the vibrating throttle beneath them. Watching red symbols track across a screen was a poor substitute for the actual sight of the enemy raid.

Over the tactical net, he could hear the Hornet pilots snapping at each other, chivvying to be the first in line to top off from the tanker and get into the fight. The longer-legged Tomcats were already underway to the fight. Had he been able to come up with an excuse—any decent excuse would have done—he'd have been up there with them. But, as CAG had reminded him, it was time to turn the fight over to better eyes, faster reflexes, and the next generation. His place was here on the ship. The harder job, perhaps, except for the dying— watching it instead of doing it.

"Admiral! S-3 SUCAP reports a visual on a periscope!" the flag TAO said.

"Where?" he demanded.

"Thirty miles to the east, sir. DESRON is vectoring them in for the intercept." The TAO paused, and a frown crossed his face. "Lost it. It went sinker as soon as the S-3 got overhead."

"I'll save DESRON the trouble of asking the next question. Tell that Viking he's weapons free, and to watch out for those Grails," Tombstone said immediately. The TAO nodded, and passed the word up five decks to the DESRON.

If he'd had any doubts about the Chinese intentions, the sudden appearance of the submarine had cured them. No matter whether it was a Kilo or a Han-class boat, it had just surfaced for the last time.

CHAPTER 24
Thursday, 4 July

"Good hunting, Lieutenant," Chief Franklin said.

"Thanks, Chief," Bird Dog said absently, his mind already forty feet away in the cockpit of the Tomcat. He scribbled his name in the maintenance log, acknowledging he'd read the "gripes," the maintenance action forms, filed in the compact folder. He patted himself over one time, carefully checking that he had his water bottle, candy bar, gun, and all the other paraphernalia that pilots tucked into the pockets of their flight suit. He gave the crotch straps on the ejection harness one last tug to tighten them. As dangerous as ejection could be, loose straps could result in permanent damage.

He pushed open the hatch and felt the heat and the noise of the flight deck assault him. He scanned the deck and found Tomcat 205 waiting near the handler's shack. The plane captain, a slim, coverall-clad figure, was dogging down one last panel.

Shaughnessy! Bird Dog stormed back into the handler's office. Chief Franklin was still there, leaning on the counter and chatting with the handler.

"Chief! What's she doing on my aircraft?" Bird Dog demanded.

Chief Franklin slowly straightened up, and his face lost all expression. "She's preflighting, Lieutenant. Plane captains have their own routine for certifying the aircraft safe for flight."

"I know what a plane captain does, damn it! What's she doing on *my* aircraft?"

"Take it outside, gentlemen," the handler said abruptly. "We've got work to do in here."

Bird Dog followed Chief Franklin out of the shack and around behind it. The massive bulk of the island masked part of the screaming jet noise and made conversation in normal tones of voice almost possible.

"I don't want her on my Tomcat," Bird Dog said. "And I'm surprised you'd even consider it, Chief. What the hell were you thinking? Putting a plane captain that I'm sending to captain's mast on my aircraft?"

"What I'm thinking, Lieutenant, is that you are one arrogant, ignorant son of a bitch," the chief said. "Who the hell are you? You really think that girl would do something to your aircraft just because you assigned her some extra duty? If that's the way you think of these plane captains, you better find a new career. Because today, and every day that you fly, you're going to be depending on those people for your life."

"You've got other plane captains!"

"And let me tell you something else. Yes, I *do* have other plane captains. But Shaughnessy is the best damn one of the lot. You're the most inexperienced pilot in this squadron, sir. I don't know whether you or the plane captain missed that hydraulic leak a couple of days ago. What I *do* know is that it killed a sailor. Given that, what makes sense to *me* is to put my best sailor on the job to make sure you don't fry your young ass or kill someone else in the process. And if you've got a problem with that, I suggest you take it up with the Maintenance Officer. Sir." The chief turned abruptly and stalked away.

Bird Dog stared after him for a moment, and then started after him. As he reentered the Handler's office, he saw Chief Franklin's broad back disappearing down the passageway. He started after him.

"Lieutenant!" the Handler said sharply. "You've got a mission to fly. I suggest you get your ass out to that aircraft before your event gets canceled. And get your head in the game. You got problems with your chief, you leave them down in your Branch spaces. Don't be airing your dirty laundry up here."

Jesus, was everybody in the whole air wing out to ream him today? Bird Dog stopped short of snapping out an angry response and nodded abruptly. There was some truth to what the Handler said. Always, the mission came first.

He turned and headed for the hatch again, ready to start his preflights. He stopped abruptly as he caught sight of the slim figure framed by the entrance.

Shaughnessy. How long had she been standing there? He glared at her. Everything that had gone wrong so far had been her fault. If she'd just worn her cranial on the flight deck like she was supposed to . . .

"Just coming in to sign your aircraft out as safe for flight, sir," she said. Her voice sounded tight. "Could I have the MAF, please?"

The Handler slid the multipart form across the desk to her. She ran her eyes down it and then scrawled her signature across the bottom. "Your aircraft, sir." She started toward the hatch.

"Shaughnessy—" Bird Dog started.

"Sir. Excuse me, but I've got three other aircraft to preflight," she said, finally looking up at him. Dark circles ringed her eyes, and her face looked thinner than it had the last time he'd held quarters inspection. "Could it wait?"

"Of course," he said finally. "We'll talk when I get back."

She nodded abruptly and led the way out to the aircraft. As Gator and Bird Dog performed their preflights, she followed them around the aircraft, occasionally double-checking a panel fixture or wiping a smudge off the fuselage.

Finally, Bird Dog clambered up into the cockpit, and Gator followed. Once they were seated, Shaughnessy followed them up, stepping carefully on the pull-out steps on the fuselage. She checked to see that the ejection seat pins had been removed, and double-checked the ejection harness connections to the seat. Finally satisfied, she gave both of them a weary nod. "Good flight, sirs," she said, fixing her eyes on Gator.

Gator waited until the canopy slid into place and then said, "Sometimes you can be a real asshole, Bird Dog."

"Seems to be the unanimous opinion today," the pilot snapped. "You want to go fly or you want to share more of your exciting insights with me?"

Gator sighed. "Let's just get airborne, Bird Dog. At least I know that you know how to do that."

Bird Dog taxied forward, following the Yellow Shirt's hand signals and carefully sliding the Tomcat into position on the catapult. Halfway to the catapult, the fear hit him again.

He was so tired—oh, Jesus, was he tired! Two days of flex-deck operations, launching alert aircraft every time the Chinese sortied, struggling to get back on board the pitching deck at night, fighting not to think about the monster that grew larger every day! It was past the point of mere preference and into the issue of safety. Even the surge of adrenaline that had hit him when he'd heard about the inbound raid had faded away to a dull, aching jangle of nerves.

Had Airman Alvarez been this tired when he'd wandered behind the Tomcat that night? What had it been like—to be so

tired he hadn't seen the danger, so tired he hadn't noticed the
screaming F-14 turning on the deck? Alvarez would have been
thinking about his rack, six decks below, calling to him. Maybe
he'd even felt a momentary gleam of hope—Bird Dog's event
was one of the last to launch, and Alvarez could have looked
forward to perhaps almost an hour of unconsciousness before
he'd have been called back onto the flight deck to start
recovering aircraft. Not in his rack, no. Not with that many
aircraft airborne, due back on deck too soon. Alvarez probably
would have simply gone down one deck and stretched out
full-length in one of the passageways that crisscrossed the
interior of the carrier like a maze.

When did he realize what had happened? When the jet's
sucking pull first hit him? The second his feet left the deck? Or
had it taken a few milliseconds, long enough for him to come
fully awake only as he was hurtling through the air, suspended
in the air between the ship and the jet engine?

How many times had he stepped over the exhausted plane
captains lining the passageways? Cursed as he tripped over a
sound-powered telephone cord stretched across the linoleum to
an outlet, the earphones still clamped firmly to the plane
captain's head? Had he ever even stopped to think that the
flight deck crews had no mandated crew rest requirements
between flights, or that too few of his fellow officers ever gave
a thought to the countless bone-tired enlisted people it took to
get the elite aircrews off the deck?

"Bird Dog! They gonna start charging us rent, man," his RIO
said into the ICS.

Bird Dog was suddenly aware of the waving green lights in
front of him. The Yellow Shirt was motioning frantically for
him to move forward, to clear the way for the next aircraft.

Was he safe to fly? Bird Dog hesitated, and then slowly
eased the throttle forward. He held the image of Alvarez's face
before him for a moment, then forced it back into the

compartment of his mind that held everything not associated with the immediate mission.

Suddenly, a figure darted across the flight deck toward the catapult. Lights flashed red as the air boss called a foul deck. Bird Dog craned his neck to try to see what poor fool had just incurred the wrath of the tower.

For the third time in the last hour, he choked on Shaughnessy's name. What in the hell was she doing *now*! She'd already formally certified the Tomcat as safe for flight and turned over responsibility to the Yellow Shirt and the pilot.

The young airman was pointing at the left side of his Tomcat and making jerking motions with her hands. The Yellow Shirt shook his head no. The airman put both hands on her hips and leaned forward, standing close and screaming in the senior petty officer's ear to be heard over the noise. The Yellow Shirt shrugged, then nodded. Bird dog saw his lips move as he spoke with someone on the flight deck circuit. Finally, he looked back up at Bird Dog and shook his head from side to side.

Enraged, Bird Dog began demanding answers. "Your aircraft is down," the Handler replied. "You might have a control surface problem—we want to get it checked out. You need to move back off the cat."

"Damn it, this aircraft is fine!" Bird Dog yelled. "It feels fine! Don't you think I'd know if I had a control surface problem? Look!" He cycled the stick again.

"Off the cat, mister," the Air Boss snapped. "You want to argue, you come up here and see me!"

Bird Dog swore and backed the Tomcat off the catapult. He taxied back to the spot and shut down. He jammed the canopy back and vaulted out of the aircraft, ignoring the steps and welcoming the hard shock of hitting the deck.

"What the hell are you doing!" he swore at the plane captain. "This your idea of revenge? You just bought your ass another trip to Captain's Mast!"

Airman Shaughnessy ignored him. From the handler's shack, Chief Franklin came over at a trot and interposed himself between the pilot and the plane captain. Bird Dog tried to get around him, but the chief grabbed Bird Dog's shoulder and slammed him up against a huffer, shouting, "Hold still, you arrogant son of a bitch!"

Bird Dog watched Shaughnessy pop one panel open, then another. She hauled herself up to the fuselage, and the upper portion of her torso disappeared into the airframe, leaving only her legs sticking out. For the briefest second, Bird Dog remembered how Alvarez had looked as he disappeared into the sucking maw of the jet engine. He shuddered, part of his anger dissipated by the horrendous memory.

Gator stood by the half-visible airman, talking to her as she rummaged around in the guts of the hydraulics system, electrical lines, and avionics that controlled the Tomcat. Finally, even over the shriek of the flight deck noise, Bird Dog heard her exclaim, "Got it!" Her butt wiggled as she backed herself out of the airframe. Gator caught her waist and helped her lower herself gently down to the deck.

Her eyes shining with triumph, Shaughnessy held up her prize. Clutched in her left hand was a wrench. "It was jammed up next to the actuator, Chief!" she said excitedly. "When I saw 205 cycling on the cat, something looked funny to me. You know how it is, you get familiar with how your birds look. Just as the surface dropped, I thought I saw a little hitch. Kind of a bobble, just like a second or when it wasn't traveling smoothly."

The chief nodded. "Couldn't have caught it in your preflight, though. And if that bird had launched with it, there's a damned good chance those control surfaces wouldn't have responded when the lieutenant tried to level out after his climb. He would have been stuck at full flaps—rolled over on his back, and come right back down onto the flight deck!"

"And, sir," he added, meeting Bird Dog's eyes with open

challenge on his face, "you probably wouldn't have gotten out."

Bird Dog turned pale as the full implication of Shaughnessy's find sunk in. "I didn't know," he said finally.

Gator put one hand on the airman's shoulder. "That was damned fine work, and one of the sharpest problem catches I've ever seen. Thanks. You made a big difference today."

Shaughnessy nodded, her eyes suddenly bright. "It's my bird most of the time, sir," she said to the RIO, carefully avoiding looking at the pilot. "It's only yours when it's in the air."

"True enough. Would you please preflight this turkey again so we can get back onto the cat?" Gator asked.

"Sure thing, sir. It's your bird in five minutes." She darted off to get another MAF.

"And you," Gator said, turning to Bird Dog, "really screwed the pooch this time, asshole. The only way you could make matters worse right now is if you don't put this outside the cockpit and fly this damned mission as hot and tight as you've ever flown one. You owe these people that much."

Sun flashed off the nose of the Tomcat, leaving red specks flickering in his vision. Bird Dog blinked and waited for his vision to clear before easing the throttle forward.

Flying—any sort of flying—would have also let him escape his thoughts for a while to concentrate on the almost-reflexive actions of bonding with the Tomcat. Sitting on the flight deck, with only Gator and the chatter on the flight deck circuit for company, it was too hard to escape thinking about the Chief's words.

Arrogant, was he? He tried to summon up the anger he'd felt when the Chief said that, but all he could feel was embarrassment. Shaughnessy had just saved his life by catching the control surface problem. Bird Dog shifted uneasily, telling himself that it was the stiff new lumbar support pad that caused it.

Sure, he'd made some assumptions about his enlisted troops, probably some that weren't entirely fair. But hadn't they taught him that in Aviation Officer's Candidate School? That it was up to *him* to supply leadership and direction to his troops? That the chiefs would depend on him for guidance, discipline for the men and women in the branch? Hell, everyone swore an oath to obey the orders of the officers appointed over them, didn't they? Didn't that include Bird Dog's orders?

He thought of his drill instructor, the Marine gunny sergeant who'd shepherded him through those endless months of AOCS. Now *there* was an enlisted man who'd never disobey orders, he was certain. Shouldn't the Chief be the same way?

Probably not, he admitted. He tried to imagine giving Gunny MacArthur Cat AOLCS an order to do *anything*. But that had been different, some part of his mind insisted. Gunny was the one who knew how things worked. It was his job to turn the raw civilians he'd been given into officers.

This was different, though. Bird Dog *knew* naval aviation now. He'd had classes on leadership, courses on motivating and leading people, in addition to his bachelor's degree in psychology. This was stuff he understood, and he was right!

Yeah, and I walked right out of ground school and flew a T-34 by myself, too. Sure he had—after countless hours of dual-controls flight with an instructor, simulator training, and a careful practical walk-through by more experienced aviators.

Maybe the same principles applied to learning to be a leader. It was possible—just barely possible—that he'd been wrong.

The heat in the Tomcat's cockpit seemed more bearable than it had a few minutes earlier. When he got back, he'd go have a chat with the chief. It might be time to listen instead of talk for a while.

Bird Dog felt the Tomcat shudder, and steam pressure

immediately began building in the steam piston below the decks. The shuttle holding the aircraft on the catapult transmitted the vibrations to his bird. A Yellow Shirt darted forward and out of view under the aircraft. He came out carrying six red streamers—Bird Dog counted them carefully as the ragged ends whipped in the wind. They were the safety pins on his weapons, which were now fully operational.

Another Yellow Shirt held up a white board with greasepenciled numbers on it, giving the Tomcat's takeoff weight as it was currently configured. Two Phoenixes, two Sparrows, and two Sidewinders hung beneath his wings, a full range of ACM weaponry. Bird Dog begrudged the Phoenixes the space they took up; he would have preferred to have a full load of the more dependable Sidewinders.

Bird Dog nodded vigorously at the Yellow Shirt, confirming the launch weight. The Yellow Shirt held up his thumb, and then snapped his hand up in a salute, the signal that he was transferring complete responsibility for the aircraft to Bird Dog. He returned the salute. Somehow, the simple flight deck ceremony took on more meaning for him now. It was no longer an archaic ritual that impeded his speedy progress off the deck, but an exchange of responsibility as significant as any in the Navy. It was given and received as a sign of respect between men and women who shared similar responsibilities and burdens of serving their country, regardless of their education, background, or pay grade. It made them, for that split moment, anyway, equals.

He dropped his salute and shoved the throttle forward to full military power. A split second later, the Tomcat slammed him in the back.

Airborne!

CHAPTER 25
Thursday, 4 July

As the coastline of Vietnam slipped by below him, Bien made the call to the rest of the aircraft. "Feet wet," he said, referring to the fact that he was over water rather than land. Not that it would matter. There were no SAR forces standing by.

He then reached down and flipped the protective plastic cover off of the IFF gear. He looked down long enough to check the position of the dials that set his modes and codes, the unique set of IFF symbols that would identify his aircraft to any unit with the appropriate detection gear. He twisted the dial until the numbers his Vietnamese superiors had given him were displayed.

In the ten miles of airspace around him, every Vietnamese pilot was doing exactly the same things.

"About time," *Jefferson*'s TAO said, as a massive gaggle of hostile air contact symbols popped onto the big screen display. "I was starting to think they changed their minds." The weak joke brought a spatter of laughter from the crews manning the consoles, the only indication that tensions were at a peak.

"Sir! Breaking the IFF codes for the Vietnamese forces!" the OS said.

"Thank God," the TAO said quietly. "It looks like this crazy plan just might work."

1831 local (Zulu -7)
Flanker 11

Exactly one minute after he'd changed the IFF codes, Bien shoved his throttle forward, accelerating quickly to 580 knots. At that speed, his jet gulped down fuel at a prohibitive rate. Fortunately, he thought as he observed the fuel gauge quiver, it wouldn't be for long. He glanced behind him, watching the orderly Vietnamese formation straggle out into a ragged line of aircraft and then coalesce back into a fighting unit that followed him. He banked hard to the south and watched the others follow. Only twenty seconds had elapsed since his speed increase.

His radio crackled with orders and demands for information. All the questions were in Chinese.

And that is exactly the wrong language for answers, Bien thought grimly.

1842 local (Zulu -7)
TFCC

"There they go," Tombstone said. "Those birds breaking off and heading south are Vietnamese."

"Roger," the TAO acknowledged. "We know who the good guys are now, sir. I'll make sure *Vincennes* understands, too."

"What's she doing?" Tombstone demanded. The speed leader attached to the ship's symbol had suddenly changed directions.

"Headed south at thirty knots. Still out of missile range and screaming bloody murder!"

"Give me that handset," Tombstone ordered. The TAO turned over his tactical circuit to the admiral. "Get your ass back up north, Killington!"

"Are you fucking *insane*? You've got inbound hostile air, with only a couple of frigates around you! The FFG's standard missiles have a maximum range of twenty-five miles, you idiot! You *need* us there!"

"I also have two squadrons of Tomcats and two of Hornets airborne!" Tombstone snapped. "These are Flankers, Killington! Fighters! The only thing they carry is air-to-air missiles, not air-to-surface ship missiles! And if those Flankers are carrying anything heavier, it's a laser-guided or dumb bomb, and they're so weighed down that they're dead meat!"

"You're dead, you know," Killington said in a cold, calm voice. "May God forgive you for what you're doing to your crew."

"I may be dead, but you're relieved! TAO, are you listening?" Tombstone demanded.

A long pause, then a tight, higher-pitched voice broke in on the circuit. "Sir, this is Lieutenant Commander Carson, TAO."

"Son, get your Executive Officer up to Combat ASAP. And log it now—Captain Killington is hereby relieved of command, and ordered to report to the *Jefferson*. Your XO has command of the ship, and you are on watch as TAO until further notice. Got that?"

"Yes, Admiral."

"Very well. Now get that ship back in position. We believe you have about five minutes, at the most, until you start picking up inbound long-range cruise missiles. I'm counting on *Vincennes* to stop them. Any questions?"

"Uh, no. Admiral, the captain—" the TAO paused, and Tombstone heard screaming in the background noise "Captain Killington, I mean, is demanding to speak to you."

"Let him listen, then. Captain Killington, you are to station yourself in your helo hangar until I give the orders for your helo to transport you to *Jefferson*. Under no circumstances are you to remain in CIC, nor are you to give any orders on any subject to any member of your crew. TAO, you will call the ship's security force to CIC, and have Captain Killington removed. You understand?"

"Admiral," a new voice broke in, "this is the Executive Officer. I've heard your orders, and we will follow them. And my apologies," he said, his voice suddenly hitched up a few notes, "but the rest of this will need to wait. I'm about to be real busy." Abruptly, the circuit went dead.

"I guess you are," Tombstone said quietly, and handed the handset back to his own TAO. Plastered on the tactical screen, in single-file formation, were ten LINK tracks with missile symbols imposed over the radar, just leaving the coast of China and heading south. "Now let's see if the Aegis is all it's cracked up to be."

1850 local (Zulu -7)
Flight Deck
USS Jefferson

"Get that bastard off the cat!" the Air Boss screamed. The Hornet five decks below him waggled its control surfaces forlornly as the pilot cycled the stick again. One aileron refused to move. "We don't have time to troubleshoot on the cat. Move, people, move!"

The Hornet backed down from the catapult, pivoted, and then taxied aft of the island. Green-shirted avionics technicians swarmed over it as it rolled to a stop, popping panels off of it to find the cause of the stuck aileron. Another Hornet rolled smartly up to the catapult. Within moments, it was airborne. The JBDs, or jet blast deflectors, dropped down, and the next waiting fighter rolled forward.

"Goddamn Hornet," the Air Boss snarled. The Mini Boss carefully stifled his agreement. It was the first time he'd ever heard the Air Boss admit that the Hornet was anything other than the most superb fighter ever built. "What was our time on the alert fifteens?"

"Five minutes. Not too shabby," the Mini Boss replied.

"Not too hot, either, with a strike inbound. I sure hope to hell Tombstone knows what he's doing." The Air Boss glanced at the relative wind indicator, watching it quiver. "Tell the OOD I want another five knots of wind. We need another three Vikings airborne. If the admiral's right, we're going to have some submarines making themselves conspicuous right quick. Hunter 701 has contact on one of them, but those slimy little bastards could have a couple more in the area."

The Mini Boss toggled the bitch box and relayed the message to the Officer of the Deck. With enemy fighters inbound and the threat of submarine-launched missiles, there were a hell of a lot of things he'd like more than Vikings. The Aegis snugged in closer for instance, or more aircraft in the pattern. And maybe, just maybe, a little luck wouldn't hurt.

"Rabies! Get us the hell out of here!" the TACCO said urgently.

"One more shot," Rabies snapped.

"If we're going to get back, we have to leave *now*," his copilot argued.

"If we leave now, we may not have anywhere to go back to! You think that sub's just here for the fun of it? Don't you know what overwhelming force is all about? Those fighters are there for a reason, to distract us while this bastard takes his next shot!"

"MAD, MAD, MAD," the TACCO sang out suddenly. "That's it, Rabies! Attack criteria."

The torpedo was off the wing an instant later. Rabies fought the sudden change in weight, as the strong winds caught the now asymmetrically loaded Viking. He quickly retrimmed the sturdy jet, reestablished level flight, and circled to watch the results.

The top of the sail was already visible, a darker shape and peculiarly stable against the churning water. Half of the sail had already slid back, exposing the starkly gleaming launcher. A missile was already on the rails.

Rabies squinted. No sign of the torpedo or its telltale wake.

"She's active—*acquired*!" the AW shouted. "Homing—homing—YES!"

Three short cheers echoed on the ICS, drowned out immediately by the coldly professional recitation of the AW.

"Explosion—secondaries. Wait one—flow tones. Okay, that's it. She's breaking up."

Adrenaline surged through the pilot, making him almost

giddy. For the moment, he forgot about the eighty men below him, struggling against a torrent of invading seawater, dying quickly in an explosion if lucky, drowning slowly if they were not. Later, he knew, it would hit him, but for the moment the sheer joy of the kill sang in his blood.

CHAPTER 26
Thursday, 4 July

"Tallyho," Bird Dog heard Batman call out, confirming contact on the enemy aircraft. "Low and fast, probably counting on coming right out of the sun low on the horizon."

"You got them yet, Gator?" Bird Dog asked.

"Not yet. But I'll take those JAST avionics on our lead anytime, if he's seeing them from this range!"

"Batman's supposed to be as sharp as his bird. Not often we get to fly wing on a full captain. Let's just see if he's still got it, after pushing a desk in the Pentagon!"

The loose, orderly formation of Tomcats scattered. Bird Dog broke right, following Batman to intercept the northernmost cell of enemy fighters. The JAST bird was armed with four Sidewinders and two Sparrows, the weapons load tailored to the lead's preference for close-in kills. Five hundred feet above and behind his lead, Bird Dog's Tomcat carried the heavier and longer-range Phoenixes, as well as an array of shorter-range missiles.

"Bogey to the north, Bird Dog," Gator said. "No, wait! I lost him! This little bastard pops in and out on my screen like a—hey, wait a minute! You think this has anything to do with those ghosts we've been seeing?"

"Do I give a shit? Get me a goddamm target! You can't hold that one, pick another!"

"Getting contacts from the JAST bird now," Gator muttered as the targeting pip appeared on his HUD. "Damned tough to hold, though."

"Take a shot, Bird Dog," Batman ordered over the circuit.

"Fox one!" Bird Dog thumbed the switch and felt the aircraft jolt up as the massive missile shot off the rails. Even if it missed, it lightened the Tomcat, extending his time on station by decreasing his fuel consumption. He held the Tomcat straight on in level flight, feeding targeting information to the missile.

"Closure rate, one thousand knots," his RIO said. Already, Gator had ceased to exist as a separate presence, becoming instead a part of Bird Dog and his aircraft, a voice feeding him information.

Aside from situations allowing the use of long-range missiles such as the Phoenix, aerial combat was a battle for position and altitude. Aircraft danced through the air, darting around each other and maneuvering for position. Above and behind—the ultimate goal for position on an enemy.

Bird Dog nosed the F-14 up, sacrificing a little airspeed for altitude. With the enemy strike force approaching, he had little time to spare. Altitude was something you could never have too much of.

1902 local (Zulu -7)
Chinese F-10

"Missile inbound," the officer in the backseat howled. "Phoenix!"

"I've got it," Mein Low swore. He cut the aircraft into a sharp turn, heading nose-on to the missile to reduce their radar cross section. The F-10's avionics examined the radar signal and radiated countermeasures intended to defeat detection and targeting.

Mein Low scanned the sky, knowing the missile was too far away to see but trying anyway. Over his tactical circuit, he could hear aircraft in the strike calling out targets, dividing up the launching American fighters between themselves.

No matter. He was flight leader, and the first aircraft they saw would be his—As well as the first kill.

The long-range Phoenix missiles were not the ones that worried him most. They required guidance from the AWG-9 Tomcat radar for most of their flight, switching to individual guidance only as they neared their targets. Intelligence had told him that they often suffered fusing problems, failing to ignite, and that none had ever been used successfully in engagements. It was not enough to make him overconfident, though. Even a Phoenix that failed to detonate could do a massive amount of damage if it struck his aircraft.

The weakness in the system was the AWG-9 radar, and the need for the Tomcat to maintain a radar lock on him.

"Chaff," he ordered, and felt the gentle thumps of the canisters of highly reflective metal strips being ejected from the aircraft. With any luck, that would confuse the radar picture, and perhaps mislead the Tomcat into keeping the missile locked on the chaff rather than his aircraft.

As the chaff was shot off, he broke into a hard turn and headed directly for the missile. At its Mach 5 speeds, it was unwieldy, and would be unable to follow drastic last-minute maneuvers. As a last resort, he could always dive for the deck, although it was an option he'd prefer to avoid in this sea state. The AWG-9 was notoriously erratic on tracking targets below fifty feet. If he broke radar lock with the Tomcat before the missile acquired him, on its own independent homing radar, the missile would not pose a threat to him.

A scream echoed over the tactical circuit, abruptly cut short in midcrescendo.

"I see it!" his RIO exclaimed.

"Got it," he muttered, and concentrated on the missile's course. Wait for it, wait for it, he kept repeating to himself. The tiny speck in the air grew larger at an incredible rate. At the last moment, he dove for the deck, pouring on all the speed he could muster.

The Phoenix snapped by him, barely visible at close range for a few moments before dwindling again from sight. It would lack sufficient fuel to regain a lock on him, he knew.

Even if it were no longer a threat, it had achieved its tactical purpose—forcing him onto the defensive and throwing off his own engagement plan. Not a fatal position to be in. There was plenty of airspace, and far more Chinese fighters than American ones in the air.

1904 local (Zulu -7)
Tomcat 205

"Missile lock broken!" Gator snapped. "He slid off the scope like greased lightning. Sparrow armed."

"Okay, okay—now! Fox two, Fox two!" Bird Dog said. The lighter Sparrow shot off the rails.

"Oh, shit. Got a lock on us, Bird Dog!" The warning tone of an enemy missile lock warbled in his headset.

"Get some airspace!" Batman ordered. "He can't see me as well as he can you. I'm going to move in closer. Join back up on me as soon as you shake the missile!"

Mein Low watched the missile follow the American, grim exultation filling him. It was time for a combat kill, his first against the Western forces. The sacrifices his countrymen had made serving as operational test targets for the F-10 would be vindicated.

Suddenly, the missile lock tone wavered, then fell off into silence. Anger shot through him. Why now?

"Lock lost," his backseater announced. "Probably from the climb. It can't follow quickly enough, or perhaps the seeker head failed."

"*My* weapons do *not* fail!" he snapped.

"Jamming," the backseater added. "Probable EA-6B Prowlers. Recommend we go to heat-seekers."

Mein Low snarled his concurrence. If the American pilot wanted a knife fight, that's what he'd get. Four Flanker pilots had died trying to evade the F-10, and Mein Low had learned how to best use his fighter up close and personal. Close-in, dirty fighting—nothing beat the F-10.

"Lost it! Bird Dog, I don't think those Chinese missiles liked that high rate of climb maneuver."

"Get the word out," Bird Dog said. They'd lost some speed from the climb, but the Chinese fighter was below and in front of him now.

He watched Batman's dance through the sky and waited for

an opening to join it without spoiling Batman's targeting. His lead had already expended two Sparrows on the other aircraft, but was still out of range for the deadly heat-seeking Sidewinder. The enemy fighter was as hard to hold radar contact on as the JAST bird was.

"We're moving in closer. Sidewinder next," he said, thumbing the weapons selection toggle to the appropriate position. If he could get within range, the heat-seeking Sidewinder wouldn't care about radar cross sections. The ass-end of the Chinese fighter was spewing out hot exhaust that would pull the missile into it.

Bird Dog tapped his fingers on the control stick, waiting for the growl that would tell him the missile had acquired the target. If Batman would just clear the field of fire, the geometry would be perfect.

1909 local (Zulu -7)
Chinese F-10

"Behind us!" his backseater screamed.

"I know, I know!" Mein Low snapped. He'd temporarily shaken the Tomcat that had been dogging him for the last five minutes. Two Flankers were diving in to deal with the first fighter.

He snapped the F-10 into a tight turn and headed back the way they'd come. It was imperative that he prevent the second Tomcat from getting a clean shot at his tailpipe. By turning, he'd put the two aircraft nose to nose and increased the closure rate to almost Mach 2. The Tomcat might be faster, but the Flanker was more maneuverable. In a close-quarters, one-on-one dogfight, he'd have the advantage.

"The wingman—where is he?" he asked, remembering the predilection for the fighters to operate in groups of two. The

"Loose Deuce" formation, he thought, his mind stumbling over the uncomfortable words. American fighters normally fought as pairs, one aircraft above the other poised to maneuver into killing position while the lead aircraft fought in close.

"Two Flankers have him covered," the backseater muttered. "He won't be back."

"Good." One Tomcat alone would be easy prey. Easier, anyway. The numbers were in the Chinese's favor, at least until the Americans could get the rest of their aircraft off the deck.

1910 local (Zulu -7)
Tomcat 205

"Oh, no, you don't," Bird Dog muttered. The radar contact was approaching at five hundred knots, slightly slower than a Tomcat's max speed at this altitude. "You might want a nice look at my ass, you pervert, but I'm onto you!" He pulled the Tomcat into a tight bank, cutting across the path of the Flanker.

"Jesus, Bird Dog!" Gator yelled. "You want to give him a great beam shot or what?" As if in response, the high-pitched warble of the missile lock tone wailed in their headsets.

"Worked once, will work again. Chaff!" Bird Dog ordered. He put the Tomcat in a steep, circling climb, pulling in behind the Flanker again.

"It's still got us! Chaff away again!" Gator shouted.

"Hang on! We're going to show this fellow what a *real* fighter can do!"

1911 local (Zulu -7)
Chinese F-10

"Go, go, go," Mein Low chanted, watching the missile pip approach the American fighter. The Tomcat was above and behind him again, rapidly approaching perfect firing position for the Sidewinder. He banked hard to the right and nosed up into a steep climb, putting his aircraft between the sun and the American.

"Missile!" his backseater screamed.

"Sidewinder," he grunted against the G-forces pounding him into the seat. "Flares, chaff, more flares!" The gentle thumps were barely perceptible over the screaming engines and the high-G-force vibrations.

A wash of turbulence shook the jet, and a few sharp metallic noises bit through the roar of the engines. "It went for it," his backseater announced, relief evident in his voice.

"Now for him," he replied, dropping the jet's nose down. The Tomcat was now below him, afterburners screaming across the infrared spectrum. He toggled off a heat-seeker, then climbed again.

1912 local (Zulu -7)
Tomcat 205

"It went for the flare, Bird Dog," Gator said. "One Sidewinder left. Missile lock!"

"You'd figure. Let's see if their missiles are any smarter than ours. Flares!"

Gator popped two flares. Bird Dog wrapped the Tomcat into a ball, turning more sharply than he'd ever tried before, standing the jet on its tail.

"Guess not," he said a few moments later as the Chinese heat-seeker exploded into the middle of the flare grouping. "Let's make this last one count!"

Bird Dog popped the speed brakes, losing fifty knots of airspeed almost immediately. The Chinese fighter quickly overshot them. "Fox three!" Another Sidewinder darted forward off the wing.

"You're inside minimum range!" Gator said.

"By the book, I am. Wanna bet that the firing doctrine has a safety factor built into it?"

"You can't count on—" The explosion two miles in front of him cut him off. "—that every time," Gator finished. "Damn it, Bird Dog, those safety factors are there for a reason. See?"

Bird Dog stared at the fireball in front of him. The missile had detonated beyond the enemy fighter. The aircraft turned to meet him, putting him within gun range.

"All we got is one Phoenix and one Sparrow. No more knife fights, Bird Dog."

"And guns. Don't forget the guns."

Bird Dog slewed the Tomcat to the left, turning head-on to the other fighter, and pointed the Tomcat's nose slightly ahead of the other aircraft's course. He carefully led the enemy fighter's maneuver and squeezed off his gun. Six thousand rounds per minute streamed out of the six-barrel Vulcan 20-mm gatling-gun, stitching a ragged line down the side of the other aircraft. Bird Dog came close enough to see the windscreen shatter and chunks of the hardened Plexiglas spray out away from the airframe.

Smoke streamed from the right side of the aircraft, which was rapidly losing altitude. A punctured fuel tank, probably, he thought. At any rate, he was hurt badly enough to be out of the air battle raging above him.

Bird Dog turned the Tomcat back toward the aerial fur ball behind him. "Where's Batman?" he demanded.

"Nine o'clock, six miles. He took out one Flanker, but he can't shake the one on their tail."

"Think they'd like a little help?"

"Might come in handy. Course, Tomboy'll swear later that she could handle it alone." The RIO grinned. "It'd be nice to pull her tail out of the fire for a change."

"Tallyho!" Bird Dog said a few minutes later. "Looks like she's in trouble to me!"

Batman's Tomcat was heading for the deck, just finishing off a high altitude maneuver designed to give him tactical height and position on his opponent. It hadn't worked. The smaller, more maneuverable Flanker had cut inside his turn. The JAST Tomcat was jinking like crazy, trying to screw up the shot. The maneuvers bled off airspeed and reduced the speed advantage the JAST Tomcat had over the Flanker.

"Batman, pull up and break right!" Bird Dog ordered. Without waiting for a reply, he screamed in on the pursuing Flanker and toggled the stick back to select a Sidewinder. As soon as the Sidewinder growled its acquisition signal and Batman had cleared the field of fire, Bird Dog shouted, "Fox three!" and shot his last close-range missile.

Seconds later, the Chinese Flanker exploded into a fireball. Shards of metal pinged sharply off the skin of the Tomcat.

Bird Dog got a quick acknowledgment of no damage from Tomboy and then grabbed for altitude, heading for the next engagement.

"You only got the Phoenix, Bird Dog," Gator reminded him. "Too close quarters for another shot."

"Still got the guns."

"But not much ammo. Face it, Bird Dog, it's time for us to be out of here. Let's get up high, look down, and see if there's anything we can do from there."

Bird Dog reluctantly acknowledged the wisdom of Gator's advice. Two minutes later, Batman and Tomboy joined them, the wings of their Tomcat clean and vulnerable. At fifteen thousand feet, they circled for the next ten minutes, listening to the tactical chatter, calls for assistance, and victory screams gradually subside. Finally, the last of the adversary air had either fled or fallen into the ocean.

The rest of the Tomcat squadron joined them at altitude. Most still had Phoenixes hanging under their wings. The Tomcats turned back toward the carrier while the Hornets lined up behind the two KA-6 refueling birds, eager to replenish their tanks before attempting a landing.

1920 local (Zulu -7)
Chinese Strike Force

Less than half an hour after they'd met the American fighters, the remaining Chinese fighters turned west to head back to their base in Vietnam. Only twenty-five of the fifty Chinese aircraft survived the brief but furious ACM after being deserted by their supposed Vietnamese allies.

The aircraft straggled into a loose formation and watched in stunned silence as the Americans broke off the attack. Had the Chinese had the Americans' tactical advantages, they would have pursued the retreating enemy. Burning airframes out of the sky was a good method of ensuring there would be no counterattack.

Ten miles from the coast, the Chinese flight leader—the senior pilot left alive—began to understand *why* the Americans had not come after them.

CHAPTER 27
Thursday, 4 July

Mein Low initiated shutdown procedures on the damaged engine, holding his breath while he watched for any indications of fire. None. Good, perhaps he'd shut down in time.

The aircraft felt oddly sluggish and heavy, although one engine was more than enough to keep him airborne. Not that that mattered right now—they were out of the battle for good, limited to 370 knots on one engine and such sluggish maneuverability that they'd be easy prey for anyone.

He headed for the deck, intent on avoiding any interest from the fighters circling and maneuvering above him. After he put some distance between them, he'd climb back to a more fuel efficient altitude and pray that his remaining fuel could at least get him to within range of the carrier. If he couldn't kill fighters, then at least he could turn their flight deck into a fiery inferno. They couldn't stay airborne forever. Ruin their landing area and they'd be forced to either eventually ditch or break off immediately and try to reach land with their remaining fuel and the tankers currently aloft.

"What are you doing?" his backseater demanded. "You're way off course—we're only a hundred miles from rescue forces."

"Shut up." Backseaters. Just for a second, he smiled with grim humor. He wondered if American pilots had to put up with pushy backseat drivers as well.

1925 local (Zulu -7)
Chinese Flanker

"Bien, you coward!" the Chinese lead pilot raged over tactical. "You slimy dogs, turning tail and running away from the strike! We lost over half of our forces, escaping with barely enough fuel to make it back to base. You'll pay for this, you bastards!"

Bien clicked his mike a few times, wondering if he had the strength to resist temptation. He didn't, he decided. He'd spent too many months under the crushing imperialism of the Chinese to not savor the sweet radar picture. A ragged line of Chinese fighters limped toward the coast, eking out every last mile from their remaining fuel.

He keyed his mike for the last time on the Chinese tactical frequency and said, "Go ahead, punk. Make my day."

At that, the Vietnamese fighters broke formation and descended on the remaining Chinese fighters like starving sharks on a school of fat tuna. Only this time, the tuna didn't have enough energy to run.

1927 local (Zulu -7)
CDC
USS Jefferson

"We got contact on them while they were still in the high-altitude portion of their profile," the *Vincennes* TAO told his counterpart on *Jefferson*. "They're running about Mach 3, it looks like. Damned tough to see—if we'd stayed down south with the carrier, we wouldn't have detected them until they'd gone into the sea-skimmer mode. Ten, maybe twelve seconds warning."

"You got them targeted?" the *Jefferson* TAO asked. "Oh, never mind. Symbology just coming up on the LINK," she finished, as the NTDS symbol for a missile raced away from the *Vincennes* on course to intercept the Chinese cruise missiles. "Looks like a good firing solution. Just what do you think the range on those bastards is?"

"About two hundred miles shorter than China planned," *Vincennes* replied. "Look, I hate to be rude, but don't you have something else to do besides talk to me right now? I mean, it's okay with me—my missiles are off the rails, and it's just a matter of wait and see. But according to the LINK, you've got a hell of an air battle going on to your west."

"Oh, that," the TAO replied offhandedly. "Our part's already over. The first Tomcats are back on deck as we speak."

"So who's in that fur ball off the coast?"

"Let's just say that the Vietnamese government made some permanent choices about the future of their country," she replied. "And it looks like China's a little annoyed about it. We're standing by in case they need a hand. But from what I can tell, they're doing pretty damned well on their own."

1930 local (Zulu -7)
Niblet 601

"Well, will you look at that?" the SH-60F pilot yelled over the ICS. Angel 101 was on SAR, hovering a discreet distance from the air battle to be immediately available for rescues. "Damned fighters, letting one sneak off like that!"

It wasn't too often that the less glamorous elements of the

carrier air wing got a good look at a bad guy. Especially a hurt one.

"Doing 270 knots," his copilot said. "I make his closest point of approach less than one mile. And he's headed for the carrier."

"Let Homeplate know they got a kamikaze inbound. Give me a course to close him."

"You thinking what I'm thinking?"

"You betcha!" the pilot said. "Those damned Penguin missiles have been hanging on our wings for too long. Let's see if these suckers work as advertised."

1930 local (Zulu -7)
F-10

The carrier was only eight miles away, but it already loomed huge, blocking out most of the horizon. He felt his gut tighten and tried not to think about the next few minutes. It was his duty—his destiny, perhaps. If it meant that he must die, then so be it. The possibility of doing permanent damage to the carrier was too good to pass up.

Less than five minutes to live. He shut out the sounds of his backseater screaming. The man had figured out his plan a few minutes ago, and had been wailing ever since. Mein Low had taken the precaution of switching the ejection seat controls to front seat only. It would have been better for the backseater's karma if he'd been able to face it bravely, but then the wheel of the universe moved in mysterious ways.

"Roger, Homeplate, you heard right. Tallyho on bogey. Taking with Penguin." The pilot toggled the safety cover aside, took careful aim, and then let fly the Penguin missile tucked onto the underbelly of his helo.

"Fox—hell, Homeplate, what do I call these?" Fox one was a Phoenix, Fox two a Sparrow, and Fox three a Sidewinder. "This a Fox four?"

He watched the antiship missile close on the crippled Flanker. The first missed, but the second scored a solid hit on the windscreen. The remaining tattered fragments of Plexiglas shimmered in the air, along with remnants of the cockpit. Including, he assumed, the pilot.

"Ain't Fox four," he heard the carrier TAO reply, amid a few cheers in the background.

"Well, how do I report it?"

"Let's just call it a first, and leave it at that. You're credited with one kill, Angel One."

"Dang!" The pilot high-fived his copilot. "That plane captain's gonna love me! Bet he never thought he'd get to paint a kill on his helo!"

On the ground, the Chinese officer left in charge screamed in rage. "Cowards!" he swore, yanking his pistol from his belt. He reached for the first senior Vietnamese officer he could find, intending to execute him immediately.

As he brought his pistol up, he felt something punch him in the middle of his back. It was more than a punch, he thought, surprised at the sudden detachment that seemed to have descended on his mind. No ordinary blow could have thrown him across the room, bashing him into a GCI console. He noted that he was sprawled on the ground, partially underneath one console, and the fact did not seem surprising.

His brain, operating on what residual blood remained circulating in it through sheer momentum, finally made the connection between the hard blow, sudden mind-numbing pain, and the warm, gaping hole immediately below his rib cage. As his vision began to turn black at the edges, he tried to turn his head to see who had shot him. An impossible task, since every Vietnamese officer and soldier in the room had his weapon drawn and aimed at a Chinese soldier.

His last thought, as consciousness faded completely to reenter the great cycle of being, was that Mein Low and his F-10 had failed their final live-fire operational test.

Thirty minutes later, the remnants of the Vietnamese Flanker squadron landed at the airfield. While four of their aircraft were missing, not a single Chinese fighter clouded the skies above them.

Bien taxied to a stop near his hangar, went through the shutdown checklist, and finally climbed wearily out of the cockpit. When he'd first outlined the plan to Ngyugen, he hadn't seriously believed that it could work. Foremost among his concerns was that the Americans would use the opportunity to follow the Chinese squadron back to the coast and annihilate the Vietnamese squadron.

Perhaps the politicians have some use after all, he mused, watching the ground crew take possession of his aircraft. *And there may be some possibility that we can use this engagement to extract additional compromises from the Americans. After all, I doubt that the Chinese will be willing to continue providing us with technology and training.*

As he trudged across the tarmac, he wondered what it might be like to fly the American Tomcat. After today, it looked like his odds of finding out might just have improved.

CHAPTER 28
Thursday, 4 July

Tombstone gazed at the officers assembled in the room. Cheers echoed up and down the passageway outside the normally quiet conference room as aircrews swaggered out of CVIC, debriefed and ready to expand upon their exploits in the air. Even the restrained and professional faces of the senior officers seated around the table wore looks of quiet jubilation.

"First, the most important part," Tombstone said. "We lost two aircraft, one Hornet and one Tomcat. SAR recovered all three aviators, and there were no serious injuries. A remarkable performance. I'll be talking to each squadron later on, but you all pass my congratulations on immediately."

And it's the first combat action I've ever had to sit out, he thought, surveying the squadron COs sitting around the table. *Not a one of them even thought to question that, just like it never occurred to me when I was flying—that someday I could do more on the ground than in the air.* Again, the image of his uncle's face came to him. The old bastard could have told him what a bittersweet feeling it would be.

"You were all briefed on the plan, and it came off flawlessly.

China's key weakness in the Spratly Islands airspace has always been their lack of refueling capability. They'd counted on a quick, hard strike, with enough casualties to make us back down. They were wrong.

"Not only did their plan fail to allow for the strength of our response, they underestimated the Vietnamese government's weakness. China badly miscalculated how Vietnam would take the sinking of her patrol boat. There's a lesson in this—fight one war at a time. By taking on both the United States' *and* Vietnam's presence in the Spratly Islands, they overextended themselves. And you saw what happened. Vietnam simply waited for them to batter themselves bloody against our fighters and then picked them off when they tried to land in Vietnam."

"What now, Admiral?" the CO of VF-95 asked. "A full alpha strike on China?"

"Not this time, Speedie," Tombstone replied. "China was partially right about one thing—the United States is not ready to take heavy casualties in the South China Sea. It's one thing to bloody their noses in international waters on our own terms. It's an entirely different matter to take them on over their own mainland."

A few of the officers let out sighs of relief. The concerns about escalating military actions had been one reason Tombstone had scheduled this briefing immediately. Left to its own devices, the carrier's rumor control system would have had the battle group on the verge of World War III within a matter of hours.

"Our orders have not changed. In two weeks, *USS Lincoln* will relieve us on station. Between getting ready for turnover and keeping an eye on the Chinese, I think we've got plenty to do. You hear rumors about an alpha strike on China, you can put a stop to them.

"Any other questions?" Tombstone concluded. The officers assembled around the table shook their heads. A few yawned as the gut-wrenching fatigue that always followed combat missions set in.

"Go see your squadrons, and then get some sleep," Tombstone ordered. "Come see me if any other issues surface."

He watched them file out of the conference room, remembering how many times he'd been in their shoes, and then glanced down at the message in his hand. There was one other piece of good news to deliver, but it could wait until the morning.

Friday, 5 July
0900 local (Zulu -7)
Admiral's Cabin
USS Jefferson

"What took you so long?" Tombstone snapped. "I passed the word for you ten minutes ago. Did you forget how to get to my quarters?"

"Sorry, Admiral," Batman said. He glanced around the officers assembled in Tombstone's cabin, and a puzzled look spread across his face. All six captains on board the *Jefferson* were present, along with every squadron CO. "What can I do for you, Admiral?"

"It's customary for admirals to call each other by their first names, Batman," Tombstone said solemnly. "Although I suppose we'll need to wait a few months for the Senate confirmation to make it official."

"What? Oh, no, you don't mean it!" Batman exclaimed. Every face in the room was split with a broad grin. "Oh, *shit*, Tombstone! For real?"

"Here's the message," Tombstone said, a rare smile lighting his face. "You're number one on the list selected for promotion to rear admiral. See for yourself."

Batman stared at the message, then started to smile. The corners of his mouth pulled further and further away from each other, until he was grinning like a Cheshire cat. For once in his life, he was at a loss for words.

"And I wanted you to have these," Tombstone added. He handed his old wingman a red-and-white Navy insignia box. "There aren't many sets in the ship's stores, so I had to part with a set of my own. Bring you good luck."

Batman stared down at the two silver stars gleaming against their white cardboard backing. "Still come mounted on cardboard," he said reflectively. "Funny, I guess I thought once you made admiral, they'd be on black velvet or something."

The assembled crowd broke into a line of jostling senior naval officers queuing to shake his hand and offer their congratulations. One by one, they started filing out of the office, until Batman and Tombstone were alone.

"You had to surprise me, didn't you?" Batman said. "Couldn't let me just read it on the message board."

"You would have done it differently if our positions had been reversed?" Tombstone said gravely, his eyes still warm. "I don't think so—not after you forgot to tell me about Pamela being on that COD."

"Hell of a payback, Tombstone. You're pissed at me for the surprise, so you get me promoted just to get even." Batman shook his head. "The things you'll do for revenge."

"There're even more surprises in store," Tombstone said. "Guess who called me this morning?"

"The president, wanting to offer me his personal congratulations?"

"Almost. My uncle. You know, the old guy with more stars than both of us put together? He asked me to pass on his congratulations—and one other thing as well."

"What's that?"

"Well, seems like he's going to have an opening for a Carrier

Battle Group Commander. For *this* battle group, as a matter of fact. He wondered if you wanted your name put in the hat for it."

"He had to ask? Damn, what have you been telling your uncle about me, Tombstone? Of course I want it! It'd be my first choice!"

"I told him I'd have to get back to him, seeing as you'd gotten so fond of the Pentagon and all."

Batman snorted. "Right. If I get it, I'd be relieving you. And be back on the ship I grew up on, so to speak. Hell, I'd arrange for all the other selectees to have accidents if I thought it'd guarantee me this battle group!"

"Still up to DC, of course, but my uncle does swing some weight with the heavies. After his tour on special assignment to the White House, he got to know his way around the Pentagon fairly well. You'd have to cut your tour in DC short—"

"Yes!" Batman cried. "Oh, yes, yes, there is a God!"

"I take it you'd have no objection, then," Tombstone said dryly.

"And what about you?" Batman said suddenly. "Any idea of where you're going?"

Tombstone shook his head. "Not a clue. There've been a couple of possibilities discussed, but nothing even more than a passing thought. It won't be to sea, though. Probably DC would be my guess."

"Well, that wouldn't be too bad," Batman said thoughtfully.

"Hah! Look who's talking! You were just crowing over the chance to get out of there!"

"My situation's a little different from yours."

"How so?"

"I don't have a RIO who thinks I'm the greatest thing since sliced bread. You do. And DC is a hell of a big place, Tombstone. Big enough for one admiral and one lieutenant commander to get lost in the shuffle."

"What are you saying?"

"Just this, amigo. You've got a chance to have something very good with that young RIO of yours. These circumstances—it wouldn't work, and you're smart not to try. But you pass on this one when you get ashore, Stoney, and you're going to regret it. I guarantee it." For a second, something wistful shone in Batman's eyes. "She's a fine RIO, Tombstone, and a hell of a woman. And one of our own. Don't blow it, okay?"

"Thanks for the advice. I'll think about it."

Batman left, clutching the precious stars in his hand. Tombstone watched him go. He'd make a fine admiral, no doubt about it. And if he had to give up command of his carrier group to anyone, he'd have picked Batman.

He scowled and reached for the next folder on top of the pile that threatened to slide off of his desk. During the last week, the normal paperwork associated with running a battle group had accumulated to a daunting stack. In two weeks, *USS Lincoln* would relieve *USS Jefferson* on station in the South China Sea, and the logistical issues and lessons learned were responsible for at least half of the folders demanding his attention. Nothing short of a full alpha strike from the mainland would get him out of wading through it today.

He heard a light tap on his door and sighed. COS had extracted a promise that he would spend four hours on paperwork and had guaranteed no interruptions. Tombstone wondered who had managed to sneak past his gatekeeper.

"Come in," he snapped irritably. "And it better be important!"

The door opened slowly, and Pamela slipped in. "Maybe not in the grand scale of things, but I did want to say good-bye before I got on the COD. We leave in an hour. I promised COS I'd only take up a couple of minutes of your time."

Tombstone leaned back in his chair and tossed his pen on the desk. "So soon?" he asked. "I thought you might stay for part of the wrap-up or the transit back to California."

"The story's not out here anymore, Stoney. It's back with the politicians. I'll let someone who likes tamer stories cover that part of it. Besides, Bosnia's flaring up again."

"Some things never change, I guess." For a moment, he envied her. After the challenge of dealing with the Chinese, the trip back to the States was going to be boring. Still, he might actually have a chance to fly a bit more. How much more satisfying, though, to be able to leave when things got slow.

"Some things *do* change. Like us. It's been different this time," Pamela said.

"Has it?"

"Oh, yes, I think so." She paused, studying his reaction. "You're different."

"Think the stars make that much difference?"

"It's not just the rank, Tombstone. It's you. Seeing you here, on your ship—knowing what you do, the responsibilities you have. It makes a difference."

"This is where I wanted to be the entire time, Pamela. I thought you knew that—what it would be like."

"I knew but I didn't know."

They both fell silent. There was no point in resurrecting the perennial argument about their careers. The last time they'd met, they'd decided it would never be resolved, and they'd broken their engagement. While seeing Pamela this time had awakened all of his old feelings, he now recognized that it had been mostly reflexive nostalgia.

"Maybe sour grapes," Tombstone suggested.

"How so?"

"Being on the ship and all. As much as I'd like to, you know there's no way that—I mean, how can I expect the crew to—it just wouldn't—"

"You mean making love?" she said softly.

"Yeah."

"Tombstone, if that's all we had, it wouldn't be much, would it?"

"It'd be a real good start, right now," he said reflectively. He let his eyes run over her body hungrily.

"And a real dramatic end, if you got caught."

"There's that. But maybe an end is in order."

"After all these years, you're ready to give up? Leave the Navy?"

"People do. I've got over twenty years in. A rear admiral's retirement pay's not bad. We could get married. Try living a normal life, maybe."

"Oh, Tombstone." Pamela studied him for a moment. "If you'd made that offer ten years ago—hell, even two years ago,—I'd have taken you up on it."

"And now?"

"And now I know better. You'd have hated me for it, in the end."

"Now's different. Pamela, I haven't been in a cockpit on a regular basis for three years—longer if you count that tour of duty at the Naval War College. It's not fun anymore."

"Maybe that's the payback for all those years of flying. In those years of what you call fun, you learned something. You proved that today."

He was silent for a moment. "I'm grounded, you mean?"

"You know you are. At least, you won't be flying as much as you used to. You can't, Tombstone. It's not fair to your air wing and to the crew."

"I can't fly, and you won't marry me. Somehow, that doesn't sound like a happy ending."

"Did they ever promise you one? I thought that's what duty was all about."

"Duty means a lot of things. Right now, the only thing I can think about is whether I'll ever see you again."

"I'd count on it if I were you, Admiral," she said lightly. "When you least expect it, perhaps."

She touched her fingers to her mouth and then brushed them gently against his lips. "That's permitted on board your ship, isn't it?"

His lips tingled where her fingers had touched him. "Yes—but this isn't." He stood, drawing her to her feet with him, and drew her close. They paused for a split second, and then their mouths locked together, hungry, demanding release from the pressure of the last weeks. His hand caressed her neck, and started downward. He felt the jutting prominence of her collarbones, the soft upper slope of her breasts. Even as he felt his body responding, he knew it was the last time.

"Enough!" she finally gasped, and pulled away. "Any more and I'll miss my flight. Any second now, COS will be banging on the door, shooing me out."

"Any more and I'd be joining you on the COD. And if he thought your visit was too long, imagine how he'd feel about that," he said raggedly.

"Good-bye, Stoney," she said softly. "See you next war." The door clicked shut behind her.

CHAPTER 29
Saturday, 6 July

"Admiral?" Lab Rat asked. "I think I may have what you asked for."

"Shoot, La—uh, Commander Busby," Tombstone said.

Lab Rat groaned inwardly. The nickname appeared to be permanent, if even the admiral had trouble remembering his real name!

"It's a matter of saving face, Admiral. That's one of the most critical parts to dealing with an Asian nation. It's something I don't think we've ever understood, not completely. But I think I might have a cover story that would work."

"I'm listening."

"Here's the idea. . . ."

Fifteen minutes later, Tombstone was nodding. "Get this on the wire to your spook buddies, Commander. They may not take your suggestion, but it sounds like a fine operational deception to me. If anyone in the State Department's got a hair on their ass, they'll pull this one off. Helluva good idea!"

If Lab Rat hadn't known better, he would have sworn the somber admiral was even starting to smile. It was just as well he was sworn to secrecy—while his colleagues might be able to believe his plan, not a single one of them would have believed that old stone face had smiled.

"How are you holding up?" Bird Dog asked, glancing at the rearview mirror. "You ready for some aerobatics? Tell me if you're not—you'll be cleaning it up if you puke."

The backseater nodded.

"Use the ICS. If I'm not looking, I can't see you nod," he ordered.

"Yes, sir," the answer came finally. "I think some aerobatics would be just great!"

"Okay, Shaughnessy, but don't say I didn't warn you!" Bird Dog jammed the throttles forward, pitched the nose of the Tomcat up, and headed into an Immelmann.

She may own it on the ground, but up here it's all mine! And the more she knows about that part of it, the better she can do her job.

He'd never been too good with words, but a highly illegal and damned well-deserved ride in a Tomcat ought to make up for a hell of a lot of mistakes!

A war whoop echoed over the ICS as he reached the pinnacle of the maneuver. He felt a grin split his own face and added his best imitation of a rebel yell to her voice.

Damn, it was nice to have a backseater that appreciated the fancy stuff! Maybe it was time to talk to Shaughnessy about getting some college under her belt and going to AOCS. In six years or so, Gator might just find he had a little competition.

Then again, if her eyesight held up, she just might have her eyes on the front seat! From the way she was enjoying the aerobatics, she just might.

"Admiral? Lieutenant Commander Flynn to see you, sir," COS said.

Tombstone looked up from his desk and frowned. He'd known this day would come soon enough, and he still hadn't decided how to handle it. The more he tried to ignore Tomboy, the more he found her creeping into his thoughts. He could spot her in seconds in the crowded dirty-shirt mess in the forward part of the ship, and lately he'd taken to avoiding the VF-95 Ready Room. Every time he stepped into it, she was there.

She'd noticed, he was certain. How could she not know something was wrong when the man she'd flown with for a year, day in and day out, in combat and on routine hops, suddenly started avoiding her?

"Show her in, COS," he said. Well, absent a plan, he'd have to play it by ear.

"Commander," he said formally, while COS lingered at the door.

"Admiral, thank you for seeing me," she responded. Her voice was low and steady, although her usually light complexion looked starkly pale against the flaming red hair. She wore khakis, ribbons, and her wings, every inch the professional naval officer and pilot that she was. Suitable dress for a junior officer to see the admiral.

"Please—sit down," he said, gesturing to a chair in front of his desk. For a moment, he considered asking her to sit on the couch, to put her at ease. After all, if this meeting was difficult for him, it had to be doubly so for her.

"Thank you—I'd prefer to stand, if that would be all right

with you, Admiral. This won't take long." She paused and took a deep breath. Then she placed her hands at the open collar of her khaki shirt, slid one hand inside, and tugged. Her wings popped off and lay, shining gold, in the palm of her small hand. She looked down at them for a moment, and then sighed.

"What the hell are you doing?" Tombstone snapped. For a moment, as her hand went inside her shirt, he'd been afraid that—no, it wouldn't have been possible. Tomboy make a pass at him? On the ship? Never.

"Quitting. You won't ask me to—you wouldn't ever ask that of your own backseater. But it's obvious to me that that's what you want. I thought I'd save you the embarrassment." She stepped forward, reached across the desk, and gently placed the wings in front of him. Her hand lingered on them for a moment, as though saying good-bye. Then she stood, straight and proud, and looked him in the eyes.

"Thank you for seeing me, Admiral. I'm sorry to have disappointed you." She turned and walked toward the door.

Shock held Tombstone in place for a few seconds. Tomboy quit? Why would she ever think that's what he wanted? How could she?

As she reached for the doorknob, his throat suddenly unfroze. "Commander! Tomboy! Now just hold on one damned minute!" He was out of his chair and around his desk in a split second. He grabbed her by the shoulder and spun her around to face him. Face to face, her head barely reached his wings. She was looking down, but he saw one tear trace its way down her pale cheek.

"Sit down, Tomboy," he said, shoving her gently toward the couch. Her call sign came to his lips automatically. "That's an order."

She resisted for a second. "Please don't make this any harder than it is, Admiral. You don't know what it took to come here. I won't change my mind, no matter what you say."

"Just sit down. I'm not asking you to change your mind"—
not yet, anyway, he added silently—"I just want to talk to you
for a moment."

She nodded jerkily and walked around the coffee table to sit
perched on the edge of the couch. Her eyes were still locked on
the floor.

Tombstone sighed, berating himself for having let it come to
this. Of *course* she'd thought he wanted her out! How could
she not, when he'd avoided getting near her for the last month.

He lowered himself into the chair at right angles to the couch
and leaned back. It was his mess, and it was up to him to
straighten it out.

"I have a problem, Tomboy. Not you, me. Somewhere
between the Kola Peninsula and the Spratly Islands, you started
to be something to me besides a RIO. I don't know exactly
when or how, but I do know that's true. When I realized it, I
started avoiding you. I didn't want to put you in an uncomfortable position, I told myself. You couldn't handle it—at
least that's what I wanted to believe. The truth is that I couldn't.

"Do you know I almost called you every day while you were
on shore duty and I was at the war college? Every day I thought
about you, wondered what you were doing. I didn't, though. I
was afraid that I'd call you and hear you act surprised, or that
you'd just treat me like your old pilot. I'm ten years older than
you are, Tomboy, so I use that word literally. Or maybe you'd
feel uncomfortable with a rear admiral calling you, asking if
you'd like to go to a Patriots game some weekend. So I took
the easy way out. I was afraid of rejection."

"I wish you'd called," she said softly.

"Let me finish," he said abruptly. "In the last month, I've
been running scared. You're one of the finest RIOs I've ever
flown with, male or female. You're good, so good it almost
scares me. I'd rather fly with you than anyone else. But then
you and Batman seemed to hit it off, and—and, damn it,

you're assigned to my ship! I couldn't say anything, couldn't *do* anything. Do you understand?"

Finally, she looked up. Miraculously, the tears had cleared from her eyes. "That's not what I thought."

"I *know* what you thought, and I should have figured it out before. You can't quit, Tomboy. I don't want you to, and the Navy needs you. Those junior women pilots coming up behind you need you, too."

"And what about us? Is there an us?" she asked. "Not now, I mean. But this tour won't last forever, Tombstone. In another year, we'll both be rotating back to shore duty."

"Do you want that, Tomboy?" he asked, suddenly afraid his voice would crack.

"Yes. Very much so." Her eyes were shining, and the color had returned to her cheeks. "I can live with where we are now. And a year from now, things will be different."

He stared at her, hope growing in his heart. "You mean that?"

"You're an idiot, Tombstone, if you can't see that I do," she replied tartly. "If I'm allowed to call the Admiral an idiot, that is."

"Sometimes the Admiral is," he answered softly. "And he'd like to do something idiotic right now."

"Then I'd better be leaving before I compromise your reputation," she said, abruptly standing up. She held out her hand. "We have a deal, I believe."

He unfolded himself slowly from the chair and took her hand. For a second, the urge to pull her close to him, to feel the lithe body mold itself to his, was almost unbearable. Then he focused on the sharply pressed uniform, the rows of combat medals on her chest, and the empty spot marked with two little holes in the shirt above the ribbons. He released her hand and crossed over to his desk in one step.

"I believe you're out of uniform," he said gravely, and handed her the wings.

"It's customary for a senior officer to pin the wings on," she said, closing her hand over his.

He slipped one hand inside her shirt, feeling the silky softness of her breast on the back of his fingers. He positioned the wings above her ribbons and pressed the two prongs through the holes already in her blouse. Fumbling under her shirt, he slipped the two retaining clips, commonly known as nipples, over the back of the prongs, firmly attaching her NFO wings to her uniform.

"There," he said. "I don't know how many times I could stand to do that on a cruise. That's the last time I ever take my hand out of your shirt without getting a hell of a lot more physical. You ever try to quit on me again and I'm going to charge you with sexual harassment."

Tomboy laughed. "I won't quit on you again, Tombstone. Especially not now. Hell, with what I've got to look forward to in a year, I don't want you flying with anyone else!"

"Then get the hell out of here and let me get some work done," he snarled in mock ferocity. "And by the way—stop by air ops and see if you can get on the schedule for tomorrow. Among other things, I'm real overdue for five day traps."

"And we'll talk about the night traps later," she said.

1400 local (Zulu -7)
Kawashi Maru

"What the hell is this all about?" Third Mate Gringes asked the master of the ship, waving the radio message in his hand. "Since when did we start taking on Navy helicopters?"

"Since they decided one of their people wanted to have a little chitchat with us," the master replied. "Evidently our complaint about the fly-overs got some attention. And there's no reason why they couldn't land here," he continued, pointing out to the broad, empty expanse of deck. "When we were in the Navy, we had helicopters setting down on a lot smaller deck than that."

"Guess I'd better dig out that emergency gear," Gringes replied. "It's been a while since I was an LSO."

An hour later, following a hasty FOD walk-down, Gringes saw the helicopter appear on the horizon. The SH-60F made two exploratory circles of the deck, getting a look at the area, and got an update on relative wind from the bridge of the massive RO-RO. Finally satisfied, it settled neatly onto the deck.

One flight-suited crew member hopped out and darted over to the Third Mate.

"Hi! Commander Busby, *USS Jefferson*," the man said, offering his hand. "I gather you were expecting us."

Gringes stifled the reflex to salute. "Yes, sir, we sure were. If you'll follow me, I'll take you up to the master—uh, captain."

"Any chance you could ask him to meet us in your radio room?" the Navy officer said. "It'll save some time, and things are getting a little urgent out here."

"Don't we know it! We're cranked up to max speed to get away from you people. Guess it didn't do much good, since you were able to hunt us down so quickly. What's all this about, anyway? The Navy want to give us a permanent helo detachment?" Gringes asked, his curiosity rising to unbearable levels.

"I'll brief you in with your master, if he says it's okay. And, no, we're not staying. In fact, I've got to get back to the carrier as soon as possible. We're just coming over to ask a little favor, that's all."

"I guess we could try to pretend we're a decoy carrier,"

Gringes said over his shoulder as the officer followed him into the skin of the ship. "Don't know that our owners would like that much, though."

"Nothing as serious as that. We just want you to send a message out for us."

"A message? With all the communications gear you've got over there, you want us to send a message?"

They paused on a landing between flights of stairs, and Gringes thought he saw a flash of amusement in the other man's face.

"Let's just say that the source of this particular message is important," the officer said finally.

"What *kind* of message?"

A smile lit Commander Busby's face. "A weather report."

CHAPTER 30
Saturday, 6 July

The ambassador's stomach churned uneasily. Even with the president's words of confidence still ringing in her ears, the thought of the next few hours filled her with an ineluctable dread. She paused for a moment, and the flock of staffers and assistants behind her almost ran her over. She heard a few angry whispers, the almost imperceptible thud of elbows on ribs.

None, save her Chief of Staff, had any inkling of what was about to happen. There were no position papers, no carefully thought out amendments or resolutions. Just her own instincts, honed in years of political maneuvering and international intrigue, to get her—and the nation—through this crisis without irrevocable harm to America's interests.

She sighed and started forward again. This, as the president had said, was why they paid her the big bucks.

"The ambassador from the United States." The chairman of the Security Council recognized her. She ignored the puzzled flurry of comments from her own staff behind her.

"Thank you, Mr. Chairman. The United States appreciates your courtesy in allowing us to proceed with our message of support for our valued allies in China."

T'ing looked up sharply. His features quickly smoothed themselves back into inscrutability. He started to speak, then thought better of it.

"Support?" the chairman said doubtfully.

"Yes, of course. By now each member has probably received reports from their own sources,"—*read "spies" here, my esteemed colleagues*, she thought, allowing a faint smile to reach her lips—"and are no doubt preparing their own statements. However, we wished to be the first."

She glanced around the room. Only years of experience allowed her to read the turmoil bubbling within the other delegations. Not an ambassador flinched, nor were there any guarded whispers to their respective staffs. Instead, each one adopted the same expression as T'ing wore on his face, an air of calm knowingness.

She wiped the smile off her face. Be damned hard for them to know anything about it—since it never happened.

"I'm advised by our military staff that at 0600, during joint operations off the coast of Brunei, the People's Republic of China suffered a tragic accident. While all peace-loving nations of the world understand that such incidents are an unavoidable part of the price of freedom, we nonetheless extend our deepest sympathies to the families of those injured and killed during the incident. The ambassador from China, no doubt not wishing to slow down the work of this important body, will not mention the incident. But I feel compelled to publicly recognize the bravery of the military forces involved."

She glanced at the faces again. Still no reaction.

"This morning in the South China Sea, operational forces from Vietnam and China were performing joint maneuvers off the coast of Vietnam. According to the Master of the *Kawashi Maru*, a commercial vessel in the area," she continued, holding up a message, "winds and seas reached typhoon strength in a matter of hours, completely without warning. Fifty aircraft engaged in training exercises were lost. The United States carrier group on hand in international waters attempted to offer aid in locating the downed airmen and the sailors from the ship. Working together with our allies, a few men were recovered. As soon as practical, they will be repatriated to their respective homelands. In the meantime, the United States regrets that a tragedy of this proportion could occur, and offers its condolences to the families of the men involved."

T'ing cleared his throat and looked down, as though overcome by emotion. A staffer reached around from behind him, placing a piece of paper before him. T'ing slapped the hand away, glanced at the paper, and then shoved it aside.

"Does the ambassador from China wish to respond?" the chairman asked uncertainly.

She intercepted a keen look of distrust and anger from T'ing, a millisecond-long flash of belligerence. It was gone as quickly as it had come. Then T'ing stood.

"On behalf of my government, we thank the ambassador for her condolences. The events of this morning . . ." T'ing stopped, feigning momentary emotion, and thought furiously. If he disputed the ambassador's version of that morning, it would inevitably follow that word of China's defeat would be circulated immediately. It was intolerable—the loss of face in front of the Pacific Rim tiger nations would set China's plan for regional leadership back generations. On the other hand, her proffered explanation would buy China time, time to rebuild and rearm, time to further insinuate itself into the countries bordering the South China Sea.

He glanced at Vietnam and saw Ngyugen's almost imperceptible shrug. Whatever China decided, the Vietnamese ambassador would support. Brunei didn't even matter, and Malaysia had no proof. In that instant, pitted one-on-one against the American devil, he decided.

". . . are indeed a tragedy," he continued. "We thank the United States for her assistance and look forward to the immediate return of our airmen and seamen."

The ambassador from the United States rose again. "Those events only point out the ever more pressing need for a regional plan for the South China Sea. We must be prepared to move swiftly, to act in concert, to prevent further loss of life in future storms."

T'ing gritted his teeth and nodded. It would do no harm to agree now. Sun Tzu would have understood using the tactical advantage of peace to buy time to prepare for the next conflict.

CHAPTER 31
Friday, 6 September

Hangar Bay
In port, Alameda, California
USS *Jefferson*

"Attention on deck!" the Chief of Staff snapped.

The ranks of officers and enlisted personnel stiffened slightly, but made no other appreciable movement. Even the Navy Band detachment seemed immobilized as they struck up "Ruffles and Flourishes," only the conductor's right hand beating out the tempo.

Vice Admiral Thomas Magruder strode up the steps to the platform and returned his nephew's salute. The band finished with its final bars, and Tombstone dropped his hand. His uncle greeted old friends on the dais, then took a seat in the chair slightly to the right of the podium. The colors were posted, the national anthem played, and the chaplain offered an opening prayer.

Tombstone stepped behind the podium and adjusted the microphone. There was no need for it—his staff had checked and double-checked every detail thoroughly, rehearsing the change of command ceremony until even the most junior ensign on the *Jefferson* could have recited every line by heart.

The only part that would be new would be Tombstone's farewell speech.

He looked out over the ranks of men and women—almost two thousand of them, the remainder on watch, liberty, or leave—arrayed around the two hundred metal chairs on the flight deck of *Jefferson*. Civilians and military guests from other commands packed the space encircled by the ranks, rustling their programs and catching up with old friends. His eyes sought out Tomboy and found her standing in ranks with her squadron. A small smile passed between them.

It had been his decision to hold the ceremony on the flight deck, although they'd kept the cavernous hangar bay spotlessly ready in case it rained. The weather in Alameda, *Jefferson*'s home port, could be unpredictable in the spring.

During his early days as a junior officer, Tombstone would have tried to find some way to get out of attending any ceremony. It had seemed boring beyond endurance, standing in ranks, listening to the dinosaurs drone endlessly on about honor, duty, and courage. What possible justification, he'd wondered, could there be for wasting so much time over a ceremony? Get the new admiral on board, brief him, and get back to the routine. The constant demands of training and repairing aircraft never ceased.

It was, he realized suddenly, the final perquisite of command. No doubt his transfer from the *Jefferson* meant far more to him than it did to his staff and the crew. His relief, Rear Admiral Edward Everett Wayne, would make his own mark on the ship and staff. Even if he proved to be an impossibly idiotic flag officer—which Tombstone sincerely doubted Batman would—he would only be there for eighteen months. The staff could do that standing on their heads.

These last few moments were advertised as essential to letting the crew know who was in command. But more than that, it was a starkly poignant moment for the officer leaving command. It was the last moment he would gaze over his people—*his* people—before he would turn responsibility for their lives and well-being over to another. It was the time in which he severed the umbilical cord that bound him to each man and each woman, a point in life clearly delineated when he could finally put down the burden of their safety.

And it was a time to say his second good-bye of the day. He wasn't sure which was the more difficult, leaving his command or finally admitting that his relationship with Pamela was over.

He suddenly realized that the crowd was murmuring politely. He cleared his throat and heard the sound reverberate from the huge speakers set at either end of the dais.

"Vice Admiral Magruder, distinguished visitors, officers and crew of CARGRU 14, *USS Jefferson*, and Air Wing Nine. I thank you for your presence here today at this change of command ceremony."

He paused for a moment. He'd thought long and hard for the last week about his speech, and had finally resuscitated a number of old naval aphorisms, pasted them together with his best wishes, and committed them to memory. Now, understanding the true purpose of the ceremony, he slid his cheater notes into his pants pocket.

"I want to leave you with one thought. Duty, ladies and gentlemen. That is the essential ingredient that distinguishes military service from any other career in the world. It is an obligation to always be prepared, to learn how to practice your skills and arts for the day that they will once again be needed. It is especially difficult when your country seems not to appreciate you. But there it is. When all else fails, when you're tired, exhausted, and far from home, I want you to remember one thing—that duty demands not what is easy, not what is convenient. It requires doing what is right, time and again, unnoticed and unapplauded. It is your sacred obligation. And one that you will fulfill in the following months with my relief.

It has been my pleasure—and my honor—to serve with you.

"I will now read my orders." Tombstone paused again, staring down at the photocopy of the message traffic he'd received just hours before. He read the originator and the subject line out loud, and then continued with the text. "When relieved, report to commander, Pacific Fleet, for further assignment." A weaselly assignment, stashed in Hawaii on the PACFLT staff until his next assignment was decided by the higher-ups.

Batman read his orders, a solemn note in his voice. Tombstone tried to remember if he'd ever heard his friend sound so serious. He hadn't, he decided. He wondered whether he should tell Batman what he'd just realized about the ceremony, and then decided he wouldn't. Better that his old wingman learn it in his own way.

Finally, it was over. He and Batman exchanged salutes and formally and publicly reported the change of command to their immediate superior, commander of the Third Fleet. They followed the admiral off the podium to the sound of the "Anchors Aweigh" and headed for the reception table set up below on the hangar bay.

"They're all yours, Batman," he said quietly. For a moment, just a few seconds, Tombstone felt a deep sense of loss.

"I'll take good care of them, Tombstone," Batman said solemnly. Tombstone wondered if there'd been the same look of quiet jubilation in his eyes when he'd taken command of the carrier group. It would come within the next week, he knew. The sudden doubts, the overwhelming burden of commanding such a potent weapon. Batman would find his own way of dealing with it, just as he'd found out how to cope with his earliest doubts about his abilities as a pilot, Tombstone knew. If he had to relinquish command, it could be to no better officer.

"Any idea of what they've got planned for you?" Batman

asked as a mess management specialist filled his cup with punch.

"Not a word," Tombstone answered. It bothered him a little, that not even a rumor had leaked out of the E-ring at the Pentagon.

"I might be able to shed some light on that," he heard a familiar voice say. "Congratulations, by the way, Batman. I know you'll do a fine job."

"Thank you, sir. But have you heard anything about Tombstone's orders?"

Vice Admiral Magruder smiled. "I have, but I'm sworn to secrecy. I can tell you this, Tombstone. Just a hint. If you thought the Spratly Islands and the Chinese were a challenge — you're gonna love the next two years!"